Hallowed Halls

HANNAH ALEXANDER

Hallowed Halls

Published in Partnership with:
Christian Writers Guild Publishing
5585 N. Erindale Drive, Suite 200
Colorado Springs, CO 80918

Cover created by: Lisa Hainline

Interior created by: Steven Plummer

Printed by: BethanyPress

ISBN: 978-0-578-13707-0

Printed in the United States of America

Chapter 1

Fury surged through Dr. Joy Gilbert like a rifle shot as she shut her office door and yanked the stethoscope from around her neck, suppressing a rebel yell. She stormed to the wide windows and sucked in her breath, ready to throw open the panes and shock the world. But an inquisitive squirrel leapt from one branch to another on a tree behind the clinic.

With a comical tilt of his head the furry critter broke the force of her outrage. Joy released her breath and deflated. As a child, she'd helped Mom bottle feed an orphaned gray squirrel, and the little thick-tailed acrobat had often made her laugh.

Why scare the squirrels because she was angry with the ridiculous accusations of a hostile patient? The man was unbelievable.

Her intercom buzzed, jerking her back to complete maturity.

"Dr. Gilbert, honey, you okay in there?" It was Betty, her favorite nurse.

"Give me a sec—"

"The boss is on his way to the clinic, sweetie. I want to rush Mr. Bezier out the door before he can waylay Mr. Cline."

Joy winced. Along with half the clinic staff and several patients in the waiting room, Betty had clearly heard Frank

Bezier berating Joy for her refusal to write him a script for a half-year's supply of Percocet. He wouldn't listen when she explained that was illegal. Some people thought they were above the law.

He had, in fact, loudly accused her of using her physical attributes and other "abilities" to land her job with Weston Cline "since you're obviously an incompetent physician." The man was a bully.

"He'll just call Weston later," she told Betty. "He has clout." And Weston's personal cell phone number.

"Oh horse dumplings; the man's a legalized drug junkie and everyone knows it, including the boss. And might I remind you that Mr. Cline hired you for your ability with patients? Not anything else, and everybody here knows that, no matter what Mr. Bossypants says."

Joy closed her eyes in relief at her nurse's soothing words. No one in the clinic knew about the pains she'd taken to keep Weston Cline's hands off of her. All the struggles growing up without a daddy could teach a girl a few hard lessons, so she'd been prepared. Being accused of doing the very thing she'd always sworn never to do before marriage had felt like a stab in her gut with a butcher knife.

"You could fire him from your service," Betty said. "Send a letter and he's out the door in thirty days."

"And then I'll be out the door." Joy suspected Weston chose to advertise the clinic's willingness to take chronic pain patients in the first place because it would ensure a fast growth rate. And it certainly had. "The boss wants Bezier happy."

"If you go out the door, so will I, and so will half the staff. Mr. Cline knows better."

"I'm not so sure. He wants me to write more scripts for narcs."

"You don't want the state medical board breathing down your

neck for being overly generous with controlled substances," Betty reminded her.

Joy turned her back to the desk. She refused to become a legal pusher. Where had her brain been the day she agreed to work for a man who wanted her to put an emphasis on pain management?

No, wait, she hadn't been thinking with her brain last year. Weston Cline had the charisma of a world dictator, and for a short time she'd allowed herself to be dazed by his sweet words and the promise of a successful career—particularly after Zack broke their engagement.

If only Weston wasn't so damaged. If only his character had been as solid as she'd believed it to be in the beginning. Over the months she'd realized that the man she'd thought he was had concealed his broken character by utilizing his dynamic personality. He had plenty of that. His male magnetism that had nearly been her undoing.

Mom taught Joy long ago that sweet words and a handsome face might draw a woman to a man, but she'd better be smart enough to hold him at arm's length until she could see the character beneath. That took longer.

While watching Weston promote the clinic to the public, Joy had found that for him the game was all about making people believe in the magic of narcotics. Money was his narcotic. He'd failed the character test for Joy.

The hum of familiar voices drifted through her closed door. There was a cry of a child and the clatter of a computer keyboard, the laughter of a couple of the staff members in the break room.

"Dr. Gilbert?" Her door opened, the bottom of it brushing across carpet. She caught a whiff of Lindsey Baker's spicy perfume. The girl needed to be educated about patient allergies and invasion of doctor privacy.

While Joy's stomach growled because of a missed lunch three hours ago, she reminded herself that her hometown was just downriver, between Frankenstein and Hermann, Missouri. Not that far, really, though it seemed a world away.

"Dr. Gilbert, it's Sarah Miller," Lindsey said.

Joy turned immediately. Good. A real patient. She reached for the file Lindsey held out to her.

"She's in Two," Lindsey said in that timid, eager-to-please voice of a new-hire. This one was especially young, with rich auburn curls and friendly, dark brown eyes.

Weston encouraged an attractive appearance among the clinic's staff members.

Once again drawn into the milieu of work, Joy glanced at the information on the clipboard. She was halfway down the hall, paging through the three-inch-thick stack of notes and test results when a pair of polished black wingtips stepped into her field of vision. She looked up into the cobalt gaze of her employer.

She should have been able to sense his arrival by the suddenly hushed voices of staff, and the adoring—or possibly fearful—glances from every woman in view, depending on their status with him. Employees feared or worshiped him. Patients who recognized his city-wide fame from the billboards practically genuflected at his feet. The man had been featured in a regional magazine recently for taking his family fortune and doubling it. Who besides Joy didn't worship the wealthy?

She'd overheard a couple of women arguing in the waiting room one day over whether he looked more like Hugh Jackman or Gerard Butler. Had Joy really once shared their admiration?

"Weston, hi. What brings you here in the middle of the week?" She instinctively moved her hand to cover the name on the file she carried—Sarah Miller was a pro bono case. He would make no money from this one.

"Doesn't a man have a right to check on his business investment from time to time?" The intentionally seductive depth of his voice and the gentle expression in his gaze assured her he was presently relaxed. "I heard you haven't taken a lunch break. Why don't we have Lindsey bring you a Reuben from the deli? You can join me in my office while you eat and catch me up on today's progress."

"That would be great if I had time, but we're a little swamped right now." That should thrill him. "Rain check?"

He glanced at the file in Joy's hand. "After this one?"

"Three more."

He reached down and nudged her hand from the name. He'd taken Joy to task more than once about "wasting time with non-payers." She could almost feel the temperature drop in the room a couple of degrees.

At thirty-nine, Weston had flecks of white at the temples of his night black hair, a neatly trimmed beard and pinpoints of quicksilver in his blue eyes when he was upset.

That quicksilver gave a momentary flash. "Joy."

"This one's in pain."

He tapped the file folder. "This one's a hypochondriac."

She glanced around and lowered her voice. "I beg your pardon, but I'm the physician on this case." Since when did he get his degree? She swallowed. Had to remain calm. "I have some unique cases that—"

"As you've pointed out to me in the past, every case is unique."

"This clinic is doing so well after less than a year. It's not hurting the bottom line to help someone every now and then." She held her breath.

His gaze softened, but remained on her. The troubled questions in his eyes had haunted her for months. As Bezier just finished trumpeting to the whole clinic, Weston had hinted from time to time that he hoped for more than an employee relationship from her when he brought her to Kansas City. At one point, when they met after clinic hours to discuss strategies, she'd almost weakened. Why save herself for marriage when the only man she'd ever loved had broken their engagement? When it seemed the whole world believed in the joys of matrimony without the contract—when her own mother had obviously weakened at one point long enough to become pregnant with her out of wedlock—why had she pushed back so hard every time a man tried to push her into bed?

Just in time she'd realized that no woman could give Weston what he truly needed, because the great Weston Cline, sole heir to the Cline family fortune, had a heart so wounded he could barely function emotionally. Losing a child could do that to a parent.

Weston's ex-wife, Sylvia, claimed his heart was forged in ice and stone, but every so often Joy saw something different in his expression, heard it in his voice, sometimes in his words. There was no denying he'd been a lonely child, and she knew about the tragedy of his younger brother's death when Weston was eleven.

That might explain why his relationship with his mother was always so strained, but Joy had stopped herself from following that rabbit trail before becoming too involved with his private life. That could give him the wrong impression. Sometimes she really did follow in her mother's old habits and attempt to soothe the woes of the world. It wouldn't be wise to encourage Weston to get the wrong impression.

"I have a patient, Weston." She tried to step around him.

He didn't move.

She pressed between him and the hallway wall, retaining as much dignity as possible. How she wished this man didn't control her life so completely, as Mom had warned her he would.

Sometimes it seemed as if Molly Gilbert had ways of reaching across the distance to make her daughter pay for the choices she'd made that Mom—and by implication, God—had not condoned.

She entered the exam room, shutting Weston out so she could focus on one of her favorite patients. "How are you doing, Sarah?"

Pale of hair and eyes, Sarah Miller met Joy's gaze with a tentative nod.

A wise professor had once taught that if physicians would listen longer to the patients, those very patients could provide missing puzzle pieces for their own diagnoses. Oh, for the luxury of time. Joy loved listening. But with Sarah, Joy had realized many weeks ago that it was necessary to know more than the information on the chart.

"Haven't been sleeping?" Joy sat on the chair in front of the computer and studied the notes the nurse had made.

Sarah looked up and shook her head. Today her eyes were more gray than green, a sure sign she didn't feel well, though her vitals were solid. Her translucent skin was paler than usual, her mouth more rigid. She put Joy in mind of a prisoner who hadn't seen the sun in years.

"What's wrong, Sarah? Betty said you wouldn't talk to her about why you're here."

"That's because last time I was here I think someone told the rest of the staff that I asked for a colonoscopy; they were all snickering at me from behind the Plexiglas when I walked out the door." There was reproach in her soft voice.

Joy knew Betty wouldn't do that, but after being fired from the services of two other physicians, Sarah was gun shy.

"Tell me what's going on with you today," Joy asked, leaning forward, keeping eye contact. "Is your stomach still causing you trouble?"

"Yes, but that's not what I came for." With a sigh, Sarah pointed to her nose. "Could this be melanoma?"

Joy nudged Sarah's finger away and examined the worrisome spot. It was tiny, with even color and edges.

"Can you tell, Dr. Gilbert?" Sarah's breath sounds were irregular, with underlying fear—irrational, erratic, intense—that had characterized her visits since she'd become a patient here seven months ago. "I know how fast those things can grow."

Joy took Sarah's hands, feeling the frailness of her bones. It would take a lot of work to allay the real fears that stalked this otherwise rational, intelligent twenty-four-year-old. "What you have is a freckle."

Sarah's eyes widened. "But it's right there on the end of my nose, where the sun hits it."

"The way you slather yourself with sun block, and at your age, I don't think you'll have a problem with melanoma. I can biopsy the spot if you're horribly worried about it, but we don't want an unnecessary scar to mess up that flawless complexion."

Sarah's gamine features scrunched. "Am I being a hypochondriac again?"

"Not at all. There's a problem, and you need treatment, but—"

The phone on the desk buzzed, and Lindsey's voice came over the intercom. "Dr. Gilbert, there's a call for you. Sounds urgent. It's a Dr. Zachary Travis from—"

"Take a message, please." Joy said the words before the name registered, and she struggled mightily to maintain a professional demeanor in the presence of her patient. Oxygen refused to enter her lungs for a brief moment. Zack? Why would he be calling here? And now, after all this time?

"But he says it's important," Lindsay continued. "It's an emergency and I've got him on hold."

Joy snatched up the receiver with one hand while holding up a finger for Sarah—a silent apology. "Lindsay, remember when we discussed this a couple of weeks ago? Unless the building's on fire, all calls can wait." But everything within her wanted to take the call. Zack hadn't contacted her since breaking the engagement. Why now? "Take a message, please."

She disconnected and selected a preprinted sheet from a rack of brochures on the wall, then turned back to Sarah. "I've spoken about your situation with a colleague of mine, who is a trusted friend. I've not given her your name. I won't do that without your permission."

Sarah's face reddened. "You're not going to see me anymore."

"Yes I am. As I said, all your physical findings are normal." Joy gave her patient a tender smile. "That doesn't rule out a concern I have for you. Dr. Myra Maxwell and I attended the same medical school, and then she continued her education in psychiatry."

Those soft eyes, which had held trust for Joy after their first encounter, filled instead with hurt confusion.

Joy slid the brochure into Sarah's hands. "She and I both feel she can help you, and she's the best."

The flush on Sarah's face lightened a little as she studied the glossy tri-fold that exhibited Myra Maxwell's picture. Straight, black hair and the tanned olive tones of her skin showed a Cherokee heritage. Joy recalled the day they'd both gone to have professional photos taken. Nothing Joy did would bring a smile to Myra's face so soon after the tragedy.

There was an infinitesimal slump of Sarah's shoulders. Silence.

Joy scooted to the periphery of her patient's personal space, took in the clenched fingers, the wobbling chin. "Sarah, I found out what happened to you. Because of that, your mind can better cope with physical disorders than with the memories."

For a moment, the only sounds in the exam room were the buzz of the wall clock and the muted rainfall on the roof of the building. The murmur of voices from the outer office filtered through the closed door. Joy watched the delicate rise in the center of Sarah's throat, strong emotions trying to fight their way out.

"How do you know about that?" Sarah's voice barely rose above the patter of raindrops.

"Research. I went to the *Corrigan Times* and found the front-page story about the attack on you and your husband."

A glimmer of moisture threatened tears. The pale blonde brows drew together. The lines of Sarah's face scrunched like a child's.

"Sarah, you experienced a living nightmare."

The slender shoulders jerked in a single, powerful spasm, eyes squeezed shut tightly, hands grasping the chair arms. "I can't do this."

"You can't continue as you have. You're not dealing with the original injury, so you will persist in having physical manifestations of—"

Sarah jumped up. "I can't, Dr. Gilbert. I'm sorry." She grabbed her purse, pulled open the door, and nearly collided with Weston. The brochure floated to his feet.

Joy followed her out. "Sarah, please."

But the patient kept going. When Joy tried to follow, Weston blocked her. "You're not her mother, Dr. Gilbert."

Something cracked inside her. She gritted her teeth, knowing that if she spoke her mind at this moment she would most certainly lose her job.

He leaned close enough that his mouth was within inches of her ear. "You have paying patients waiting for weeks to get an appointment with you. If you continue your present practice of medicine, there will soon be no clinic to treat anyone."

Joy stepped away from him and met his gaze. "We both know how much money this place brings in." She whispered the words for his ears only.

His lids fluttered down for an instant, then he took a deep breath and let it out slowly. Silence filled the hallway around them. "You're forgetting who owns this place that pays your generous salary."

He was right, and she knew it. Time to tread carefully. She ducked beneath his arm and headed to her office, but she heard the sound of his footsteps as he followed her. This discussion wasn't over.

Chapter 2

Tressa Cline relished the first cramps of *that* kind she'd ever had as she stared out the side window of the school bus into a sky that had grown more pregnant with rain throughout the afternoon. Her teachers and classmates at school had complained about the unusual darkness of the sky. She didn't mind the darkness, and wouldn't mind when the invisible sun set, turning Corrigan even darker. She couldn't remember ever being afraid of the dark. She'd stopped using a nightlight when she was three.

Four years ago, she'd discovered that the darkness hiding under her bed or behind the bushes at night had nothing to do with a deeper absence of light that could attack in bright sunshine. She'd learned about this danger when Keegan died, and then afterward when her parents grew silent, began to fight, and then dragged her with them through a divorce battle, blaming each other for her brother's death.

So now, at fifteen, Tressa feared only the darkness that dwelt in the human soul and attacked and destroyed families.

Dad called her a drama queen when she wrote her angst-filled poetry about Keegan. She no longer showed him her writing. Mom said Dad was an idiot not to realize that their daughter was "gifted." Tressa would have appreciated the supportive term better if she wasn't so sure Mom simply welcomed any excuse to call her ex-husband an idiot.

They never saw the darkness in which they wallowed.

And because Tressa was on her weekly trek to Wednesday night visitation—which was a joke, since Dad didn't know how to visit—she couldn't help thinking about all of it, especially after she'd sensed some of that same darkness between Dad and Joy in the past few weeks. It scared her. Until Dad brought Joy Gilbert to work for him at the clinic—one of several Cline Family enterprises that Dad controlled—Tressa had come to dread visitation nights and weekends, and she knew Dad had dreaded them, too. Not that he didn't love her. And she loved him. But she knew she reminded him of a time in his life when he'd lost the only good things he'd ever had.

When Dad started spending time with Joy last year under the pretense of helping her settle into a new environment, he just happened to invite her to join him and Tressa for dinner on Wednesday night after work. Practically from the first night, Tressa wanted Dad to see more and more of Joy. He'd made it pretty obvious that he hoped the same thing. Joy never fawned over Dad the way his other women had. Joy was her own person.

Still feeling the cramps, Tressa stepped off the school bus and walked sedately through the rain, across the parking lot, and into the clinic. She never used an umbrella.

Dad said that was because she was rebellious. Mom said it was because she was a strong person who loved to embrace the elements. Joy never mentioned it; one day she simply stepped out from beneath her back patio and joined Tressa in the rain.

She loved Joy for that. Her friend. Tressa had decided many months ago that if Dad and Joy got married, all would be well. That was a dream that wouldn't come true, and Dad was beginning to realize it. Joy spent more time with Tressa than with Dad on visitation days, but whose fault was that? He was the one who disappeared into another room for "just one business call" that turned out to be five or six calls and additional time on the computer. If only he would admit to himself that being with his own daughter depressed him.

But Grandmother had raised him to believe real men didn't get depressed. She had also raised him to blame himself for his little brother's death.

As soon as Tressa stepped into the clinic office, while she brushed the rain from her hair, she felt it. The darkness. For a moment she couldn't figure out what was wrong, she just didn't want to move forward.

Seconds later, she saw Joy's closed office door at the end of the wide corridor that divided the treatment rooms from the business office; Joy's door was almost always open.

The staff was silent for once behind the glassed reception window. Dad usually complained that they talked too much and too loudly and someday would get the clinic into trouble when they discussed the wrong patient at the wrong time, federal regulations being impossible to comply with.

Tressa shrugged her book bag from her shoulders and strolled toward Joy's office until she heard Dad's voice from behind that door. The darkness had already entered it.

One of the nurses gave Tressa a curious glance, so she stepped into Dad's seldom-used office and set her book bag into the corner, making no noise. With only two days before summer vacation, she wasn't going to touch the books, anyway. The teachers were tired, the kids were tired. Time for a break.

She sank to the floor and crossed her legs next to the vent, not because there weren't any comfortable chairs in this clubby, dark, manly office, but because the vent transferred voices better from Joy's office next door.

"...promised me when I came to work here that the clinic

would be reaching out to patients of all economic levels." Joy's voice, usually mellow and harmonious, held anger. Her words were clipped. "Now I'm in trouble if I bring in more than two pro bono cases a week?"

"I make the financial decisions about all my businesses." Dad's voice had that irritatingly reasonable quality it always did when he was about to shoot holes through someone's argument. "Was that promise in the contract?"

"Since I thought you were a man of your word, I didn't ask you to write it into the contract."

"Then you've learned one of life's lessons the hard way. Always get your expectations in writing. Contracts can be negotiated. Did you even read yours?"

Tressa could picture Joy seated at her desk, arms folded in front of her, dark brown eyes extra dark, as they often were lately. Mostly sad.

"I read it three times," Joy said softly. "But in my world, the spoken word was as good as a contract. I care about those patients. All of them."

"You're killing yourself to keep up, while the time you spend with each case makes other paying patients wait too long. You need to speed up your game or find another line of work."

Tressa tensed and closed her eyes. No! How could he even suggest that?"

"You can take the staff time and supplies out of my pay." Joy's voice held a sense of urgency. "The pro bono cases I take matter a lot to me. I'll work even more hours."

Dad gave a heavy sigh. "Didn't you hear me? You're already working too much. Obviously I don't matter to you anymore." He said it softly, with almost as much urgency as Tressa had heard in Joy's voice.

"Weston, we're discussing patient care."

"I haven't been able to miss the long hours you spend here,

including Saturdays and Sundays, and lately I've suspected you did that to avoid me."

"Do you have any idea how much time it takes to keep files updated? I don't have that luxury when patients are being run through every fifteen minutes five days a week from eight to six. I spend my lunch breaks making referrals when other offices are open. I can't afford to get behind—"

"I'm talking about you and me now, Joy."

The silence stretched.

"Once upon a time I thought there was going to be an 'us,'" he said.

"I...I'm sorry, Weston."

Tressa held her breath, but Joy gave no words of reassurance.

"I waited patiently," Dad said. "I even respected your desire to postpone intimacy, and that's never been an issue for me before. Do you know how difficult it's been?"

"I'm sorry. I had no intention of leading you on. There was a time when I also thought there might be more between us, but I've discovered we are two very different people."

Tressa cringed. There was compassion in Joy's voice—something she probably used for patients whose cases were hopeless.

"Why?" was all Dad asked.

No voices reached her from the front office. It was as if the world held its breath for Joy's reply.

"I realized my mother was right about at least one thing," Joy said. "Business and romance can be tricky things to balance."

"You're angry about Sarah Miller. I understand that, but are you so angry you'd be willing to sacrifice your job?" Dad's voice was almost too quiet.

"What you need to do is learn to leave your work here at the clinic and stop attempting to rescue all the needy Sarah Millers of the world," Dad said.

There was a soft sigh from Joy. "Sarah Miller got married

two years ago. She and her husband were on their honeymoon when three men out for a good time—three beasts high on drugs—broke into the honeymoon cabin." Joy's voice tautened. "Two of the men used a serrated butcher knife to stab her husband repeatedly."

Tressa covered her mouth with her hand. She was going to heave. Her stomach was already feeling queasy.

"While Sarah's brand new husband bled to death," Joy continued, "the monsters raped her. His final experience on earth was watching these men abuse his wife."

Tears stung Tressa's eyes.

"Then she went to doctor after doctor with a silent cry for help, and she got the brush-off because she didn't know that her emotions were causing physical illness."

"Then you're sending her to the right place. End of story."

Tressa cringed at her father's callous words.

"Excuse me?" Joy snapped. "The end?" There was a squeak of a chair, as if maybe she had stood up. "I spend hours a week writing scripts for people who don't want to bother getting to the real issue for their pain, and here's one patient who—"

"Who's also not seeking help for the real source of her trouble," Dad said. "Remember, I saw her refuse your advice. So what's different about her? Everybody has pain, sweetheart."

It was quiet for a moment, then Tressa heard a heavy sigh. "Maybe you're right. If I can't do my job the right way, then I might as well get out of the profession."

Joy stared into the silvery sheen of Weston's blue eyes as she remembered watching a tornado form in the air one stormy spring day. She'd heard the wind, but couldn't feel it, couldn't see movement on the trees or vines around her. She saw the clouds moving above her head, as if they were being stirred and shaped into a circular crucible by an invisible pestle.

It didn't occur to her until later that day to be afraid for herself. Her first thought was for the vineyards where her mother worked. Joy never forgot the awe she'd felt, the silent waiting. That tornado didn't touch down.

Would this one?

She studied the curve of Weston's lips, the gaze that had weakened many a woman's defenses—had almost weakened hers while she was recovering from her broken engagement. How glad she was now that she'd avoided that mistake.

Before she could say a word, her intercom buzzed. "Dr. Gilbert, call for you on line two. It's Dr. Travis again."

Weston spread his hands, and she could see the jealousy in his eyes.

"Dr. Zachary Travis? You and your fiancé are communicating again?"

"Ever heard of physician referrals? He might have a paying patient for us."

Weston's eyes snapped at her sarcasm. "Wrap it up and get back to work."

Just before Joy pressed the line button, she heard a soft footfall—that telltale creak of floorboards beside Weston's desk in his office next door—and she wondered who might have overheard their conversation.

She glanced at the clock, and her heart contracted. Tressa. Weston's beautiful, breakable daughter.

She answered the phone softly, as if, by her tone of voice, the effects of her words to Wes might be diminished in his daughter's ears.

"Joy Marie, is it really you this time?" came a deep, long-familiar voice that, to her surprise, still held the power to cause a deep ache inside after all these months.

"It's me," she said. Only Zachary Travis had ever used Joy's middle name.

"You're a hard one to reach," Zack complained in the southeastern Missouri drawl that he still occasionally fell back on when stressed. Was that from calling her?

"Sorry. Crazy-busy day. What's up?"

"Joy, you need to come home."

"What? Why?"

"It's Molly. She had some chest pain, and it was bad enough to convince her to come to the ER. Don't panic. I've checked her out and nothing shows on the monitor."

Joy steadied her breathing. Mom was sick? "What about cardiac enzymes?"

"Not even close to elevated, but for once she allowed your cousin, Dawn, to talk her into coming. For Molly to agree to that, the pain must have been bad."

Mom took on life like a warrior and no one bested her. The thought of her suffering in a hospital bed sank Joy into her chair.

"Molly hasn't lost any weight since you left," Zack said.

"Since I left? I've visited several times, believe it or not." She closed her eyes and willed her voice to soften. Time to be a doctor. "What are her numbers?"

As he read them off to her, Joy memorized them while she made mental notes about what to pack, wondering what Mom's reaction would be when she arrived.

Joy preferred to call her mother constitutionally substantial. Others weren't so kind, and so Joy's proud, beautiful mother had gradually begun to withdraw from life after their first major adult conflict last year. That conflict created a wall that separated them emotionally when Joy left Juliet after Zack broke off the engagement. How tempting to blame the fiasco of these past months on Zack, but that wouldn't be fair.

"Think you can come?" Zack asked. "Her animals need care. I'll be able to pinch hit, but I'm working so many hours—"

"Of course I'll be there." Mom's rescued strays had become her preferred companions: cats, the occasional batch of discarded puppies, a goat, a miniature horse, and no telling what else by now.

It had once been Mom's dream to help Joy establish a small family practice in Juliet. Instead, Molly established her own care center for abandoned animals.

"The electric company turned off her power," Zack said.

Oh, just great. "That's crazy. Why would they—"

"Your cousin Dawn just told me in the hallway a few minutes ago that Molly lost her job."

"Mom? Why didn't she say anything to me?"

"Seriously? You think your mother's going to step down from that pedestal you placed her on all your life?"

"Dawn usually keeps me informed. Why didn't she—"

"Because Molly threatened to dump her next batch of abandoned puppies or kittens on Dawn's front porch if she told you anything."

Joy recalled her last visit with Mom a couple of months ago. Their sharp words and thorny silences had been like navigating through a field of cactus. Molly wasn't the only one to blame for their awkwardness when they were together. Joy contributed.

Poor Mom. How she must have struggled to keep up a strong front. Why would Dusseldorf Vineyards let her go?

"Dusseldorf went under," Zack said, correctly guessing Joy's thoughts.

Joy groaned.

"So Molly isn't working and didn't have the money to pay the electric bill," Zack said. "Dawn didn't know about it soon enough to sneak a payment."

Joy shook her head. Her mother would take in any stray

animal that came her way, but take a single dollar from family? Molly Gilbert's besetting sin was pride.

"How long has she been out of a job?" Joy asked.

"The vineyard had a major layoff last month, when the late freeze killed all the new Vignoles shoots. Molly worked at a reduced income since the company began having financial difficulties last November. They hired a bad accountant."

"Dawn told you this?"

"Nope. I heard old man Dusseldorf, himself, talking about it at the bank. Two weeks ago Molly started using a generator for power in her house."

"Well, thank the Lord that it's May and not August, or she'd be roasted to a burnt nub with no AC. So you think the chest pain's from stress."

"I do, but I won't take any chances with our Molly."

Joy loved the way that sounded. How she'd missed their old rhythms of conversation. If she could overlook the fact that this time they were talking about Mom, and Joy was freaking, she could almost convince herself she and Zack could still read one another's thoughts. She trusted Zack to do whatever was necessary to take care of Mom.

"Just a warning," Zack said. "She told me to tell you not to come, but—"

"It's time I used some vacation days."

"I might have to hogtie her to a hospital bed. She's worried about her animals, but I promised I'd check on them after my shift is over."

Tears smarted Joy's eyes. "Oh, Zack," she whispered. "Of course you'd do that." How she'd missed his natural kindness and giving spirit. What a contrast to the man who had just marched out of her office. But then, Zack had broken their engagement without an explanation.

"Another warning," Zack said, "you know that chicken

house she has on the property? She's begun bricking it by hand."

"I don't believe it."

He chuckled. "She has the whole town mystified. The latest word is it's for her animals."

"A brick cat house?" Mom was, for sure, a source of entertainment for Juliet.

"She's out of power and she goes and does something like that." Admiration filtered through his voice. He'd always had a soft spot for Mom. "She told me she's using brick she collected from the old high school, hauling it in that old pickup truck of your grandpa's that doesn't run half the time."

Joy sighed. "She's always had some sort of reputation in town. Since it's no longer obvious she's a single mother I suppose she had to find some other way to shock the citizens."

"She keeps life in Juliet interesting."

"Any idea how much she owes the electric company?" Joy asked.

"No, but Wilma Rush threatened to make her pay the five hundred for a set-up fee even if she does pay her bill."

"Wilma's never forgiven Mom for butting heads with her when they were both on the town council," Joy said. "Bless her heart, the woman's got little enough to do with her time, she might as well make life difficult for the rest of us."

Zack chuckled. "And right now you're considering ways to make life difficult for Wilma."

Joy grimaced. When had she lost her forgiving spirit?

"I'm glad you're coming," Zack said.

Joy closed her eyes, conflicted. "Why?"

His silence told her he hadn't expected that question. "You're needed here."

"That wasn't the impression I received when I left Juliet. Mom was fine, though furious I was leaving and ruining her plans for me; you had already broken our engagement and moved on." Might as well trot out that ol' elephant into the room while she was feeling talkative.

"I didn't go anywhere, Joy. I stayed right here."

"Oh, you left, all right." She said the words softly, then swallowed. It wasn't wise to start an argument with the physician in charge of her mother's care.

"Anyway," she said, before Zack could reply, "I'll do whatever it takes to get Friday off. Tomorrow's my regular day off. Tonight will be a late one, but I'll get there." What would Weston say when she told him she'd be gone a few days? Particularly since he would no doubt realize she was leaving in response to Zack's call.

"Your cousin Dawn said you could stay at her house," Zack said.

"I think I'll risk Mom's menagerie. They'll need feeding, and Dawn's five kids in a four bedroom house is crowded enough already."

"You're coming…alone?"

The question surprised Joy. "Of course. Who do you think I'd bring with me?"

There was a long hesitation. "I thought…perhaps Weston."

She closed her eyes and took a quiet, deep breath. She could still read every inflection in his voice. "My employer doesn't make a habit of traveling on personal business with those in his employ." She couldn't prevent the sudden coolness that settled in her voice. "And I haven't changed as much as you seem to believe. I'll be there sometime tonight." Hopefully long after Zack went home. "Right now I have patients to see and charts to complete." After a quick goodbye she disconnected.

Her first concern was Mom, the consummate control freak, at least about her own life. Now she was out of work, in the hospital and couldn't pay her bills.

And Zack. In all these months since their breakup, he'd never attempted to contact her. Now she thought she might know why. Could he truly believe she'd taken this job with Weston for reasons other than financial need?

Chapter 3

Zack replaced the receiver with slow deliberation. Nurses and techs chattered around him as more patients were being brought back—the sounds were commonplace now that he practically lived here. It was time to get out, keep in touch with people who worked outside the hospital, particularly the Gilbert clan. Perhaps if he'd spoken more often with Dawn, the self-ascribed Gilbert family information center, he could have warned Joy before Molly's collapse.

Joy. He smiled. She wasn't "with" Weston Cline. She'd called the man—the devious manipulator who'd snatched her away from Juliet—her employer. Nothing more.

He needed to jump back into action and give a few more orders, but he couldn't wipe the smile from his face, and for this moment, he couldn't focus.

He wasn't going to over-analyze how he felt about this surprise information. He didn't need to. He knew exactly how he felt. *Stupid.* And he didn't care about that, either, because he also felt like dancing a jig across the room.

Since the only entertainment patients expected in this hospital was a private television, he settled for a soft chuckle as he did a quick-step instead of a two-step to Molly Gilbert's treatment cubicle.

Joy's mother lay quiet for once, her long lashes heavy against her pale skin, her dark, wavy hair mussed across the pillow. Zack sank onto the chair beside the bed and rested his hand on Molly's.

His older patients had told him she'd once been one of the most beautiful women in the county. She'd had an hourglass figure, a quick laugh, and gentle kindness in her gaze. Her dream was to become a physician, and she refused all invitations to dinner, movies, chances to get to know the most eligible men in town more personally.

Molly returned home pregnant two months after leaving for University of Missouri, Columbia. She never attempted to defend herself or her reputation.

The community, the Gilbert family, everyone she knew was stunned, and possibly more outraged than if she'd been an ordinary person. Like Joy, there was nothing ordinary about Molly. According to Juliet grapevine, Molly went into seclusion and deep depression while she carried her baby to term, but after Joy was born Molly focused all the energy she would have placed into med school on her much-loved daughter.

Zack studied the determined curve of the woman's lips as she lay sleeping. Joy was going to be the hometown family doc Molly didn't get the chance to become. For years they made plans and dreamed.

How did one person manage to interrupt the rosy life Molly and Joy had planned? How had he managed to destroy Zack's and Joy's dreams, as well, for the wedding, for the cottage above the Missouri River?

Weston's family money had built the research wing that connected the hospital with the small medical school, but until early last year Weston had left the research to others. Zack had no doubt that one introduction to Joy had set the stage for change. Joy's beauty transcended even that of her mother's. Had Weston expected to woo her with his limitless finances?

My fault.

Though Weston didn't know Joy well enough to know the lure of wealth would never affect her, Zack had known. He should never have doubted himself. Should never have listened to Weston Cline. Had he allowed his jealousy, and Weston's goading, to destroy his dreams with Joy?

"Are you that unhappy to see me, or did you just talk to my daughter on the phone?"

Zack snapped from his reverie as he met Molly's wide-open gaze and allowed her smooth alto voice to float through the room.

"Brace yourself, Molly. She's coming."

The deep brown eyes widened. "Please don't tell me she's dragging that hideous man with her."

Zack resisted a grin as he checked the monitor and blood pressure. Rock solid. "Does she ever bring her employer with her when she visits?"

Molly adjusted herself on the bed so she could see the monitor numbers. "No, but she's brought his daughter on occasion."

Zack felt a quick drop on his elation meter. "His daughter?"

"Kid's a doll. Nothing like her father. In fact, I have trouble believing Tressa's connected to the same gene pool."

"Joy is close to Weston Cline's daughter?"

"Why should you care?" Of course Molly could read his mind. He had an expressive face and couldn't do a thing about it. "I told you last year to confront Weston and tell him to stay away from Joy after hours. You blew it."

Zack felt like a child being scolded, and he felt a frisson of compassion for Joy. Prickly was an understatement when it came to describing Molly Gilbert.

"My numbers are fine," Molly said, reaching for the blood pressure cuff on her arm. "Time for me to go home."

"No it isn't. I want to do an echo."

"I can have that done outpatient. If you'll recall, I don't have insurance right now."

"You know you don't have to—"

"I'm leaving now." Molly unhooked herself from the monitor and walked around the bed, the edges of her hospital gown flapping behind her. "If you don't want me walking out like this, you'll go check on another patient so I can get dressed."

Zack wisely stepped out and closed the door behind him. He had an AMA form to prepare. Joy wouldn't like this at all.

~

When Joy entered Weston's office, Tressa was plopping into the chair behind her father's desk as she simultaneously opened an American literature textbook. The guilty grin on her face made it obvious that she knew she'd been caught in the effort to conceal her dubious activities.

At fifteen years of age, Tressa was almost a mirror image of her mother, but with more open, trusting eyes, a wider smile and an extra dimple in her cheek... and a few small blemishes on her face. It was the smile and friendliness that drew people to Tressa and helped them overlook her penchant toward an occasional gloomy, cynical outlook on life—the typical angst of a creative teenager with the history of loss she'd suffered.

"You're not supposed to eavesdrop." Joy sank into one of the dark brown chairs in front of the desk. As the butter-soft leather hugged her body, her stomach growled. Loudly.

They looked at each other, and Joy saw the humor in Tressa's beguiling blue eyes—the only hint that she was Weston Cline's daughter.

Tressa pulled a sandwich from the side pocket of her backpack and slid it across the desk. Joy wanted to snatch off the wrapper and swallow the sandwich whole, whatever strange ingredients might have been used to concoct it—with Tressa's creative mind, one never knew what to expect. The girl had once used caviar and almond butter in a meatloaf recipe and failed to reveal that information until Joy was reaching for her second slice. Joy had less exotic tastes.

"Where's yours?" Joy asked.

"I ate it. I made this one for you. Every Wednesday, when we're supposed to be spending time together, you work late because you're behind as usual, and then you're starving, and Dad uses that as an excuse to take us out to some expensive restaurant for dinner so he can sit close to you."

As Joy unwrapped the sandwich—it appeared to be organic cheese and tofu with alfalfa sprouts on gluten free bread—she felt a wave of sadness. She wasn't the one who should be spending time with Tressa, but the girl needed someone to talk to, and she couldn't communicate with Weston.

Soon after Joy joined the father-daughter evenings and weekends, Weston had left the visiting to Joy, as if Tressa carried a disease he didn't want to catch.

In an effort to effect a better communication between father and daughter—and prevent Weston from becoming a hermit in his home office—Joy had begun to invite them to have their visits at her house. Weston tried to take part in their conversations. Joy could see his frustration when he failed to connect with his daughter. Then his cell phone would chime, and he'd end up spending the remainder of his evening on a conference call, or his frustration with his failure to communicate with Tressa would send him fleeing to Joy's exercise room to hone his toned physique while catching up on the latest news in the world of economics.

Long ago, Tressa had stopped sharing important things with her father because he tended to lecture. On visitation weekends, Tressa spent the majority of her time alone with Joy, who had learned that if she wanted to avoid Weston all she had to do was mention Tressa would be there. She now preferred the daughter's company to the father's.

Joy treasured those moments with her lively, lovable friend. They discussed everything from the state of the English language, to movies, to the silliness of other girls Tressa's age.

As Joy sat in luxurious leather she ate quickly, like a starving woman, as Tressa had clearly suspected.

"I've been learning in our nutrition class at school about compensatory weight gain," Tressa said. "If you don't want to turn out like Molly, you should plan ahead of time for little meals throughout the day that you can grab between patients."

"Are you saying I'm fat?" Joy asked with a half-full mouth.

"No, but someday you will be if you don't learn to eat right."

"I know I should."

"If you and Dad got married and I lived with you, I could pack these sandwiches for you every day, and I'd use the gluten free bread and grapeseed oil mayonnaise and organic pickles."

"Tressa, if I lived in the same house as you, I'm sure I would become a bean sprout." This wasn't the first time the dear child had suggested a change of address for both of them, and Joy needed to steer the conversation away from that sad subject.

"I'm not that bad," Tressa said.

"I'd also be worried all the time that you were eavesdropping on my...um...spirited discussions with your father," Joy said, "like the one you just heard."

Tressa closed the textbook and slumped back into her chair. "Those aren't discussions, those are fights. I heard enough of them between Mom and Dad. At least you don't shout like Mom does."

"You shouldn't be eavesdropping at all."

"How am I going to be mistress of my own world when I don't know what's going on with the forces that shape it?"

"Miss Tress, you *are* of your own world."

Tressa stuck her tongue out.

As Joy finished her sandwich she regarded Tressa with narrowed eyes. "You're looking a little pale. I hope our argument didn't freak you out too badly."

The lovely lines of the girl's face turned downward. "You dumped him."

Joy couldn't think of any words to soften the blow, but surely Tressa had realized for some time that there could be no lasting relationships for her father unless he sought help.

"Be careful, Joy."

"Meaning?"

"What if he fires you?"

Joy had thought of that, of course. "Legally, he can't fire me for refusing to have a relationship with him."

Tressa sighed and leaned forward, arms crossing her stomach. She obviously had something else on her mind.

"Out with it," Joy said.

Tressa patted her belly, grinning suddenly—though for some reason, the grin didn't fit her face. "I got it. Finally. Cramps and all. You never warned me about the pain."

Joy shot a fist in the air. "Yes!" She knew Tressa had begun to worry if there was something wrong with her when all her friends had begun their menses years ago. "Does Sylvia know?"

Tressa's smile vanished. "When would I have a chance to tell her? And why would she care?"

"Oh, believe me, she'll be thrilled. Maybe the three of us can have a girls' day out, do some mani-pedis, maybe facials."

Tressa shrugged. "I don't think Mom's up to it."

Joy winced. "How are things with Porter?"

"Nothing's changed. He comes over almost every night. I bet he's there now." She closed her eyes. "Probably won't leave until after breakfast."

Ah. That was the subject uppermost in Tressa's mind.

Weston's ex, Sylvia, was blond, fit, well-endowed. She had friendly green eyes and she could be a lot of fun when she wasn't allowing bitterness and desperation to color her world and her daughter's. She'd never been able to endure being without a man, and Sylvia's pain flowed from the same fountain as Weston's—their son's death.

The woman's unfortunate choice of male company was a source of deep concern for Tressa, and so she was given carte blanche access to Joy's home at any time, with her own key, unbeknownst to her parents.

Before Joy could finish the sandwich, she heard the muted buzz of the phone in her office next door. "I'd better get back to work."

"When are you going to Juliet?" Tressa asked.

Joy put her sandwich wrapper down. "You heard that, too?"

"When do you leave?"

"Tonight."

"Let me go with you."

Weston's phone buzzed less than a foot from Tressa's right elbow and she jerked.

"Dr. Gilbert?" Lindsey's voice came through the speaker.

Joy nodded to Tressa, who pressed the speaker button.

"I'm here," Joy said.

"Mr. Cline says you need to get your—"

"Thanks, I can imagine what Mr. Cline says." Just great. Now he was issuing orders via the new-hire. "My four o'clock appointment needs blood work. If that isn't done yet, would you have Lynn go ahead with it? I also need a bone density." Joy hit the button and nodded to Tressa. "Go say hi to your father, Miss Tress, if he's still in the building. Then take a brisk walk. That'll help with the cramps."

"It's raining."

"Use one of the treadmills in the exercise room, but don't overdo it."

"And your trip?"

"You have two days of school left. I don't want to contribute to the delinquency of a minor."

With a long, dramatic sigh, Tressa relinquished her chair, relinquished her claim on the room, and resisted, with obvious reluctance, the urge to linger and talk.

"You have the key to my house, Tressa. Even if I'm not in town, it's not a long walk from your home to mine. But don't walk through the woods. There are worse things than poison ivy in that area."

Tressa's slender shoulders had just the right slump to portray utter dejection. But there was a dimple in her cheek as she cut a look of mischief at Joy before closing the door.

Joy glanced at the phone and considered calling Dawn for information about Mom, but she didn't want to set her cousin up for a brood of unwanted puppies to add to her brood of children. Mom followed through on her threats.

The Gilbert relatives were a boisterous clan who took interest in one another's lives, particularly the juicy details. Joy had never understood this tendency. She battled enough difficult details in her own life, and she didn't often share them. Her closest adult friend, Myra Maxwell, lived in Tiffany Springs, and though they met for lunch on weekends when they could fit it into their schedules, Myra had her own psychiatric practice to build.

Joy knew she shouldn't place the burden of reciprocal friendship on a fifteen-year-old girl starving for adult interaction, but the sassy kid was pretty much Joy's best friend in Corrigan. How sad was that? For both of them.

She would call Myra later about Sarah Miller, but she wouldn't call family until she reached Juliet and read the emotional climate for herself.

How she dreaded the coming storms.

Chapter 4

Tressa stuffed a zip bag of granola into her backpack. Tears dripped down her face. She'd been warned about fluctuating hormones, but this was crazy. Not that she didn't have good reason to cry.

Tonight, when Dad dropped her off after dinner, she'd seen Porter's car still in the driveway. Dad didn't even ask about it, or remark on the fact that there were no lights on in the house. She refused to sleep in the same house as that creepy man for another night.

Sniffing, she folded her favorite clothes and placed them into the backpack Joy had given her for her birthday eight months ago—soon after they met. It was a real backpack, big enough to carry supplies for a week in the wilderness.

She focused on memories of the week they'd tested the pack on Christmas holiday in Death Valley, when she discovered that she had a lot to learn about backpacking, camping and making it in the wild. And bugs that bit.

That was the first time she'd ever roughed it, but she'd go with Joy the next time she asked.

It was also the first time she'd made a best friend. Girls her own age just didn't get her. Not her real self. People hung out with her because Dad was rich. Joy was the one who knew and understood Tressa deep down where it counted.

The friendship was forged and honed in Death Valley when their clothes began to stink after a week in the wilderness without running water. Joy was the only person in the world who knew how bad Tressa could smell and how scared she was of snakes. And she'd never told a soul.

The backpack weighed probably thirty pounds by the time Tressa settled it over her shoulders and buckled the front clasps. She stepped to her mother's bedroom door and listened. All she heard was Porter snoring.

Later, after Mom was deeply asleep, Porter would wake up, wander through the house to the kitchen for food, and then he'd wander to Tressa's door, which Mom still didn't think needed a lock.

He just wanted to talk, while his washed-out brown eyes would never meet Tressa's, but would take in every other part of her body.

Tressa cringed as she thought about him. But if he left, then Mom would be lonely again, and she'd start to interfere in Tressa's life again, start depending more heavily on Tressa, or stay out late at night. The next man she picked up might be worse.

Tressa grabbed an apple and a bunch of grapes from the kitchen counter on her way out the back door. She couldn't always count on finding nourishment at Joy's house or at Dad's. Dad didn't know what a skillet looked like, and Joy used too many prepackaged foods to save time because she worked too many hours at the clinic.

After locking the door behind her, Tressa slid the key into the front pocket of her jeans with the key to Joy's house and stepped into the nighttime shadows.

Another bout of tears blurred Tressa's vision, and she

stumbled over uneven ground. Today's fight between Dad and Joy replayed through her mind. Dad might not have started the fight if last Sunday hadn't been Keegan's eighteenth birthday.

Four years ago, the counselor had warned Mom and Tressa about the grief that could attack them far into the future. Too bad Dad hadn't attended those sessions. Maybe then he'd realize he shouldn't be taking his pain out on everybody around him.

After Keegan died, Tressa had to stay with Grandmother Cline for a few days—not comfortable at the best of times. Grandmother loved her immaculate house more than she loved people, and Tressa tracked too much mud inside. She also talked too much, and she'd broken an expensive vase one day…not good. If it was possible for someone to kill another person with coldness, Grandmother Cline could do it.

While at her grandmother's house, Tressa began to understand her father better. He was the kind of person she'd have expected to emerge from the Cline family. Dad wanted to be able to show love, she could see it sometimes when he looked at her, or at Joy. He was great at business transactions because he knew how to play on the emotions of others, but he didn't allow himself to experience those emotions. Not that he was a sociopath or anything. He just seemed afraid to feel since Keegan's death.

A car cruised by the house as Tressa stepped past the kitchen window. She glanced into the kitchen. Porter stood there with his head stuck in the refrigerator.

Before crossing the dark street in front of the house, Tressa glanced over her shoulder toward her room. She hadn't bothered to make it look like someone was in the bed. Porter might check on her, but Mom wouldn't. When he discovered the bed empty, what was he going to do? Go wake Mom up and tell her? And what would he say when she asked him what he was doing in her daughter's bedroom?

The night wind rustled leaves high in the trees as Tressa crossed the street. She wouldn't use her flashlight until she reached the woods Joy had told her not to enter. This kind of darkness was her friend.

Tressa dreaded to think about what life would have been like if Dad hadn't hired Joy. Like Mom was doing, he'd taken a few women out before he met Joy, but even though he took whatever they offered, he didn't care for them. It was as if he was trying to quench his thirst with seawater.

Soon after Joy moved to Corrigan and met Tressa, she'd invited Mom and Tressa out to lunch. To Tressa's surprise, Mom accepted.

They went to a tearoom on the Plaza in downtown Kansas City. Mom dressed in her prettiest amethyst silk dress that made her short blonde hair glow, and she wore her most expensive pearl necklace and earrings.

Joy walked into the tearoom in her scrubs, straight from the clinic. Her shiny, dark brown hair was pulled into a smooth knot at the back of her head, the way she wore it at work—that was before Dad began to insist on more formal attire in the clinic.

Tressa could tell that Mom was relieved that she looked better than "the competition." Those were the words Tressa had overheard Mom tell a friend over the phone that Saturday before leaving for the lunch. Mom would never admit it, but something inside her couldn't let Dad go.

The tearoom that day had the best food ever. That was when Tressa decided to teach herself how to cook like that chef so she could remember the day: the warm shallot and asparagus salad with chopped Brazil nuts, the prosciutto and cheese custard, the little dishes of dessert bites: tiny servings of chocolate coconut cheesecake, warm mocha brownie, strawberry-pomegranate sorbet. The memory made her mouth water.

While Tressa focused on the food that day, Mom and Joy talked about everything except Dad. They smiled and laughed together, as if they might be discovering they could be friends...if things were different. Tressa was finishing her last bite of custard when Joy put her fork down and leaned forward.

"You're an amazing mother," she told Mom. "Tressa is a delight."

For a moment, Mom chewed silently on her miniature orange spice muffin, as if weighing Joy's words, judging them for any insincerity.

She took a sip of her rooibus tea, looked up and held Joy's gaze. "Thank you, but she's the mature one. She's been through a lot, and she's strong."

This admission surprised Tressa. She didn't want to be the strong one.

"No one can be constantly strong when they suffer so much loss in such a short time." Joy's hand reached halfway across the table, as if she would touch Mom's hand, but she drew it back.

"He told you about Keegan?" Mom never called Dad by name, only by pronouns, as if he was the only man in the world. Or maybe because she hated him so much she had to keep him at a distance. Or both.

Joy nodded. "He mentioned your son once, and he didn't give details. I'm sorry. You don't need to be reminded about—"

"Actually, I do," Mom said. "My kids were my reason for living."

Tressa paused with a spoonful of sorbet. *Were*?

"So few people are comfortable with the subject of Keegan, and talking about him makes me feel as if he's alive for a little while."

Tressa stared up at her mom. Did she forget she had a daughter?

"Then tell me all about him," Joy said.

So Tressa sipped her spiced decaf latte on that fun-weird Saturday afternoon while she learned about her brother along with Joy. She learned about how Keegan had loved to sing to Tressa when she was a baby, and how he'd always wanted a puppy but didn't sulk when he didn't get one.

With a glance at Tressa, Mom leaned across the table, holding Joy's gaze. "I was three months along with Keegan when his father married me. You'll surely hear all this from someone, so you might as well hear it from me."

Joy didn't look surprised, she just listened and nodded while Mom talked.

"The Clines offered to hire a nanny and send me to college with Tressa's father. I refused. I wanted to stay home with my baby. It's what I did best."

"That's obvious," Joy said.

"Keegan was almost fifteen when he died." Mom paused and took a quiet, deep breath. "Cocaine. It stopped his heart. We never even knew he was using."

"He wasn't really a user." Tressa spoke the words aloud in the darkness of the woods, startling something that skittered away with a crackling of old leaves. Keegan had gotten the drugs from a guy at school, who promised they would keep him alert while he studied for finals. He was super smart in an accelerated program in school and worked hard to stay there. But Mom and Dad had never listened to Tressa.

Keegan's death had drawn lines around Mom's eyes and mouth. All the time Mom talked that day last year, Joy listened with compassion and interest, asking questions that encouraged more talking. Afterward they developed a friendship.

Tressa stepped from the darkness of the woods, easily

scaled the fence—what good was a gated community if the fence couldn't keep people out?—and stepped into the glow of the security light at the end of the cul-de-sac. She stopped and stared at the pearl white Mercedes in Joy's driveway. Why was Dad here?

After overhearing their fight today, and feeling the tension between them at dinner, she was pretty sure this wasn't a romantic meeting.

Tressa reached into her pocket for the key to Joy's front door. She didn't hear anything when she stepped inside the entry hall, but before she could call out to tell Joy she was here, words flew at her like shrapnel from an explosion.

"...not only undermined my authority in the clinic in front of my staff, you humiliated a powerful man whose influence could make or break the continued success of the clinic."

"Weston, Bezier asked me to break the law. What was I supposed to do? And I did nothing to humiliate him. What I said to him I said in the privacy of the exam room, whereas he followed me out into the hallway and loudly accused me of sleeping with the boss to get my job. If all I'm here for is to be a punching bag and make drug addicts out of everyone with a pain problem, then I'm in the wrong place."

There was silence. Dad didn't reply. Why didn't he say something?

Tressa slunk back out of the house and locked the door behind her, hugging her arms against her chest and staring down the street, hearing the echo of their words. Something horrible was going to happen soon.

Chapter 5

Joy tried to ignore Weston's intimidating presence in her bedroom as she folded her softest pair of jeans and laid them in her suitcase. They were the ones Mom had given her three years ago for Christmas.

Mom always provided the best she could afford for her daughter. She'd sacrificed everything for Joy, doing a man's work at the vineyard for many years. She'd had so many night classes that by the time Joy entered medical school, Mom lacked just a few credits to become a certified medical assistant—one who would likely know as much about medicine as any physician she could work for. She'd accomplished all this while saving money to help Joy through med school. Joy had earned scholarships for college.

Was it any wonder she'd grown up in awe of Molly Gilbert?

Joy leaned hard against her suitcase, annoyed that Weston had invaded her bedroom—as if he had free run of the house because his clinic account had made the down payment. She zipped the case before it could fly open and redistribute all her carefully folded clothes. She would have him paid in full next month.

"I thought you were going for an overnight stay, not an

extended vacation." Weston gestured to the bulging sides of the soft-sided case.

"What I said was that since tomorrow's my day off, the staff won't have too much schedule to rearrange. Just Friday, hopefully." Trust Weston to hear the words he wanted to hear.

"'Hopefully'?"

Her hands clenched. "I have to get things squared away at home, and I don't know how long it'll take. Sorry for the short notice, but the staff is handling it."

"Home?"

She frowned at him.

"You're saying Juliet is still your home."

"It's my hometown, yes. As in family. Mother. Grandparents, aunt, uncles, cousins."

"Zachary Travis." His voice held a challenge, and his eyes glittered.

She picked up her e-reader and slid it into her purse. Weston stepped to her side, reached out, caressed her chin.

She withdrew and continued packing. A few minutes ago he'd been castigating her for her supposed ill manners today. Now he hoped to seduce her? He had that much regard for the power of his charms?

He left the room and she grabbed another travel bag. He'd be back. Weston Cline never gave up that easily.

Last year she'd been so much more naïve. What woman wouldn't be tempted to have the pain of a recent breakup assuaged by the attention of a dynamic man like Weston Cline? He'd lavished attention on her, shown admiration for her as a woman and a physician since the first day they'd met.

With a shudder, she recalled the few kisses, the caresses he'd attempted to give her a few weeks after she arrived here. Some men had charisma, some had physical advantage. Weston had both. After Zack, however, mere physical attraction—even the magnetism that Weston exuded—wasn't enough.

From the time Joy was twelve, Mom had drilled into her head how vital it was not to allow oneself to be trapped by physical attraction. As an unwed mother, Mom knew what she was talking about. Her whole future changed with one bad choice.

As expected, to Joy's distress, barely five minutes after Weston walked out his shadow fell across the room again. There was a heavy sigh, and Joy caught a whiff of the atypical but disturbing aroma of an intoxicant on his breath—not the mild, sweet aroma of wine or port from the Düsseldorf cellars, but the reek of hard liquor, which she'd seen him drink two or three times since she'd known him.

She turned and saw him lurking in the doorway, his broad shoulders drooping, gaze lowered. "Joy, I'm sorry. We shouldn't fight."

He needed to leave. Now. Why had she allowed him to cosign for the mortgage on this house? She'd never wanted a place this size, anyway. His name on the papers gave him the idea that he had a right to every room at any time, though seldom had he invaded it as thoroughly as he was tonight.

"This is such a bad time for you to leave. If you would delay the trip for two more weeks the schedule won't be so—"

"The schedule will be just as full. This isn't the kind of trip that can wait two weeks." She stepped into her dressing room to pack her cosmetics case.

Amazingly, he followed her there, watching in silence as she accumulated the few containers of makeup she used daily. If she'd followed Myra's advice and kept a travel case packed at all times, she'd be out of here by now.

Weston picked up a small bottle of shampoo. "Do you know one of the things I liked about you when we first met?" His voice and his alcohol breath seemed to press in on her from every side, as did his image in the surrounding mirrors, lit well from above and below.

She looked up at him and saw the softening blue of his eyes. Not the stiletto silver of irritation, but the tender side of him that he seemed able to turn on and off at will. She would prefer the irritation right now.

He spread his hands to his sides. "I loved your compassion. And your passion. It reminded me so much of my own ideals years ago." He sank onto her dressing stool. His presence minimized the size of the room.

His movements were languid, his speech slow and precise. Not slurred, thank goodness. He hadn't reached that point yet.

"Why do you resent me for those same qualities now?" she asked.

He studied the shampoo bottle as if attempting to draw an answer from it. "You pulled away. I can't seem to reach you, and my natural response is to do battle. It's why you haven't seen me at my best these past weeks."

She hid her surprise at this show of honesty—though she'd been pulling away for months, not just weeks. Had he only begun to realize how little they had in common?

"Tell me what it is I've done," he said, leaning closer. "I thought we were…I thought this was going somewhere between us. The very first time we met, I knew, beyond doubt, that there was a promise of something powerful between us, which is why I've been so patient."

"I was engaged when we met, Weston."

"I decided to establish the clinic that first day. For you."

"Not a logical decision," she said.

"Making you the inspiration for the clinic? Perfectly logical. I realized that, with your bedside manner, brilliance and compassion, you were bound for greatness. I wanted to be the one to launch your career. Admit the inspiration worked for the clinic."

"The promise of narcotics worked for the clinic." She recalled their first meeting, when he'd taken her hand and stared deeply into her eyes. When his thumb grazed the diamond ring on her finger, instead of backing off, he'd appeared fascinated.

"You realize, don't you, how much I've invested in you?" he asked.

"You invested in the clinic. You just said so. And it's up and running."

"Then forget the clinic for a moment. Forget my financial outlay. Why are you abandoning me?"

"Are you saying that my job came with strings attached? Any connection you or I might have imagined didn't develop."

His eyes narrowed. As if she'd just challenged him to prove her wrong, his gaze touched her face, then slowly studied the length of her modestly clothed body with such deliberation she cringed. He took her by the shoulders, and when she tried to resist, his fingers dug in. He turned her to face the dressing mirror as he stood behind her.

"This is who I saw when Dr. Christopher Payson first introduced us. Look at yourself, Joy Gilbert." His voice caressed her. "You were the most beautiful woman I'd ever seen, and I'd already heard about you from Dr. Payson. How could I not have been captivated by the dark depths of your eyes?" He touched her hair, which fell past her shoulders. "What man wouldn't want to tangle his fingers in this softness?"

She closed her eyes at his ridiculous purple prose. He sounded as if he was writing ad copy to sell her to the public. One inappropriate touch, and he would lose the chance at any future children.

He slid his fingers down the side of her face, and she had to suppress a shudder. The only emotion she could feel for him was pity. She stepped away from him and slid her cosmetics bag into her smaller overnight case

"Joy." With longing in his gaze, he put his arms around her. His lips began to lower to hers.

"Stop!" She broke from his embrace and swung away. "When I return, I'm putting this house up for sale. I'll rent an apartment I can afford, and our relationship needs to be strictly professional."

As if slashed away by a scalpel, his languorous expression disappeared to reveal, for a half second, the suffering man beneath.

"I've given plenty of notice for the staff to reschedule," she said more gently. "Dr. Hearst has several openings." She strapped the overnight case onto her larger suitcase, sure she'd missed something, but she couldn't focus.

"Your patients want you, not Hearst." The ice in his veins had apparently frozen him again. He wavered as he angled toward the bedroom door.

She watched him disappear down the hallway, praying he didn't return to his bottle. Thank goodness he'd taken Tressa home.

Sometimes she couldn't help comparing him to Sarah Miller. So many unhappy people in the world appeared to be clinging to life for lack of a better option. They found escape any way they could.

Some people mellowed with intoxication. Some used alcohol as a key to unlock a gate around a psyche that needed to remain permanently incarcerated. Joy intended to escape before the gate swung wide tonight. The last time Weston brought a bottle of liquor to her house, he had spent the night in emotional turmoil, either picking fights with her, or berating himself for his own words, and insisting that she stay up with him. It was during these rare times of suspended inhibitions that he'd spoken of Keegan, and of his own upbringing—tools of construction on the man he had become.

Myra had asked Joy during one of their weekend lunches—which Joy called her mini-sessions with her shrink—why she didn't give notice and leave Corrigan. But if she did, what would become of her patients? Of Tressa? The girl needed at least one stable adult in her life, even if it wasn't a relative.

"But at what cost?" That question, voiced by Myra months ago, had been lodged in Joy's mind.

She hefted the suitcase from the bed and placed it on the thickly carpeted floor. Voices reached her from a distant room in the house as she extended the telescoping handle of the case and rolled it from her bedroom and down the hallway. Her steps slowed as she neared the media room, where Weston sat on the sofa nursing an oversized glass of Dewar's. She saw the bottle on the wet bar. He was watching a DVD of It's a Wonderful Life on the plasma screen.

Joy braced for a renewed confrontation, but as she walked past the doorway he continued to stare at the screen, as if trying to steep himself in the blurred edges of a distant past.

Something within him had looked to her for relief from the loneliness in his life, and tonight she'd told him in concrete terms that he would have to look elsewhere.

She loaded her suitcases into the back of her Expedition and raised the garage door, then glanced over her shoulder to find him standing in the doorway that connected the garage to the rear vestibule.

She stepped past him into the kitchen for the sandwich Tressa had made for her. It was tofu, goat cheese and gluten free bread.

"Think you're irreplaceable?" The Dewars engulfed her as she pressed past Weston to return to the garage.

She stopped and looked up at him. "No one is."

"You're fired."

She forced herself to keep her voice steady. "Tell me that when you're sober."

He closed his eyes and took a deep breath, then opened them again. "I'm sober enough, Joy."

"We have a contract."

"I took care of that." He turned and stepped toward his car.

Was he leaving? With a shake of her head, she locked the garage door behind her and went to the Expedition, checked to make sure the hatch to the cargo hold was latched, and climbed inside. She had her headlights on and was about to close the overhead when she heard a shout through the window. She glanced in the rear-view mirror and saw Weston standing beside his car, waving a sheaf of papers in his left hand.

He didn't come to her, but stepped into the garage and gestured for her to join him beneath the dim overhead light.

She hesitated. Curiosity won out. She slid from the SUV and left the door open, engine running. He held the papers out to her. She took them, but he retained his grip. She met his gaze.

"I tried, Joy." He sounded accusatory. As if she hadn't. "I know you don't believe it, but I tried to be what you wanted."

"What I want—what I've always wanted—was to be a doctor."

"But you can see why this arrangement isn't working for either of us," he said.

Under the dim light, she looked at the top sheet, and bit the inside of her cheek. These were papers for dissolution of her contract. It was dated today.

"I wasn't drinking when I had this drawn up." Cool control. "Due to insubordination and breach of contract for not giving the required amount of leave notice, you are no longer employed at Cline Medical Clinic." His eyes became pinpoints of iridescent radiance.

She took a breath, lost it. Took another. "What act was that in my dressing room tonight?" She forced her hands to remain at her sides, not caring that her voice carried across the neighborhood. "That attempted seduction? One last ruse to see if you could get me to bed?"

He didn't respond. His eyes remained cold.

"Despicable," she whispered. And stupid. "I'm having a family emergency, and not only don't you have the common decency to give me one day off, you fire me because you can't seduce me. What kind of vile snake does that?" She wanted to punch him in the face with the force of her sudden fury.

"Our business standards are wildly divergent. We both knew this wasn't working." He reached up and touched her cheek.

She slapped him hard, wishing it was his nose, then drew back to try again. Something prevented her, some whisper of warning.

He smiled at her. "You're fired."

Chapter 6

Tressa's nose itched, but she couldn't scratch it. In fact, her whole face itched, and she remembered some leaves brushing across her left cheek when she was walking through the forest. Couldn't be poison ivy. Could it?

She had her right cheek pressed against the scratchy floorboard carpet, and was afraid to do more than blink for fear Joy would hear her.

The only voice Tressa had been able to hear was Joy's when she shouted, and that was enough. The darkness had been triumphant tonight. Judging by the size of the suitcase Joy had hefted into the SUV's cargo hold, it seemed she'd be gone for a while. But then, Joy always packed half the house for any trip.

There was a noise from the front seat. A sniff. The vehicle turned right, then left, then the speed picked up. Another sniff, this time more watery. The SUV swerved sharply to the right then straightened as Joy pulled a tissue from the box on the passenger seat, her hand maybe ten inches from Tressa's nose.

There was a quiet sob, and then a sudden slamming of brakes, shoving Tressa hard against the back of Joy's seat. A horn echoed through the darkness from another vehicle as Joy muttered a soft apology.

Maybe wasn't such a good idea. What was Joy trying to do,

kill herself in a car accident? Maybe it was time to speak up, if for no other reason than that Joy needed a friend right now. And maybe to save both their lives.

Tressa's intention had been to slip away with Joy to Juliet, spend the weekend, or however long it took to get Molly back together, and then return home. This was bold. This was making a statement. Mom and Dad might listen to her when she got back, after showing them she had a mind of her own, and that their fighting and Mom's sleeping around did affect her. She was sick of it.

If Tressa revealed herself now, though, Joy was sure to turn right around and take her back home. Dad wouldn't want her at his house, and she couldn't go back home where Porter wandered around from room to room while Mom slept.

"Myra." Joy's voice startled Tressa. "Home."

Ah. Voice activation on her cell.

It wasn't until the dialing commenced that Tressa realized Joy had her Bluetooth engaged in the car.

Okay, Tressa admitted she was an eavesdropper, but this was personal. She cringed, wishing she could plug her ears.

"Joy?" The velvety smooth voice came through the speaker system. "That you?"

"I need a consult." Joy's voice cracked.

"Honey?" Immediate concern. Like a best friend.

Sometimes Tressa felt a little jealous of the tall, confident woman with the long black hair and skin the color of Tressa's favorite almond torte. Joy probably talked to Myra about things she would share with no one else. The two doctors had known each other for so long, they sometimes seemed to talk a foreign language.

Not that Tressa disliked the woman. She just didn't actively like her.

"I'm no longer employed."

Tressa gasped out loud, but Myra's exclamation of surprise covered it.

"What did you do?"

There was silence except for Joy's quiet crying in the front seat—and the squeal of tires as she took a turn too fast and nearly plopped Tressa onto her face.

"Honey, where are you?" Myra's voice came through more vividly, as if she were standing inside the speaker.

"I'm on my way home."

"Home where?"

"Juliet."

"He kicked you *out* of that overpriced house he practically forced you to buy in the first place? Why, that dirty—"

"He didn't kick me out of my house, Myra, but he may as well have."

Tressa bit down on her finger to keep from crying.

"He fired me."

Tressa's face grew wet, her nose dripped, and she could do nothing about it. This was not the time to reveal herself. Not now, when she had more reason than ever to remain hidden. She wiped the drips on her shirt collar.

"You sure you didn't put this idea into his head? I thought he worshiped you."

The sniffling up front turned to sobs, and Tressa had to hold on tightly as the Expedition took another curve too fast.

Joy was a cautious driver. Except for tonight. Tressa wished she could sit up front invisibly so she could see the road. Sick despair settled over her as she listened to the conversation between Joy and Myra and wished, for once, that she wasn't in a position to eavesdrop. Her father was dirt.

"He thought this through, Myra."

"Oh, I'm sure he did. He thinks everything through, the seduction scene and all."

"He caught me as I was leaving. I had no warning, no chance to contact Tressa and break this to her, and it's too late at night to go by the house and see her."

"Then come stay with me tonight. You can't leave without a word to her. You know how that child adores you. This will break her heart."

Tressa braced herself. *No Joy, don't stay.*

"It's breaking mine," Joy said.

"Get a job nearby, then."

"Can't. There's a non-compete clause in the contract I signed. I'll call Tressa from Juliet tomorrow after she gets out of school. I'll talk to Sylvia. I'll—"

Another squeal of tires. Tressa's butt hit the door.

"You don't need to be driving in this state of mind," Myra said.

"I'll be fine."

"Oh, yeah? And what if you aren't? What's that going to do to Tressa?"

Okay, maybe Myra wasn't so bad.

"I feel as if my world is crumbling. I'm out of a job and I'm returning to face a mother who wouldn't even allow me inside the house the last couple of times I visited. She's removed herself from the world. I have no idea what to expect when I get there."

"Right now, we need to focus on you. Come on, talk to me. Fill me in on the details. We knew Weston wouldn't take no for an answer when it came to you, but if he fired you because you wouldn't be his lover, then that's grounds for a serious lawsuit."

"Not going there."

"You say that now, but you're in shock. You need to keep your options open."

Tressa's face itched and motion sickness crept over her, but she listened and learned. She suddenly knew far more about her father than she'd ever wanted to know.

~

Dried tears caked Joy's face, and the feeling of loss lingered when she entered the city limits of Juliet three hours after leaving Corrigan. Why had she argued with Weston so often? Why couldn't she have shown more compassion when she knew about the sharp edges of his boyhood?

She still didn't understand why a man whose family assets totaled more than a billion dollars was so insistent on making a financial success of one small part of his holdings. Still, she had no right to tell someone else how to manage his wealth just because she would do it differently.

When he'd first decided to promote her as a pain specialist, she'd protested. She wasn't board certified in pain medicine or anesthesiology, she was certified in family medicine. So he'd sent her to every pain specialty seminar he could find in the country, stating he didn't have time for her to complete another residency.

Weston's motto was that appearance was everything.

Mom's motto had always been that appearances could be deceiving. And once again, Mom was right. Weston's clinic would likely thrive without Joy. Her career, however, was back where it was last year, only now she had more debt.

Why hadn't she asked him more questions about the job he offered to her? How was she going to face her mother?

It wasn't until Joy saw the Quick Mart at the main entry to Juliet that she realized her hands gripped the steering wheel so hard that her shoulders ached. She was almost home, and most likely for good this time. She had never felt so bereft in all her life.

Even though her fuel gauge said empty, the warning light hadn't come on yet, so she drove past the convenience store. The lighted sign of the emergency department of the Juliet Medical Center cast its glow over the street head of her.

She pulled close to the sign and parked, staring at the emergency entrance. It was the only way to get into the building this time of night, and if Mom's habits remained as they always had, she'd still be wide awake, fretting over the safety of her animals.

With reluctant movements, Joy pulled herself from the SUV and stretched stiff muscles. There were no other vehicles in the patient parking lot. The small, touristy town of Hermann to the east, and the state's capitol of Jefferson City to the west, drew far more patients than this hospital, since those had the nearest bridges crossing the Missouri River.

Joy inhaled the scent of the river, the moisture mingling with blooms and spice that had always intoxicated her this time of year. She allowed that scent to comfort her. How many times had she stared toward the river from her office window in Corrigan, homesick for the familiar rhythms of Juliet? Now she was here.

A breeze lifted the heavy hair from her neck. She shivered, but instead of reaching into the driver's seat for her jacket, she wrapped her arms around herself and stepped to the perimeter of the glow of security lights.

Home. Even the peeping of frogs seemed to carry a different song here in Juliet. Everything here spoke a different language. Though the medical school and teaching hospital gave the settlement a different ambiance from others along the river, Juliet was still a farming town at heart.

Despite all the times she'd returned to visit over the eight months she'd been away, this night felt different. She breathed the air, gazed up into the multitude of stars in the sky, the full moon, yellow tonight, and she once more claimed them as her own.

She could almost pretend that this past year had never been, but what would she learn from that? Time to take tonight's nasty lesson to heart and move forward.

The breeze grew stiffer, and Joy returned to the SUV, hand extending toward the door to get her coat. Before she reached the handle, she saw a movement in the backseat.

She jumped away with a cry. For a wild moment her mind darted to the notion that Weston had somehow slipped inside the car when she did. But that couldn't be right; she'd glanced at his miniature figure in her rear-view mirror as she drove away. But someone was in the car!

How? She'd never stopped. There'd been no time…

The door swung open. Joy shrieked and stumbled backward.

A blond, bedraggled teenager burst out. Tears and red splotches covered her face. "It's me! It's okay, it's just me."

Joy couldn't catch her breath. "T-Tressa?"

The girl was nearly doubled over, arms crossed over her abdomen. "Just me."

Elation, concern and shock scrambled for precedence. "Tressa!"

"Man, I thought we'd never get here! I've gotta pee so bad. Don't you ever stop for anything? Where's the bathroom?"

Joy stared in disbelief at the sleepy face and mussed hair while Tressa moaned with discomfort.

Tressa looked at the lit hospital emergency entrance. "Got to be something in there. I'll be back and you can yell at me then."

Tressa's cramps eased as she walked inside and found the bathroom sign at the far right corner of the waiting room in the ER. She waved at the reception window, where a woman with gray hair watched.

"Sorry, can't wait," she called over her shoulder. She thought she heard a soft chuckle, and was glad she returned with Joy to this charmed town, where people had class.

Okay, yes, she was in trouble. Bad trouble, probably, but at least Joy wouldn't take the rap from Mom and Dad. No way. She hadn't even known she had a hitchhiker.

After washing her arms and hands in the scrupulously clean bathroom, Tressa scrubbed her face with soap and water to get whatever poison ivy oil might still linger on her skin. She rinsed with cold water and splashed it on her face to battle nausea and cool the heat. Joy didn't need another patient.

But Joy did need to know that she didn't have to face all this alone. It would be okay. Tressa had been praying most of the way here.

With her wet hands, she ran her fingers through her hair, scrunching some of the bedhead out of it. Her face was puffy and itchy. Not that Joy would care what she looked like, but she didn't want to scare anybody.

After explaining to the nice lady at the reception desk that she and Joy were here to see Molly, and that she'd be coming back in a minute, Tressa returned to the SUV. Before she reached it she saw Joy walking to the edge of the lot with her cell phone. She spoke into it, "Sylvia. Home."

"Don't!" Tressa raced across the corner of grass, grabbed the phone from Joy and snapped it shut. "You don't want to do that."

"I have to, honey. I've traveled from Kansas to Missouri with a minor. Your mother needs to know as soon as possible."

"Mom was already asleep when I left, and Porter was wandering the house. Waking her up won't help, and she won't even care that I'm gone as long as I'm with you. Don't you even think about calling Dad."

"Not calling would be worse, honey." Despite everything, Joy's voice and expression held tenderness. "They need to know you're here, and that I'll take you back home tomorrow."

"I'm not going back."

Joy stared at her. "Honey, what's wrong with your face?" She touched Tressa's cheek. "You're hot. Are you feeling sick?"

"Just car sick."

Joy's hand moved to her forehead. "Something else is going on." She squinted. "You're splotchy."

Tell the truth. No way around it. "I broke the rules."

Joy dropped her hand to her side. "You went through the woods."

"I didn't have a choice. It's only a mile to you through the woods. The long way around would've taken me through traffic."

"You could've called me."

Tressa grimaced. "Um, well, I didn't know if you'd left yet." Tell the truth. "Okay, I thought if I talked to you face to face you'd be more likely to let me go with you. Porter's practically living with us, and there's no way I'm staying with Dad after what he did to you tonight."

Joy closed her eyes with a soft sigh. "You heard me talking to Myra."

"I know it all, including what a bad driver you are when you cry. Don't do that again."

"I wish you hadn't overheard—"

"I'm not supposed to see Dad again until next Wednesday night. When he does find out, though, I'll tell him what I did. That way he can't use this against you."

"About my conversation with Myra—"

"Good ol' Dad. He tried to have sex with you, then he fired you."

Joy buried her face in her hands. "You don't need to be dragged into—"

"I'm not a little kid, Joy. Dad's kicked you out, you don't have a job, and you're dependent on family for a place to live right now, because you can bet he'll freeze your bank accounts first thing in the morning, if he hasn't already done it. I heard you tell Myra how much you owe him for paying off the school loans and the down payment on the house. You think he won't take advantage of that?" Tressa watched the expressions travel across Joy's face. The hurt. The need to disagree with Tressa, but the disappointment when she realized she couldn't.

"You know him," Tressa said. "I know Mom's warned you about some of the things he tried with her during the divorce."

Joy's eyes teared up again.

"But you're not losing me," Tressa said. "I'm sticking to you like superglue."

Joy gave her a wan smile. "I'd love to have you, but I have no parental rights. You've got school tomorrow."

"Two days until I'm out for summer? Right, like that's going to mess up my 4.0. If I want to spend my summer vacation with you, Mom will let me. She'll be glad to get me out of the house a while."

Joy's wince marred the refined lines of her face, the dark eyes darker in the shadows, long hair whipping around her neck with the breeze.

Tressa waited, willing Joy not to reopen her cell phone. "Please. You know how I love Molly, and you know she likes me."

"She adores you." Joy was wavering. It bled through her voice.

"At least wait until tomorrow before you decide."

"It's not up to me."

"You're right. It's Molly's house. She should be the one to decide."

"Your *parents* will decide."

"And they're both either asleep or drunk or both, so this can wait."

Joy closed her eyes, nodding. "First thing in the morning."

"Yes!" Tressa flung her arms around Joy. "I'll help you with Molly. I'll—"

"You'll probably be on your way back home tomorrow, so don't start making any plans." But Joy returned the hug, holding her close for an extra few seconds. "Now I need to go find Mom's room in the hospital."

"Let me go first. She likes me better." The words were out before Tressa could edit them, and it was her turn to wince. "Sorry, I didn't mean that the way it—"

"You're right. I know she loves me, but lately she doesn't like me very much."

"I saw an ATM machine inside. You'd better pull out as much money as you can right now, before he freezes it."

Chapter 7

Zack stared at the empty slots in next month's schedule and knew he'd be pulling more than one 24-hour shift. At least he'd finally convinced the new administrator to hire mid-level providers so he could get a few breaks during the busy days. If the nights remained slow, he might survive, but he needed help, and with the extra payroll expenditures for their new nurse practitioners, there wasn't enough money in the coffers to lure even the shift-hungry residents from Columbia. The physician shortage was reaching epidemic proportions.

A soft knock echoed at his open door. It was Mrs. Matthews, her silver-white hair cut in a short, perky style that became her. At 70 years of age, she outworked every other secretary this department had. "Dr. Travis, I just received word from a young lady that Dr. Joy's here to see her mother. Do you want me to break the news to her, or are you feeling brave?"

He dropped his pencil. "Goldy, you're a tease." The lady knew he was staying late tonight specifically for Joy.

Goldy chuckled, eyes lit with fondness. "Smitten, I tell you. I could see it in your eyes when I noticed Molly was a patient. Sorry I couldn't talk her into staying. She usually listens to me. I taught her in Sunday school, you know."

He pulled open the middle drawer of his desk, pinched up a piece of broken candy cane he kept there for times such as these, and slid it between cheek and gum like a bona fide tobacco chewer. "How does she look? Have you seen her?" He stood to follow the secretary into the hallway.

"I haven't seen Joy. She was announced by a young girl with blond hair. If you ask me, the child looked as if she needed a once-over. Bad rash on her face."

Joy didn't come alone? Who was her traveling companion? And why hadn't he at least taken time to comb his hair and press down the wrinkles on his scrubs? Joy would understand he'd had a long day, but still, a good visual impression would be nice considering their parting words last year.

She was just walking through the ER entrance with a young, blond-haired teenager when he reached the reception window. Hmmm. She looked a bit disheveled, herself, her hair longer, tangled around her shoulders, mascara smudged beneath her eyes. Baggy jeans. She'd lost weight. He remembered those jeans.

He paused. She'd been crying?

Something was up. He knew how much she loved her mother, but he'd assured her today about Molly's tests. What else was going on? Now that he thought about it, he'd picked up something in her voice this afternoon. Too bad there'd been no time to press for answers then.

She looked up and saw him when she reached the window. A winepress clamped down on his heart. How could he have forgotten how beautiful...?

He motioned for her to stay where she was, then rushed through the door where the patients entered the ER proper. He joined her and her companion in the empty waiting room and gestured toward some chairs in the far corner. "Freshly sanitized. Ordinarily I'd have you come back to my office, but we're good here." It took everything he had not to lunge forward and give her a hug. She wasn't dating Weston. The man was still just her employer. And all this time…

"Hi, Zack." She met his gaze with those coffee dark eyes that, always before, had reinforced the name her mother chose for her. Now they looked weary.

"Just get to town?"

"Entered the city limits maybe ten minutes ago." Joy slumped into a chair between him and her travel companion. "My car's on empty, but I didn't stop for anything."

"That's for sure," her splotchy-faced friend murmured.

"Wish you'd been here a few hours ago," he said. "Maybe you could've talked Molly into staying."

Joy groaned. "She left?"

"You know your mother. As soon as she saw the test results she checked herself out and promised to return for outpatient follow-up. I tried everything I could to keep her. I'd have driven her home, but we got busy." He didn't mention that Molly smashed flat every effort he'd made to retain her in less time than it took to reach for her gown and start to strip.

"I came as quickly as I could." Joy gestured to the girl with her. "Zachary Travis, I'd like you to meet my traveling companion, Tre—"

"Hi, I'm Tressa, a friend of Joy's." The girl reached around Joy and gave him a firm handshake, giving Joy a quick look apparently meant to relay some silent message. Most likely to conceal her last name.

"Tressa Cline, right?" he asked.

She deflated. Just how much did this kid know about his history with Joy? And if she knew enough not to reveal her lineage, perhaps Joy had been talking about their engagement.

Oh, dream on, brother.

"I stowed away," Tressa said. "She didn't know I was in the

back until we got here. Didn't you hear the scream outside a few minutes ago?"

He chuckled. "You made Joy scream? I wish you'd told me ahead of time. Last time I heard her scream was when one of our anatomy partners sneaked into the lab late at night and hid a cow's tail tied to a fishing line. The next morning, when Joy was getting ready to make her first incision, our partner tugged at the line and that cow's tail came leaping across the tile floor like a hairy toad."

Tressa burst into laughter, and the blotches on her poor face reddened.

"She never dropped her scalpel." Zack gave Joy a look of approval as he basked in the knowledge that things were definitely not well between Weston Cline and Joy. Or between Weston and his daughter, apparently.

He couldn't help being touched by the glance Tressa shot Joy. It was a look filled with affection.

"My office is isolated from windows or doors, so I don't hear many screams back there." Zack studied the girl's splotchy complexion. "Is there poison ivy in Joy's floorboard?"

"No, just in the woods I went through to get to her place. My tender flesh is a siren song for poison ivy everywhere," she told him in an overly dramatic, self-deprecating voice.

Joy gently touched a splotch on Tressa's chin. "You could probably use some help with that, honey."

"No problem. I've got steroid cream in my pack. Mom makes me carry it everywhere." Tressa looked at Zack and gave him a high-wattage smile. "Why don't I call Molly and warn her we're on our way?" Without waiting for a reply, she jumped up, tugging her cell phone from her hip pocket. She waited for the entry doors to slide apart and stepped outside.

Gentle humor lit Joy's eyes as she watched Tressa. It was that same look of tenderness she reserved for her closest friends.

Despite the girl's charm, and the obvious difficulties that existed between Tressa and her father, Zack couldn't help wondering how Joy had become so close to the man's daughter. What was that about?

In any case, if Zack had ever suspected he might have recovered from the breakup, those suspicions disappeared with the onset of a jealousy so fierce he wished he had a likeness of Weston's torso for target practice.

"So... Tressa?" he asked.

"As she said, she stowed away, estranged from parents who are estranged from the world. This little stunt might get me into trouble with my former employer."

"How's this going to affect Dr. Payson?"

Joy gave him a pointed look. "My latest former employer."

"Oh?" It finally registered. "What do you mean 'latest'?"

"Weston fired me tonight, and Tressa just happened—"

"What? Fired! No way."

Joy spread her hands, holding them up as if to staunch his words. She shot a glance out the window toward Tressa. "I'm in a mess, Zack, all because I took the wrong job with the wrong person. And Tressa... we've become so close, and her situation is practically unbearable. She needs a stable adult friend. It's a long story, and I can't get into it right now, but I can't abandon her. She thinks she's tough but she's so fragile, and—"

"And she's Weston's daughter. That means this could be a volatile situation."

Joy nodded. "I've befriended her mother. There's been great tragedy in that family, and it's ripped them to pieces. I'm afraid Tressa might suffer more from the fallout than her parents. Weston can't get me for taking Tressa across state lines, but he would if he could. One doesn't mess with a man with the power and tenacity of Weston Cline."

There was no missing the moisture gathering in the corners

of her eyes. Zack resisted his first, second and third urges and kept his hands to himself; he made no nasty cracks about Weston, and didn't even move closer to Joy, though an unseen magnet drew him.

"All I wanted to do after you and I broke up was get out of Juliet," she said. "You'll never know how that…how devastated I was."

"Oh, but I do. I was just as devastated."

Was that disbelief he saw flash across her face? He met her gaze and held it. Had he truly let her down last year? Could he have listened to the wrong person?

"When the research project shut down I no longer had a job, so—"

"So Cline lured to you to his lair." Zack bit his tongue and cleared his throat.

A touch of warm humor transformed her expression. "I forgot you took drama and speech and debate in high school. Something you and Tressa have in common."

He wasn't up to debating their breakup last year, and he doubted Joy was, either. "Before we started dating, we were friends," he reminded her. "Beneath all the hurt feelings and doubt and immaturity, we had a solid friendship." Maybe she'd allowed Weston to lure her…but who'd left her open to that temptation in the first place? All the emotional acid that had burned through him last year returned with a vengeance. It didn't help that he'd been right about that slithering lizard who'd eased past Joy's defenses. Though her mother had preached to her all her life about the dangers of men, Joy had little experience to guide her. It was one of the facets of her personality that attracted him.

"The job was legit," she said, obviously reading his expression. "And it was only a job for me, no matter what everyone here said or thought. We disagreed on my treatment methods."

"Pain clinic. Tell me he didn't try to turn you into a legal pusher."

"The last thing I feel like doing right now is defend him, but to be fair, he paid to send me to every pain management conference, seminar and course in the country until I was somewhat up to speed with the options available. I rely—excuse me, I relied—as heavily as I could on non-narcotic alternatives, but I wrote more than my fair share of class three drugs, some class two, and I hope the state board doesn't come after me."

As Joy talked on about her practice the past months, about the patients for whom she'd been able to help find permanent pain relief, he watched her face light up with the passion she'd always had for medicine and caring for others. Despite the shadow of Weston Cline, Zack's old admiration rose to the surface. With Joy, it was always about stopping the suffering. It was one of many things he shared with her.

"Unfortunately for Tressa," Joy said, "she's avoiding an awful situation."

"With her father?" Zack couldn't help himself.

Joy shot him a look. "She lives with her mother, who has custody. Anyway, she landed in the middle of my dismissal tonight. I'll have to call Sylvia tomorrow."

"You'll go to Molly's tonight, then?"

"I need to make sure she's okay. We might end up sleeping on the floor with fifteen cats, but—"

"Not at all. I helped her haul two twin beds up the stairs myself last week."

Joy paused, dark brows raised. "You?"

"What, you don't think I can do it?" He playfully pumped a bicep, and was rewarded by a tentative grin. So much for soliciting admiration for his new workout program.

"Stairs?" she asked. "Since when did that house have stairs?"

"Since Molly built them."

Joy groaned and rolled her eyes, but Zack thought he caught a glimpse of humor. "She's a carpenter now, too?"

"She's kept herself busy since you left."

Joy winced, and Zack was sorry he said that. But maybe there was a way he could help her situation. She needed a job. He needed a doctor.

"So you and Mom remained friends after…you broke our engagement," she said.

"Sure did." Was it time to start blaming himself for leaving her open to Weston Cline's influence? If so, he'd be kicking himself enough to have a permanently bruised bum.

"Don't get me wrong," Joy said. "I'm glad Mom still has at least one friend left."

Zack laid his hand over Joy's fidgety ones until they grew still. "Juliet has some rumor mongers, but it's also filled with decent people who love and respect Molly Gilbert. Just because she's going through a tough time doesn't mean she's lost friends. She just hides from them now."

The outside door opened and Tressa walked through. If anything, her face looked more blotched than it had a few minutes ago.

"Tressa, why don't you dig out that steroid cream and use it now?" Joy said.

"It's in my pack out in the car. I'll do it on the way to Molly's." The girl reached a hand out and beckoned. "She's waiting."

Joy's fair skin turned pale as she stood and joined Tressa. Zack realized that, at least for now, the source of her anxiety wasn't the fact that she no longer had a job. The thought of facing her mother with that news was the origin of her stress.

He didn't have time to offer her a reprieve, however, before she and Tressa said their goodbyes and were out the door.

Chapter 8

JOY OPENED THE left passenger door and shook her head at the full backpack Tressa had left in the floorboard. "You really did plan to come with me, didn't you? Tell me where the ivy cream is."

Tressa reached over from the front passenger seat and pulled a tube from a side pocket. "I like your guy."

"He's not my guy."

"He's still watching through the window."

"Would you stop?" Was that heat spreading over Joy's face? Couldn't be. "You sound like one of those boy-crazy girls at school you're always making fun of."

"Boy crazy? What does that even mean? Who says that anymore?"

Despite herself, Joy glanced toward the glass wall of the hospital ER, and since Zack could probably see her outlined in the overhead light, she waved. He waved back. "Don't get any ideas, he's just protective. He's watching to make sure we're safe until we get into the car."

"Really? He does that with everyone who leaves the hospital at night? I bet that cuts into his patient care time."

Joy fought a smile. Sometimes she felt fifteen, herself. She dusted her hands and climbed into the driver's seat.

"How long since your breakup?" Tressa asked.

"Eight months, three weeks, six days."

Tressa whistled. "And you and Zack still haven't managed to extinguish the flame that kindles between you."

"Save the poetic verse for English class."

"I'm fifteen, and even I can see he's still your guy. No wonder Dad—" Her voice caught briefly. "No wonder he never had a chance." She rubbed the cream over her neck and face.

Joy sighed, reversing into the dark street that skirted the campus. "For a long time..." She paused. Perhaps the truth would load the child down with unnecessary guilt.

"What?" Tressa asked. "For a long time what?"

"You and my patients have been my reason for staying in Corrigan."

There was no missing the quick catch in Tressa's breath, or the sparkle of tears in her eyes. "I wanted you to stay forever. You might want to take a blow-dryer to your floorboard, or at least take the mat out to dry. You weren't the only one who cried most of the way down here."

Lately, Tressa was the only one who could make Joy smile.

"Sometimes parents stay married for the sake of the kids," Tressa said. "You're not even married to Dad, and yet you never missed a visitation night or weekend. Why do you think I came with you? Nobody loves me more than you do."

Joy clenched the steering wheel and focused on breathing quietly, inhaling serenity, exhaling confusion and angst. What kind of response did she give to a remark like that? She recalled something Mom told her often when she was growing up. "How blessed I am to have you in my life." And it was true now.

There was a wet sniff. "Thank you."

"You're also a blessing to your mother and father."

"Try telling them that."

"Though Keegan's death and their divorce left them lost,

you're the most important person in both their worlds." Maybe that was a burden for Tressa, but Joy had found that being unconditionally loved by Mom had given her courage to pursue her dreams.

"How can I be important to them when they don't even see me?"

"I told you, they're lost right now. They don't know how to reach out."

"You mean like you with Molly?"

Joy bit her tongue. She'd earned that comment. "Kind of."

"On the drive here I realized I wouldn't wish my father on you just to have you for a stepmom."

"Since Mom practically has her own petting zoo, I learned years ago to be cautious with wounded animals. I carry scars from the times I ignored those lessons. Today I did it again."

"You're saying Dad's a wounded animal."

"A dangerous one, but if he finds a way to heal you just might get your father back."

Tressa turned in her seat and waved out the back window toward Zack, whom Joy could still see in the rearview mirror. "That guy, though. He's not wounded."

"Maybe a little. Nothing like your father. And don't start matchmaking, okay?"

"You loved each other once."

"I was a different person then." Thanks to lessons learned from Weston Cline, she no longer felt like that person.

"Dad spent a lot of time here in Juliet about the time Zack broke it off with you," Tressa said. "I've seen my father in action. I know what he's like."

Time to redirect this conversation. "You know what he's like now, but what was he like before Keegan died? Was he a good father then? A good husband?" The death of a child caused irreparable damage to families. Joy had prayed often that she would outlive Mom because she knew instinctively that Mom would never recover from the loss of her only child.

Tressa stared out the window into the darkness for a moment. "I remember being happy when Dad came home at night, and I remember him helping Keegan and me with homework. Especially math. He used to just sit and talk to us. I remember falling asleep at night to the sound of Mom and Dad talking and laughing in the other room."

Joy clenched the steering wheel as she imagined the agony they'd suffered. When she'd known Weston was suffering so deeply, why had she caused him so much trouble?

Of course, he wasn't without fault. She had an impression that Zack had been very unhappy about Weston's presence in the research lab with her, though he'd always trusted her until Weston's arrival at the school. Several times, she'd wondered if Weston had something to do with her broken engagement, but every time, she'd dismissed the idea. Perhaps that was a naïve assumption.

She cruised down the quiet street gazing at the outline of the small medical school campus that was attached to Juliet Community Hospital. Her school, her hospital, where she'd completed residency in the small family medicine program.

Tressa pointed toward the newest wing of the school. "My grandfather's name still engraved there?"

"Sure is. He was the one who made that whole wing possible."

"If not for that, we might never have met," Tressa said.

Joy studied the graceful outline of the building. "Oh, I don't know. I think some people are just meant to be friends. Somehow, it would have come about."

Tressa's paternal grandfather, Dr. Richard Cline, had funded much of the wing's construction a few years before his death. After losing his sister to MRSA he'd been pivotal in helping the school establish the department with the express intention of searching for a cure for the hospital acquired staph infection. What a tragedy that Dustin Grooms, Myra's fiancé, died conducting that research.

Returning here was always a bittersweet experience for Joy. She'd loved her job in the lab, despite Dr. Payson's often overbearing attitude. Mom's surprising protests over the job continued to echo along the hallowed halls of medicine—or was that just in Joy's mind? She still couldn't understand how Zack could allow himself to be dragged into the middle of a mother-daughter conflict.

Despite the coolness of the night, Joy lowered the driver-side window as she reached the edge of town. The scent of the water was more pronounced here atop a cliff overlooking the Missouri River and the lush valley beyond it. She turned onto a narrow gravel drive that cut through a dense thicket of trees.

The frogs sang more loudly here, and the breeze stirred the trees with the floral-spicy scent of late spring blooms. A fully waxed moon shaped eddies of fog from the river into glowing spirits. Joy remembered staring out her bedroom window at night during full moon, when the sky was clear and the whole countryside appeared outlined—platinum overlaying onyx.

"This place is like a beautiful dream," Tressa breathed as they broke through the trees into the clearing around the house.

Joy smiled, pleased at sharing the nighttime beauty she had always loved. "Mom's been offered some hefty sums for these ten acres and the house."

"She'll never sell?"

Joy shook her head. It was a good thing Mom had paid the house off years ago. "This is more than just property to her. It's her life. Her refuge." Mom had planted her own vineyard and fruit trees, shade trees and privacy evergreens. The house was no longer visible from the road, or from the bordering properties. Only a couple hundred feet from the cliff's edge, the wide front porch faced toward the river for a spectacular view.

"Molly emailed me that she's done a lot of gardening lately," Tressa said.

"Good. Maybe she's been able to use the food dehydrator I gave her for Christmas."

"I hope she's been able to save some of the produce from the deer, raccoons, rabbits, birds—"

"I doubt she's even tried." Mom had a soft spot for the wildlife that found refuge on this acreage.

"Does she still have those raccoons?" Tressa asked.

"What raccoons?"

Tressa didn't reply, and in the glow of the dash lights Joy saw her young friend turn and watch her silently. "You don't know which raccoons I'm talking about."

"You've got me there." Tressa knew more about Molly Gilbert's life than Molly's own daughter did. It stung more than she would have expected.

"She told me about three little ones she found out by the road, where their mother had been killed by a car last month," Tressa said. "She had to bottle feed them. Don't you and Molly ever talk about anything?"

"Sure we do, but the subject of raccoons didn't come up."

"What did you talk about?"

"Why are you suddenly so interested in my conversations with my mother?"

"How am I going to be mistress of my own world when I don't even know what kind of situation I'll be walking into?"

Why was the kid digging so deeply into things that were not her business?

A brief silence, then, "So what do you two talk about when you visit?"

Joy suppressed an impatient sigh. It was late. She already

dreaded this visit, and she wasn't up to an interrogation, particularly about such a sore subject. "She gives me a rundown of community affairs, which she gleans from the local paper and updates from family. I tell her about interesting medical cases. She's always loves those."

"She never calls or visits you."

"Not since Christmas. She doesn't wish to intrude in my life." Though Joy didn't intend for the sarcasm to bleed through her words, she could tell by another sharp glance from Tressa that it did.

What Tressa didn't know was that their tiny, two-woman family Christmas had been a dance around the subject of Joy's relationship with Weston and whether or not she'd followed in her mother's footsteps. Joy now dreaded the holiday season.

"She's awesome," Tressa said, almost reverently.

Joy grimaced.

"Well, she is," Tressa said. "Just because you don't get along with her—"

"I took a job with your father and I've been paying for it ever since. Neither you nor I are especially gifted in that area, so don't try preaching to me about getting along with my mother."

That shut Tressa up for about three seconds.

"She told me about the orphan fawn you and she raised," Tressa said.

"That was about fifteen years ago. We had to keep Bambette all her life, because she became so trusting of humans, sending her out into the wild would have been a death sentence."

"I can't believe that name. Bambette. Really? A feminine form of Bambi?"

"Well, excuse me for not having your creative genius. My mother seemed to like the name at the time. In fact, she used to let me name all our animal refugees."

Joy thought she saw a faint, golden glow emanating from one of the windows. Had her cousin managed to talk Mom accepting help after all?

"She sounded all excited when I told her we were in Juliet," Tressa said.

Of course Mom was excited. Tressa was coming for a visit. Tressa was someone else's responsibility. Easy to have a good relationship with someone when one did not have the responsibility of care—or whose life Mom didn't wish to control.

Sometimes being loved had its down side.

"She wants us to stay for a nice, long visit," Tressa said.

"Visit? You didn't tell her I've been fired, then."

"Thought I'd leave that part to you."

"You didn't tell her we were here to bail her out of trouble."

"She knows you, Joy. She didn't exactly say it, but why else would you be driving down here in the middle of the night?"

Joy thought about the thousands of dollars she was carrying on her person, both from home and from the ATM machine she'd given Tressa permission to rob. They made a good team.

Tomorrow, Joy would get a safety deposit box in hers and Mom's name so Weston couldn't attach to it. Would Mom accept financial aid from her own daughter?

"That's got to be the cathouse." Tressa pointed toward the outline of the long building, kissed by the moon where it hovered behind the main house. Multiple windows reflected the headlights. "Molly told me about it. She's bricking it and everything. I can't believe she's finishing it herself, just following directions she found online."

"And I can't believe she's doing it for the cats. The place is bigger than the main house. She refused to even talk about it last time I visited. I asked if she was planning to raise chickens." Joy pulled up to the side of the small, white house with green trim and ample windows. She and Mom had always loved those windows. "When I was growing up, I thought my mother could do anything."

"Well, then she can lose weight and get back on her feet financially," Tressa said.

Joy studied the side stoop and concrete steps.

"What's that thing at the top of the steps?" Tressa asked.

"It's the live trap she uses to catch strays." Few people left a live-trap on their porch, baited, no doubt, with cat food, or even tuna that could very well be needed by the owner of the house. The kind of food Mom fed the cats was probably higher in protein and nutrition than what she ate herself.

"Why catch them? Why not just place food for them outside?"

"She never feeds a stray until she's taken it to the vet for a health check. Then she has it neutered or spayed."

"Are we going in, or are you just going to sit here and stare at the house?" Tressa asked. "She's expecting us."

Joy no longer saw the glow from inside. It must have been a reflection of the headlights.

Tressa scrambled out the door before Joy turned off the engine. The girl's hair shone in the moonlight like burnished gold, her movements belying the lateness of the hour and the fact that she'd lain cramped in the floorboard all the way here.

To be that young again... with the opportunity for a do-over.

Joy had nearly reached the first concrete step when Tressa gasped, then screamed and rushed back down the steps, grabbing Joy's arms. "Snake!"

"What? Where?"

"On the concrete."

Joy put an arm around Tressa's shoulders and edged her back toward the SUV. "Stay here."

"Don't go up there!" Tressa's grip tightened. "It could be a copperhead or—"

Joy squeezed her young friend's hand and smiled. "I'm my

mother's daughter. I know how to handle wild things." But the creature moved when she started up the steps, and there wasn't enough light to see clearly.

Tressa tugged on her arm. "Front door, Joy. Come on!"

Before they could retreat, an eerie orange glow emanated through the window of the door, brightening until a flame appeared. Kerosene lantern. And above the lantern hovered a caricature of Molly Gilbert's face, stretched out of proportion by the sculpted glass.

The door opened with a squeak of hinges.

"Screaming?" Mom stepped out onto the porch, arms crossed over her belly. Joy thought she saw a gleam of humor in those dark eyes from the glow of headlights, but she must be mistaken.

What Joy wanted to do was run up the steps and grab Mom in a tight hug, rest her face on that solid shoulder, and weep about the failure that was her life.

But Mom was the one in trouble this time. Joy's turn to be strong.

"Most people knock to get my attention." Mom merely nodded toward Joy, her newly acquired form of greeting since their falling out last year.

"Snake!" Tressa called. "On the porch. Be careful!"

Mom raised her lantern and looked at the snake, then tsked. "Oh, that Prissy Lou, always bringing me presents. She thinks I prefer to finish them off myself. I mean, what self-respecting cat wouldn't? And since I'm alpha cat around here…"

She set the lantern down and caught the poor reptile by the tail.

Tressa's screech echoed from the surrounding foliage. "What are you doing?"

"Putting the little thing out of its misery. Pity, too. King snakes keep the copperhead population down."

The snake writhed and undulated, but judging by the damage done, it was obviously beyond help.

Tressa gasped, pressing close to Joy's side as they leaned against the porch railing. "I hate snakes. Molly, please don't tell me you've started collecting them, too."

"No, but Prissy Lou's a great hunter, and she likes to show off." Mom carried her burden out to the edge of the yard and quickly disposed of the wounded reptile where Joy and Tressa couldn't observe.

"Welcome to the world of Molly Gilbert," Joy said softly to Tressa. "Still want to stay? It'll be like lodging in a zoo."

"I like animals."

"Good thing you're not allergic to cats."

Tressa looked up at Joy, her expression earnest in the mingled moonlight and the overhead glow of light in the car. "This is better than watching a parade of men come in and out of the house at all hours."

Joy drew the child close.

Tressa laid her head on Joy's shoulder. "I can't do it anymore. And Dad doesn't want me, you know that. Why couldn't you have been my mom?"

Joy got tired of defending the actions of Tressa's parents, but she knew from talking to Tressa that they hadn't always been that way.

"You're the only one who wants me." Tressa paused. "You and Molly. Why shouldn't I be with my best friend?"

"I'll call Sylvia tomorrow. Since school will be out in two days, we might be able to arrange something."

Tressa hugged her. "Thank you."

Joy returned the hug, but for Tressa's sake she almost hoped Sylvia would refuse.

Chapter 9

Molly brushed her hands together as she rejoined her daughter and Tressa on the steps. What she wouldn't give to go back in time and take her only child into her arms and hold her and never let her go again. Instead, she felt imprisoned by regret.

"Here to save the day?" She cringed at the gruffness of her own voice.

Joy eyed Molly's hair. "Cute cut. Do it yourself?" It was her tendency to try hard to keep their conversations light.

"Looks that bad, huh?" Molly shook her head and enjoyed the feel of freedom and added coolness, which she especially appreciated when hot flashes hit. Tragically, a pair of sharp scissors couldn't free her from the thick layer of extra flesh that incarcerated her. Just walking to the edge of the yard left her breathless.

"You did a good job," Tressa said. "Joy said you always cut her hair."

Molly eyed her daughter, trying to think of something nice to say for once. "You look good with your hair longer. Enjoy it while you can. Someday, when the hot-flashes begin, you'll want that stuff off your neck." She glimpsed shadows that looked like luggage and backpacks behind the front seats of

Joy's SUV. "Your timing's good, since I only just got some beds upstairs."

"Zack told me." Joy hesitated. "I hoped you wouldn't mind taking in two more strays."

Molly drew Tressa into a hug. There might be a moat of ugly words separating her from Joy, but Tressa was still safe. "How's my buddy?"

Tressa clung to her tightly. Too tightly. Something was off. Molly caught Joy's gaze and saw the anxiety in those eyes. She released Tressa, and for the first time since Joy discarded their carefully laid plans last year, Molly reached for her.

Joy paused, then entered Molly's arms and held on tightly, as if gripping a stanchion in the middle of a raging river. "Sorry to get you up in the middle of the night like this."

"Nonsense." Molly held her for as long as she dared, relishing Joy's nearness. When she tried to step away, Joy held on a second longer. What was up?

Molly had to clear her throat before she could speak. "Get your stuff. I stay up half the night and sleep half the morning. Guess I'm turning into a cat, myself. It may take some getting used to, if you mean to stay a bit." She retrieved her lantern and ushered them up the steps and through the door. "You might as well see what I've been doing. I wanted to get all the mess cleaned up before giving a tour."

Joy and Tressa followed Molly through the tiny mudroom, the kitchen, and into the dining room.

Tressa gasped. "Wow!"

Joy's mouth fell open. "Mom, tell me you had help with this."

"How can I keep it secret if I ask for help?" Even in the gloom of lantern light, Molly saw Joy's disapproval. "You don't like it?"

Tressa, bless her, had said little when she called from the hospital, but at least she'd been thoughtful enough give Molly a few minutes' warning. Dishes were now stacked in the dishwasher—which wasn't working presently, due to the fact that there was no electricity. Thank goodness for city water and a gas cook stove and water heater.

Molly knew she should be relieved by her daughter's arrival. The lights would be on first thing in the morning, thanks to Joy coming to the rescue. When had the roles been switched?

Molly wanted her daughter to truly see her heart and soul in this haven she had provided for other lonely beings. She'd been denied the chance to assist Joy in a practice helping people, but she and Joy probably couldn't have worked together, anyway; they were both too strong-willed.

Tressa entered the former family room, now transformed by Molly's handiwork. "You really did all this, Molly?"

Molly held her lantern high to provide them a better view. "I've always been interested in carpentry, so I checked out some books from the library and did an online search."

She watched Joy gaze around the room, her attention resting first on the new cathedral ceiling, the newly constructed stairway to an upper floor that had once been attic, the patchwork carpet samples that had been fastened together to cover two of the dining room walls. For a moment, Molly could have sworn she saw a rare look of admiration fill those eyes that looked so much like the ones that met her in the mirror every morning, but who could tell in the dim light?

Molly mentally prepped herself as she gestured toward the walls, the shelves she'd built and covered with carpet and hammered into the structure's frame throughout the circumference of the room. A total of twelve cats graced their favorite ledges, viewing the newcomers with various levels of interest. Trippurr, the fat, gray tabby who often seemed more like a friendly, adoring dog, appeared ready to jump from her shelf and greet Tressa and Joy.

"How many hours did you spend on that tall, rickety ladder of yours?" Joy asked.

"Not as many as you might think. I'm a fast learner." Molly drew Tressa on a brief tour of the 15x15 room. "Cats love to be up high. It's an instinct they use to protect themselves, and my poor little rescue animals especially need to feel safe. These guys were always jumping onto the furniture, knocking down vases and covering my dining room chairs with hair. I thought I'd experiment a little. So now they have this room all to themselves, except for my reading chair." She gestured to the recliner, where she spent time enjoying the company of her little friends and staring out the window to the view of lush farmland across the river.

"You built these shelves for all the cats?" Tressa asked.

Molly nodded and glanced toward Joy, who continued to hover in the doorway.

"I thought the brick cathouse was for them," Joy said.

Molly smiled. So she'd heard the rumors. "It isn't finished, and I'm using it mostly for storage…for the moment."

Tressa stepped to the middle of the room and did a 360 by lantern light. "No dining table or anything?"

Molly gestured to the feeding and watering stations she'd fashioned with molded clay all along the far wall. "My kitchen has a table and chairs; why do I need two rooms for eating?" She spread out her arms to emphasize her girth.

She expected at least polite laughter, but Tressa gave a sad sigh and looked away.

Joy continued to gaze around the room. "What if you'd fallen while standing on a ladder? You're all alone out here, and the cats can't pick up a phone and call for help."

"Honey, you sound like me."

Joy sighed, shook her head, said nothing more, but something odd was going on with her. There was a darkness in her eyes that Molly hadn't seen since Zack broke their engagement last year.

Heartache for her mother? Fear for her? Molly Gilbert, the fat zoo lady. What an embarrassment it must be to have a mother like that. If only Joy could understand that there was no shame in making a home for the lost and rejected.

Tressa reached up to one of the highest ledges and pulled down Prissy Lou, Molly's tiny, tailless calico. Tressa loved Priss the most, and Molly loved her for it. The cat curled comfortably in Tressa's arms, the soft hair and markings on the small cat's face giving the appearance of a permanent smile.

"Know what happened to her tail, Joy?" Tressa asked, turning back to the doorway as she nuzzled the cat's head.

Molly grimaced. This was one of the many bits of information she hadn't shared with Joy these past months.

"Her tail must've gotten caught in a trap or something," Tressa said. "The vet had to remove it, and told Molly that Prissy would never be a house cat, because cats born with tails need them to control their sphincter muscles."

Molly chuckled and took Prissy from Tressa. "Wouldn't you know, that was when Prissy decided she would become the very thing the vet said she couldn't. You can't imagine the days I followed poor Priss around the yard, trying to teach her how to use new muscles to make a good... well, anyway. Good thing the neighbors couldn't see me from here. It worked, too. She stopped wetting the bed about six months ago... for the most part."

"How much was the vet bill?" Joy asked.

Molly closed her eyes, unable to conceal her disappointment.

"I'm sorry," Joy said. "But your electric's been cut off."

"Dr. Carol does her work at cost." Molly gave a frustrated sigh. She should be grateful for her daughter's concern. "She appreciates my efforts to help keep the stray animal population down in Juliet."

"But it seems to me that the cost of that tail removal would have paid your electric bill for a month," Joy said.

"Not at cost," Molly snapped "Would you have preferred I put Prissy out of her misery the way I did her prey tonight?"

"Of course not, but why do you always have to be the one to come to their—" Joy stopped, sighed, closed her eyes. "Never mind. I think I know. You don't think there's anyone else in town who will."

Molly allowed Prissy to climb back onto the carpeted ledge. She should be proud, she supposed, that Joy had taken after her so well. If she'd checked a mirror last year, during her first big battle with Joy, she'd have had that same glow of indignation in her eyes. And she'd meant well, as her daughter did now.

That thought helped defuse some of the tension that could return her to the ER if she didn't calm down.

Joy gave a soft sigh, still lingering in the doorway as if afraid to step into the center of the room. Did she have such low opinion of her mother's ability to remodel a sturdy house?

Molly caught a surreptitious glance between her two visitors, an undercurrent of something she wasn't privy to. Time to drop the self-pity get some answers.

"Zack did tell you my chest pain probably wasn't heart related, didn't he?" she asked Joy.

"How could he know for sure? You didn't stay long enough to complete the testing."

"You're the one who's worried about spending too much money. An unnecessary overnight stay could have cost me a year's taxes on this place. Anyway, I'll follow up and all will be fine." She sidled closer to her daughter. "So, how's the pain business doing?"

"Oh, it's a hit, all right." Joy's voice drawled sarcasm. She glanced at Tressa, and once again that look passed between them.

"What aren't you two telling me?" Molly demanded.

Joy held a finger up. "First, I need to check my messages and let Myra know we arrived safely." She turned from the doorway and disappeared into the night.

Tressa reached for the half grown black and brown kitten on a lower shelf. "Let me guess, this is Worf you've been telling me about in your emails."

Molly watched Joy's retreat, then allowed herself to be distracted. "Dark amber eyes, black face, prominent forehead. I'd been watching reruns of my favorite Star Trek series when I found this baby perched atop a semi tire—attached to a semi—one morning in a parking lot."

Tressa carried the purring cat over to Molly and held him out. "You look like you could use a cat hug."

Molly wrapped her arms around her youngest refugee and let him nestle into her neck with a healthy purr. "What about you, sweetie?" she asked the girl, barely able to contain her growing alarm at the undercurrent of tension. "I gathered from your latest post that things weren't the greatest at home."

"You're still getting my emails?"

"I still have enough spare change for a cup of coffee so I can sit and use my computer in the shop. So. Out with it, Tressa. What's happening?"

Tressa turned away and shrugged. "Bad stuff. I didn't get to tell you about it, because... there wasn't time."

Molly returned Worf to his perch. "Then tell me now."

Tressa turned, but she kept her gaze on the half-grown kitten. Gone, suddenly, was the broad smile that had characterized the girl's expression the two times she'd visited with Joy before.

"Your eyes are red." Molly peered closer, then straightened in alarm. Drat the electric company! She should have seen this sooner. "Actually, so is half your face. Are you breaking out in a rash?"

"Poison ivy." Tressa gazed around the kitchen and strolled past the recently-cleared counters. "I've got steroid cream on it." She opened a cabinet door, and out fell one of four bags of potato chips. Tressa picked up a bag. "You'd satisfy your cravings and be healthier if you ate nuts instead."

Molly felt like an AA member whose bottles had been discovered. "Nuts cost more. We'll get to my diet later. Let's hear what else is going on with you."

Tressa replaced the bag and closed the cabinet door, then turned and slowly made her way back to greet Trippurr, the huge gray and black tabby whose two most prominent characteristics matched her name. "Be gentle with Joy tonight, will you?" Tressa asked softly. "A lot's going on."

"Obviously." And Joy was taking her sweet time about telling her. "You okay?"

Tressa shook her head. "Neither of us is."

Molly's anxiety grew. This visit wasn't a rescue operation. At least, not exclusively. "I'll let Joy talk to me in her own time." Though, knowing Joy, that time may never come. It had been so long… "I want to know about you, Tressa. I know you love Joy, but if she's having trouble of her own somebody needs to be there for you. Everybody needs to have someone to confide in from time to time."

"You never need anybody."

"Of course I do." Molly swept her arms out to encompass the cats. "Maybe they're not the best listeners, but if I'm hurting or feeling low, they'll climb onto my chair with me and purr until I'm feeling better."

"You sure you're not having more chest pains?" Tressa asked. The girl had such a gentle soul.

"So far, nothing a little cat therapy can't ease."

"What about the babies?"

Molly smiled. "I'll let you meet the raccoons in the morning.

They're out in the shed for the night, probably prowling around in search of a way out. I made the mistake of sleeping with them the first few nights after I found them. Believe me, raccoons are nocturnal animals."

"So how's it going with the other building?"

Molly chuckled. "I've got half the town in an uproar about my plans for that place. After all, who bricks a cathouse, right?"

Tressa hefted Trippurr into her arms and buried her face in the fat cat's fur. "Everything will be better now. I know it will."

Molly didn't hear even a hint of hope in that assurance.

Chapter 10

Joy felt her way down the concrete steps in the darkness. When she reached the SUV she turned the key and switched on the headlights. The glow would offer at least a little light into the house while they got squared away for the evening. She had four flashlights in the cargo hold that would get them by until she could pay the electric company first thing in the morning.

She should've called the company today as soon as she found out Mom's situation. Self-recrimination dogged her movements as she pulled her largest suitcase from the cargo hold and hefted it to the ground. How could she have spoken so callously to Mom, knowing how proud she was of this ongoing rescue operation?

And yet, when was the last time Mom had shown such tender patience with her own daughter as she did with her rescued animals? Of all things, following a cat around the yard to teach it how to use different muscles to potty.

And what would Mom's reaction be with tonight's events?

Joy's real reason for stepping outside was to put off the truth a little longer, but she checked her messages so she wouldn't be an out-and-out liar. Two calls were from Weston. She deleted them without listening. When she reached the first message from Myra she immediately redialed.

"Joy Gilbert, you'd better have a good excuse for this," Myra said by way of greeting. "Do you know how worried I've been—"

"I received four calls on my way here. I wasn't up to talking."

"Oh? I only tried twice. You've had a busy night, but I wish you'd answered. For all I knew you could've been smashed up at the bottom of some ravine, and—"

"The ravines are clear between here and Corrigan," Joy said with a smile.

"You okay?"

"I'm breathing. We arrived a few minutes ago. Mom had already checked herself out of the hospital by the time we got there."

"We?"

"Long story, but Tressa was crouched directly behind my seat while I talked to you tonight."

"Oh, glory be. I know we picked her father apart, poor girl. It's a good thing I didn't reach you again, then, or we'd have a HIPAA breach."

Joy strolled toward the cliff overlooking the river, where the full moon touched the flowing water in hues of silver and gunmetal. "I didn't know we had patients in common."

"We do now. I need a consult."

"From me? I'm not sure I'm legal for you to talk to, since I no longer work for the clinic."

"She's your patient, not the clinic's. She was admitted to the Davidson Center tonight for a ninety-six hour suicide watch. She claimed that I was her psychiatrist, though I've never seen her. She wouldn't even have been admitted to the facility if she hadn't given your name as her physician. Unfortunately, the hospital reached Dr. Hearst instead, and she's the one who suggested our patient was suicidal."

Joy shivered as she breathed in the moist air rich with loamy soil. "Dr. Hearst doesn't even know yet that I've been fired."

"Poor thing does now. She tried to reach you, couldn't, so she called Weston. Needless to say, she's a little freaked now that she knows she's the sole physician for the clinic."

"Which patient?"

"She's young, widowed, claims doctors won't take her seriously. You tried to refer her to me today."

Joy gasped. "Sarah Miller."

"Dr. Hearst knew Sarah walked out in the middle of her appointment with you today, hence the silly conclusion."

"What happened?"

"She rammed her car head-on into a concrete buttress."

"No! Was she injured?"

"Not a scratch. Couldn't have been going that fast. She was a little upset when I saw her, swore she wasn't trying to hurt herself." Myra said. "Did Dr. Hearst try to call you?"

"No. Weston. I deleted the messages without listening."

"Are you nuts? If he has any sense he's decided to rehire you."

"I'm more concerned about Sarah right now. You've spoken with her?"

"Yes, and she'll be fine. I'm telling you, honey, that clinic's going to collapse without you there. Your former colleague has neither your intelligence nor your common sense."

"There've been some uncomfortable days in the past few months when more and more of Dr. Hearst's patients requested to have their records transferred to me."

"I'm not surprised."

"Sarah must've been wearing a seatbelt," Joy said. "No one wears a seatbelt when they're trying to commit suicide."

"I'm teaching you well," Myra said.

"Simple logic."

Myra snorted. "Dr. Hearst could use some of that."

"I appreciate you seeing Sarah."

"I'll visit her again in the morning before work. I'll have four days to convince her to come to me for outpatient counseling."

"She works in a flower shop, not the greatest of pay, and the only insurance she carries is the barest of necessities."

Myra chuckled softly. "Sweetheart, you're not the only doctor with pro bono cases."

"Thanks. I know you can help Sarah."

"I'll do my best. It's late, and we both need to get to bed, but honey, tell me how you're really doing."

Joy took another deep breath of richly scented night air and listened to the sounds of crickets and frogs. She relished the touch of a fragrant breeze on her skin.

"Joy? You okay?"

"Part of me feels as if my whole world is flying apart." She glanced over her shoulder toward the house, where the glow from Mom's lone lantern barely outlined the windows, and the headlights placed in sharp relief the fresh coat of paint on the house and stair railing.

"What about the other parts?" Myra asked.

Joy thought about seeing Zack for the first time since she'd left. She thought about the feel of her mother's arms around her. She gazed across the river and listened to the night sounds. "The rest of me feels free again. I'm home."

~

Molly heard the bounce of the wheels on Joy's suitcase coming through the mud room and felt the familiar tensing in her neck and shoulders. She glanced at Tressa, who once again held Prissy in her arms as if the cat were an infant. "You and Joy must be hungry. The freezer still has unthawed food."

"No need." Tressa replaced the tiny cat on her ledge. "I've got some good stuff in my pack out in the car. I'll go get it." She started out, then turned back. "I hope you meant it when you invited us to stay awhile." She passed Joy, gave her a nudge in the arm, and kept going, leaving Molly and Joy alone. Joy's face looked haggard, eyes even more red-rimmed than Tressa's.

Joy gestured to the carpeted walls, cat perches, the feeding station. "It looks like an expert spent a lot of time and creative energy in this place, Mom. Sorry I didn't say so earlier. Was it hard to knock out the ceiling?"

"Not really. I just imagined the faces of a couple of my least favorite people and went to work with a sledgehammer."

"I don't suppose Weston's face helped?"

Molly grinned as the praise straight from her daughter's heart warmed her. "A time or two. Now you know why I didn't invite you in last time you visited. The place was covered in dust for weeks."

"There's obviously more room this way."

"And I'm cheap labor."

"Grandpa always did say you could squeeze a quarter until it squealed."

"Bet you didn't guess I had muscle lurking under all this flab. I hope you trust my handiwork, since your beds are up there." Her daughter seemed to have come to some kind of understanding with herself while she was outside. "You ready to tell me what's wrong?"

Joy closed her eyes, and then turned away, shoulders hunched. "Maybe."

"How about if I promise not to say 'I told you so'?"

"That works. Weston fired me."

Molly sucked in her breath as if she'd been kicked hard. Outrage and relief fought a fierce battle in her gut, and she knew that would be ongoing for a while. "I just thank the Lord you didn't marry the man."

"Please give me more credit than that."

"When did this happen?"

"As I was pulling out of the driveway to come here. And no, he didn't fire me because I was coming to see you."

Some of this afternoon's chest pressure and shoulder pain returned, and Molly found herself clenching her hands. Time to calm down, but how could she? Not only had that pernicious man seduced her daughter away from Juliet, Molly suspected him of being instrumental in breaking up Joy's engagement with Zack. Not that Zack had ever told her.

"You still have a house in Corrigan, don't you?"

"Yes, one that I'll have to sell immediately because I can't make the outrageous mortgage payments."

Molly closed her eyes. "And Tressa's been dragged into this mess."

"Not my decision."

Stung by the heat in Joy's voice, Molly opened her eyes. "Of course not. She's here, though, isn't she?"

They glared at each other for a few seconds, then Joy averted her gaze toward Trippurr, who had jumped from her perch to wind her way around their legs.

"Don't forget I named her for a reason," Molly warned.

Joy shook her head. "Things weren't going well for Tressa at home—something she can discuss with you later if she decides to—"

"She already has."

Joy flicked a glance at Molly. "So you should understand why she came with me. I didn't see her until I stopped at the hospital. That's when she called you. Don't worry, we'll contact her mother in the morning and work things out. I can drive her back to Corrigan if I need to."

Molly gestured to the large, fully packed suitcase Joy had managed to squeeze through the door. “Zack must have convinced you I’d need help for a while. I’m sorry for the scare. I didn’t want him to call you, but you know how convincing he can be.”

“I’m glad he did. You didn’t cause this problem with Weston, Mom. He and I have been clashing a lot lately about patient care. Tonight it finally came to a crisis.”

“Has the financier suddenly decided he’s a doctor?”

A hint of a smile touched Joy’s lips. “It appears I have a few things to learn about conducting clinic business. Pro bono is so passé.”

“You’ve never had a head for accounting. You’re a doctor. You take care of people whether they have money or not.”

“Not when I work for Cline Medical. Apparently, I tend to take after my mother.” Joy gestured around the room at the stray cats. “I don’t intend to change.”

Maternal pride blanketed Molly like a thick comforter. She swallowed hard and looked away, not wanting Joy to see the sudden moisture in her eyes. It was late. None of them were at their best.

“You’ve got a place to stay and a roof over your head for the rest of your life. You know that.”

“Thanks, Mom. I know.”

Molly was accustomed to caring for the discarded. She’d never dreamed, however, that this would include her own strong and capable daughter.

“I’ll need a job,” Joy said.

“Not to worry.” Molly spread her arms and drew Joy into their second hug of the night—of the year, actually. “I know of an opening or two.”

Joy laid her head, for just a brief few seconds, on Molly’s shoulder. Then she stiffened and pulled away. “There aren’t that many openings for doctors in Juliet. You're not talking about the ER, are you?"

"Don't tell me you're still avoiding Zack after nearly a whole year."

"Of course not, but he's never attempted to contact me before today. I don't think he'd be interested in hiring me for a position."

"He needs someone to keep him from working himself to death, and you do have experience. When the resident program was discontinued the PRN pool dried up, so they're short of help a lot."

"If you're such a recluse, how do you know all this stuff when Dawn Shoemaker doesn't even know yet?"

Molly hesitated. How much could she tell Joy without betraying herself? "Because your dear, nosey cousin didn't remain friends with Zachary Travis after the engagement was broken."

"You mean after Zachary broke it."

"There's more to that than we know right now."

"Are you saying you think he had another reason for breaking up that he didn't tell me?" Joy's raised voice made Molly's heart squeeze a little. "Did he tell you something?"

Molly silently prayed for Tressa to come back inside. "Of course he wouldn't tell me anything he wouldn't even tell you. I just think you might want to give him some leeway. Last year was hard on everyone."

"We fought. For some reason, neither you nor Zack wanted me working in research. I never understood why, and I wasn't about to marry a man who would try so hard to control me."

"Then I would think you'd have been the one to break the engagement."

"Well, I wasn't," Joy snapped.

To Molly's relief, the back door opened and Tressa came in carrying her backpack and another case.

"Anyway, I think he'd be glad for your help in the emergency department." She turned to take the case from Tressa and pointed up the stairs. "Trust me, it's solid. It'll take the three of us to heft that trunk of yours up there, Joy, but we'll manage. We need to have a quick snack and let you two get some sleep. I have a feeling tomorrow's going to be an interesting day."

Perhaps it would be wiser to retreat back into her silence. Otherwise, she might inadvertently spill secrets she desperately needed to protect.

Chapter 11

THURSDAY MORNING THE smell of bacon lingered in the house long past breakfast. Electric lights glowed softly through the remodeled cat room, and Joy squeezed her cell phone so hard she expected it to shock her in protest. "Sylvia? Did you hear what I said?"

"I'm not sure." The woman sounded as if she'd been on an all-night bender. "You mean she's not at school?" Though Sylvia had never touched a cigarette, her voice had the deep croak of a heavy smoker this morning. "She usually leaves for school before I get up. I just thought she was...you mean she just left?" Bewilderment colored her voice.

Joy couldn't help wondering for a moment if the woman might be using, but while Sylvia's addiction affected Tressa profoundly, it wasn't drugs.

"I think she just did it on impulse," Joy said. "You know how she likes my mother, and Mom was in the ER yesterday."

"The ER? Is she okay?" Sylvia had only met Mom once, briefly, last Christmas, but the two of them had taken to each other as quickly as Tressa and Mom.

"Just a little heart scare. She checked out before I could even get here, but Tressa was worried about her."

"But she came home last night. When did she leave again?"

Joy had no idea how to reply. "That's probably something you two will want to discuss. All I know is she burst from the backseat of my car when I stopped at the hospital. She nearly scared me out of my skin."

"She hates Porter, you know," Sylvia said, surprising Joy by her willingness to at least allude to Tressa's concerns. "Hated every man I've dated since Day One."

"She loves you, though, Sylvia. I can drive her back to Corrigan today if you wish." Joy strolled over to Trippurr, who sat on a ledge at shoulder level. The hefty cat watched Joy's every move with wide, inquisitive eyes framed with black lines against gray. "Or she's welcome to visit with Mom and me in Juliet for a few days."

Sylvia was silent for a moment. Joy stepped too close to Trippurr's ledge. Eager to share her affection, the cat head-butted Joy's nose hard enough to injure cartilage.

"She's got what, a week left of school?" Sylvia asked.

Joy stepped back to recover from the attack of the cat's affection. "Tomorrow's her last day." Who ever said house cats were safer than dogs?

And what was wrong with Sylvia? Was she so absorbed in her own pain that she couldn't keep track of her daughter's school days?

More silence from the other end.

"Her father doesn't know about this, by the way," Joy said. "Not yet. I haven't called him. Again, I'd love to have her stay with me if it works for you."

A long sigh, then, "It works for me, Joy." Such defeat in that tired voice.

"Look, Sylvia, I'm going to put my doctor coat on for a moment and make a suggestion if you don't mind. Have you been to your therapist lately?"

There was a soft puff of disgust. "That quack. You know

what he told me on our last visit? He actually said, 'Sylvia, you know things will get better, since they can't get any worse.'"

Joy grimaced. Of course, that therapist had been one of Weston's choosing. More than once, Weston had insinuated that his wife was mentally ill, and not in a kind, caring way. "I'm your friend," Joy said. "I'm worried about you, and I think your daughter is, too. If you don't like Dr. Higgins, I have a colleague who is excellent—"

"Not today, okay?"

Joy wasn't surprised. "Would you at least consider it for later? For your daughter's sake? And for mine? I care about you, too, you know." It was frustrating to see the number of hurting people who could get help, but instead they allowed the stigma of mental illness to frighten them. Didn't anyone realize that nearly half the country's population suffered with some form of it?

"You and I both know she's better off with you, anyway." A tone of pique entered Sylvia's tired voice. "She obviously prefers you."

Joy allowed Sylvia a moment to brood, and then braced herself. As Tressa's mother and legal guardian, Sylvia had a right to know that Weston might complain bitterly. He might even try to cause trouble, depending on how angry he was with Joy. Now she wished she'd at least listened to his voice messages last night.

"There are some circumstances you're not aware of that may impact your decision," Joy said. She dug her fingers into the thick fur around Trippurr's neck and felt the vibration of the cat's loud purr. "I'm sure the news will spread soon enough." Though Corrigan was a suburb of Kansas City, it had the character of a small town.

"What?"

"Weston fired me yesterday."

There was a gasp, and then Sylvia called her ex-husband a few unsavory names. As she spoke, her weariness seemed to dissipate. "Why? What was his excuse?"

"We disagreed on patient care."

"I bet that's not all you disagreed on. What's the matter, couldn't he seduce you?"

Tressa was right, Sylvia knew her ex-husband pretty well. "It's nothing I'd be able to prove in court."

"I knew you were smart enough to see through that scumbag and his huge ego." Though Sylvia's voice didn't sound exactly gleeful, Joy imagined that somewhere deep in the woman's mind there was a quiet unfurling of relief. She wasn't the only woman to be discarded by the son of the wealthy and influential Cline family.

"I wouldn't want him to take his irritation out on you when he discovers Tressa's staying with me."

"He doesn't care, Joy. Don't you see? If he tried to prove me an unfit mother, he'd be saddled with the responsibility of her care, and though she practically raises herself, keeping her wouldn't be convenient."

Joy couldn't argue.

"I'm just sorry you won't be there for her on their visits anymore." Sylvia sighed. "I thought if you married him...but you read him too well."

"Perhaps we could take this situation on a daily basis. Any time I need to, I'll drive her home."

"None of this would be happening if he had the human compassion of a toad."

Joy had to clamp her lips together. "I'll tell Weston I have your approval to keep Tressa for a while."

"Don't tell him a thing. Why don't we wait and see how long it takes for him to even realize she's gone."

"Do you think that'll be good for Tressa?"

There was a sigh, and a long pause. "See there? A good reason she should be with you right now. Even in the middle of your tragedy—" Sylvia said the word dryly, as if, in her opinion, moving Weston Cline out of her life would be a major relief "—you always think of others first. Me, I sleep late, lose track of my daughter overnight, and obviously don't even rate a good-bye. Why couldn't she just call me herself?"

"Because I need your permission to administer an injection for her poison ivy."

"What? She's got it again?" A heavy sigh. "She cut through the forest again?"

"Afraid so."

"I bet she looks like a wart-faced rat this morning."

Joy winced at yet another reason Tressa no longer wanted to return home. "It's worsened overnight, but I wrote a script and picked up a couple of vials at the pharmacy already. Do I have your permission to treat? I know she's had them before."

"Of course you have my permission. You shouldn't even have to ask, since you've treated her at the clinic."

"But I'm no longer an employee of the clinic, and I don't want to take any chances." Now was not the time to mention that she'd already given Tressa the injection, and she actually needed another witness to this phone call to make it legal. Joy was a stickler for rules, but when she saw Tressa's face this morning she couldn't wait.

There was a noisy yawn at the other end of the line. Joy glanced at the clock. "I'm sorry, Sylvia, did I wake you?" At ten forty-five in the morning?

"If you hadn't, I probably would have slept all day. It's all I seem to be doing."

"Depression does that, Syl. I can write you a script for—"

"No antidepressants. You know I hate that stuff. It might help with the sadness, but it keeps me from feeling anything."

Joy promised to call in soon and disconnected, relieved that Tressa had her mother's blessing for her to stay here, and glad that, despite everything, Sylvia had legal custody. Would Weston even notice if his daughter didn't show up for visiting hours? Tressa had most likely wondered the same thing.

Soon they would find out.

~

While Joy spoke on the phone to Tressa's mother, Molly led Tressa to the fenced lot behind the long shed. Tressa's gasp of delight at the sight of Captain Kirk, the thigh-high chestnut horse, warmed Molly's heart. The diminutive Captain swung his head over the top of the low-slung fence and greeted Tressa with a soft nicker.

"Isn't he a doll?" Molly chuckled. "He's a Lilliputian gelding. He was a sickly runt when I first heard of his presence at an exotic animal ranch west of here. The owners wanted to euthanize him, but Joy's cousin, Dawn, heard about him and called me."

"I could hold him in my arms!" Tressa exclaimed.

"Only if you could hold a great Dane in your arms. Kirk's heavier than he looks."

Tressa dropped to her knees to look the horse in the eyes, and then glanced up at Molly. "Dawn's the one with five kids, isn't she?"

"Yep. Sweet little Dawn also has the Gilbert heart for strays. She and her husband adopted a complete family of orphans when she discovered she couldn't conceive." Despite the busy life, however, Dawn never hesitated to interfere in the lives of others if she thought she could help—whether she could or not.

"How long have you and Joy been mad at each other?" Tressa asked suddenly.

Molly blinked. "What makes you think we're mad?"

"Oh, I don't know, maybe discovering that you never email her like you do me. She was worried about coming here last night. And you two never exactly talk to each other."

"We talk."

"You snip."

Molly grimaced.

"So... how long?"

"Honest answer? Since she took a job with a man who could have destroyed her career, and I'm not talking about your father."

"Dr. Payson?"

"Yes. Until the research project took a dive, I was afraid she would switch residencies."

"So you're mad because she isn't living your dream?"

Okay, that stung. But Molly had discovered Tressa's tendency toward the bold truth early on. It was something to admire. "I'm still trying to remember when she developed a mind of her own."

"That's a bad thing? My dad thinks it is, but then, he's Dad."

"Talks to you a lot, does he?"

Tressa pressed her forehead against Kirk's and seemed to stare into the tiny horse's dark eyes. He didn't move a muscle. Tressa had a way of charming anything or anyone in her path, even with reddened splotches of poison ivy marring the beauty of her face. "He talks to me when he wants something from me, or when he feels it's his job to meddle in my life." Tressa snorted, startling Kirk. "As if he knows anything about my life now."

"Amazing how we get our priorities all out of whack sometimes," Molly said.

"No wonder you prefer animals."

"Not over you, kiddo. Not over my own kid, even if she is a pain in the—"

"You like each other, don't you?" Tressa gave Kirk a final rub on his forelock and stood.

"Do you always like your mother?" Molly asked.

Tressa grimaced. "I love my mom, but I hate what she's doing right now."

"I hear you there, sweetie. I'm pretty sure Joy feels the same about her own mom right now."

Tressa shook her head. "No way. I see the look in her eyes when she talks about you. You're her hero."

Molly stood perfectly still and basked in the brilliant, beautiful young girl's wise words. How amazing they felt. How badly she'd needed to hear them.

"Well, okay," Tressa said, "she's freaky about your trip to the ER yesterday, but that's because she worries about you."

Molly turned to walk with Tressa back toward the house, studying at the fifteen-year-old's fluid profile. Little Tressa had always seemed like an old soul, with occasional insight beyond her years. That could be due to her feuding parents, or it could be heredity. Probably a lot of both. Other children in similar situations would rebel. Of course, wasn't this visit due to a little acting out?

"How well did you two sleep in the balcony last night?" Molly asked.

"I stayed warm. Not a hard thing to do with all those cats."

"Prissy Lou loves to cuddle up to a warm body. She didn't pee on you, did she?"

"Nope. Neither did Trippurr or Worf. Teddy Bear cuddled up with Joy, I think. It's a good thing you have those beds up there."

"It is." Molly stepped up onto the front porch and turned to gaze upon her favorite view, where the morning sunshine outlined the rows of grapevines on the far banks across the Missouri River. "We might need to consider a more permanent arrangement, such as doors and walls, stuff like that, if you plan to be here awhile. I can't plumb for a bathroom until I've studied more, but there's easily space for two bedrooms up there, and doors will keep the cats away in the summertime when you won't need the warmth."

"Really?" Tressa asked, sounding delighted. "So you're keeping us?"

Molly chuckled. "I like strays."

The screen door opened and Joy stepped out to join them.

Molly caught a look of trouble in her eyes.

"Sylvia has granted permission for Tressa to stay," Joy said.

"For how long?" Molly asked.

Joy placed an arm across her young friend's shoulders. "We might get to keep you for the summer, honey. Would that be okay with you?"

The poor child flinched as if she'd just been slapped.

Tressa knew Joy didn't mean for her announcement to feel like a kick in the stomach. She pulled away from Joy's arm and turned her back on the two women, hugging her ribs. Did she even have a mother anymore? Had she ever? It seemed she could remember good times with Mom, but that had been so long ago, maybe she'd imagined it. Maybe she'd been hatched in a bird's nest.

She swallowed back tears. Mom must be glad to have the freedom to collect her boyfriends without any disapproving eyes watching. Was this how it felt to find one's adoption papers in a previously locked drawer? She felt cut loose from her identity.

"What...did she say?" The sound of her own trembling

voice embarrassed her. So much for being mature about the whole thing.

A hand came across her right shoulder, another across her left—Joy on one side, Molly on the other, and they both moved close. But she didn't want them hugging away her pain. She stiffened.

"This isn't what you're thinking, honey." Joy's breath fell warm and soft against Tressa's cheek.

"What am I thinking?"

"That Sylvia wants it this way. She doesn't. Over the phone, she sounded resigned. She knows you don't want Porter there."

"So she chose him over me."

"Oh, Tressa, no."

Tressa blinked, irritated by her tears. What was she supposed to think?

"These past four years have knocked her to her knees," Joy said. "We have a unique opportunity right now to allow her some space to discover for herself what's really important to her in life."

Tressa sniffed, feeling her face collapse. Didn't Mom know if her own daughter was important or not? "Everybody's worried about Mom and Dad healing from Keegan's death. It's like he was their only child. But I lost him, too. I lost everyone the day he died."

She stepped away and closed in on herself. "You know what we did after Keegan died? Dad drove us home from the hospital, and all three of us went straight to Keegan's bedroom. Dad opened the door of the walk-in closet and drew Mom and me to the foot of the bed and held us while we cried and sniffed the scent that was Keegan drifting out to us. We were all so desperate to connect with him, and his scent, being surrounded by his things, was all we had."

Joy and Molly joined her again and both wrapped arms around her, ignoring her stiff posture.

"They love you," Molly said. "Who wouldn't love you madly? You're the most precious child."

"Your mother's problem," Joy said, "is that she thinks she's the unimportant one."

Molly released her long enough to dig into her pockets. "Sorry, I'm out of tissues. I'll go get some paper towels."

Tressa grabbed for Molly's arm, shaking her head. She suddenly needed human touch more than something to soak the tears right now.

Molly hovered. "Honey, remember three months ago when you flew to Seattle to visit your Aunt Carolyne?"

"Sure."

"Remember those oxygen masks the cabin attendants explain to the passengers? They always tell the parents to make sure their own masks are good to go before helping their kids. That's so they'll stay alive to help the kids."

"That's what we can do for Sylvia," Joy said. "We help her get her bearings, because she still feels cut off from life."

"Far be it from me to give my daughter the big head," Molly said, "but Tressa, you've had Joy in your life these past months. You have her strength, and now mine, to lean on. Your parents don't have that."

Tressa looked up at Joy. "If Dad hadn't fired you, and if he'd treated you the way you deserved to be treated, he'd have that." She looked at Molly. "And what about you? You got your electricity turned off. You struggle a lot, but you don't sleep with every man you can find."

"But look at my weight, honey. I have my own addictions."

Tressa looked at Joy again. "Your life's a mess but you're still a virgin. You still know how to remain true to your faith and values."

"I never lost a child," Joy said quietly. "I've never been divorced. Sylvia's endured both."

"A broken engagement, a lost job? Maybe a lost career?"

"Career?" Molly exclaimed.

"I heard Joy talking to Myra on the phone when she was driving like a crazy woman on the way down here," Tressa said.

Joy grimaced, glancing at Molly. "Thanks for tattling to my mother about my poor driving skills."

"Sorry. You told Myra that you worried about the number of narcotic prescriptions you'd written could bring the state board down on you."

"I was just blowing off steam."

"You also said the only reason you took that job with Dad was because you were rebounding from your broken engagement to Zack."

Joy shot Molly another uncomfortable glance. Molly raised her eyebrows. Both shared a look of understanding. They didn't know what goodness they had in their lives. And at least for a short time Tressa hoped she'd be a part of that.

"You also told Myra you probably never stopped loving Zack," Tressa said.

Molly erupted with a burst of laughter that echoed to the trees and back. She slapped Joy on the shoulder and, still chuckling, waddled back into the house. "You girls carry on without me. I need to make a telephone call, unless somebody's decided to disconnect my phone service today."

Joy gave Tressa a pretend scowl. "Thanks a lot."

Tressa threw her arms around Joy. "I still wish you were my mom."

Chapter 12

On Thursday afternoon, balancing on the edge of frustrated ire, Joy pulled into the visitor's parking lot nearest the hospital's ER and allowed the engine to idle while she fumed. Molly Gilbert would never change. She always had to be the one in control; it was why she resisted help from anyone. Joy had half expected her to refuse help with the electric bill this morning. She probably would have if she didn't have lodgers.

With three minutes to spare, Joy switched off the engine, got out and strolled slowly toward the hospital entrance. She studied the stately, granite and brick building set amongst mature oaks, pines and grape arbors and regretted the passing of an earlier age in those hallowed halls of medicine. When she worked here as a resident, the community had been able to support a seventy bed hospital, complete with specialists and a resident program that drew patients from all across central Missouri.

When funds dried up, the new hospital administrator was forced to reduce the operation to a twenty-five bed critical care access facility. Though the school kept them supplied with updated equipment, help was more difficult to find.

As Mom said, there were no longer money-starved residents vying for moonlight hours in the ER. Hence, this appointment.

Joy couldn't help wondering what Zack would think about her mother making this appointment for her, as if she didn't have the nerve to do it herself. Mom knew her too well.

Still, Zack had been a brilliant and supportive anatomy lab partner, where they first met in med school. Despite his brilliance, he'd never patronized his classmates. As a resident, he'd cared more for patients than for the procedure notches he could place on his belt. He was calm under pressure, and had graduated number one in their class.

Throughout med school, he'd been one of Joy's best friends. Even after they became engaged during their third year of residency, he'd never tried to seduce her—though she knew there were times he'd struggled for control.

She been unable to force thoughts of him from her mind. She'd often been pelted by silent questions, gripped by doubt. Myra had told her often enough that it was natural to experience self-doubt after a rejection like the one she'd experienced, but still...why?

She thought about Weston, and the papers he'd handed her last night. Certainly she took more time with patients than he preferred, but if anything, that special attention drew more to their clinic. It was why he'd seen it necessary to hire another physician in such a short time.

Had he hired Joy in the first place simply because of his attraction to her? It was no secret that he thought her beautiful; it was why he'd plastered her picture everywhere. He'd claimed several times, in moments of irritation when she rejected his attempts at intimacy, that if not for his skills in marketing and her exquisite exterior, she wouldn't have a job.

She was proving him wrong. She might not have a job with him, but she would most definitely be working as a physician.

On hindsight Joy realized that Zack's major concern might well have been the amount of time she'd spent with Weston.

As the financial sponsor for the research project, Weston had returned to Juliet multiple times and invited Joy and Dr. Payson out to dinner to discuss their research. Often, Dr. Payson had left as soon as the meal was finished, with Weston promising to take Joy home later.

All this time, Joy had resented Zack's lack of trust in her. In retrospect, what fiancé would fail to protest such behavior? If only she'd seen it coming sooner. Why couldn't she have been more considerate of Zack's feelings?

As she neared the ER entrance, she felt her stomach tighten. The nervousness irritated her. She and Zack were both adults, and she was in desperate need of a job. She knew Zack would never attempt to humiliate her.

In the ER, she saw several familiar faces, greeted some old friends, hugged others, endured some curious stares from staff members she didn't know while the secretary buzzed Zack. He arrived within a couple of minutes. All chatter stopped.

She swallowed, forcing herself to relax. Good thing they'd broken the ice last night. Now, however, she wasn't meeting with him as his equal, but as a prospective employee. She held her hand out, and he took it, looking into her eyes with a warm smile. She knew for a fact that he was four and a half inches taller than her five foot seven, but at the moment he seemed to tower over her.

He squeezed her hand gently, then released it. "Good to see you again so soon."

Oh, and it was so very good to see him. "Tell me you don't actually live on the premises."

He grinned. "Feels that way to me lately. We could've had this conversation last night, but you were worried about Molly, and I think I was too tired to focus. At any rate, I forgot to ask you to apply for this position, which was my intent last night. I just got... distracted by seeing you again." He winked.

Her fingers retained the warmth of his grasp after he released them. His words reminded her of the honesty with which he lived his life. That was another of his personality traits she'd missed all these months, especially when Weston played his word games to keep her off balance. Zack didn't play games or tricks.

The tension in her gut eased slightly. As she'd noted last night, his dark blond hair was shorter now. It suited him. And though there were new shadows of fatigue beneath his eyes, she still appreciated the firm planes of his face, the strong jaw line, the broad shoulders beneath the navy scrubs and white lab coat. Everything about him spoke of strength and safety. It always had.

"As it happens, we're not too busy right now, so would you like to come back to my office?" he asked.

She glanced through the reception window to the nurses and techs trying without success to conceal their curiosity. As Mom had said this morning, every human, dog, cat, and even some chickens were acutely aware of the broken engagement of Dr. Zachary Travis and Dr. Joy Gilbert, so they might as well get accustomed to working in a fishbowl.

She waved to everyone and turned to follow Zack down the wide hallway toward the old ER director's office. Zack's office now. Indeed, she could feel the eyes of the staff on her. If Zack's obvious fatigue was any indication, she was a shoe-in for the job. This hospital didn't require emergency medicine certification for the ER docs, and she was thankful.

She focused her attention on him again. He still wore spectacles at work, though they didn't dampen the inquisitive vibrancy of his eyes. She didn't know if he needed prescription glasses now, but he never had before. It was simply an obsession of his for protection. He requested, though he didn't demand, that his staff do the same. Joy would do so if she got the job.

Joy and Zack shared the memory of Dustin's contamination through the blood splash last year. From then on, Zack had taken safety precautions as seriously as a soldier in the trenches.

When she entered the office behind him she perched on a chair in front of his desk—the one closest to the door. Unlike last night, she couldn't quite get past the specter of their breakup for some reason. His rejection. Perhaps she was being too presumptuous to think he would offer her a job.

He turned to look at her and a glint of humor entered his golden brown eyes. She'd never forgotten the warmth and kindness of that gaze—the total sanity that ruled his life. How attractive that was to her right now, in this man who had broken her heart.

Instead of sitting behind his desk, he took the seat next to hers, turned it to face her and sank down, so close their knees nearly touched. "Joy, I really am glad you're back in town, and don't worry, I won't bite. I didn't last night, did I?"

She swallowed, embarrassed by her continued edginess. "Thank you for agreeing to meet me at such short notice."

"You're kidding, right?" His lips twitched. "Don't tell me we're going to keep this strictly professional. I'll always make time for my friend and anatomy lab partner."

Might as well address the presence of the elephant, just as he had. "I'm not concerned about those people, just the former fiancés."

The light in his eyes dimmed a bit as his gaze settled into hers. "It's hard, I'll admit. I'll never forget the worst day of my life."

"It was mine, too."

"Think we could work around it until it gets more comfortable?" he asked.

"To be practical, I need a job and you need a doctor. People can do a lot of difficult things out of necessity." As soon as she said the words, they sounded hostile, and that wasn't what she intended. "What I meant to say was—"

"Joy. I'm still me. I don't think you could have changed character so completely in the few months you've been elsewhere. We were good friends for a long time, and I know the good qualities you could bring to this department."

"You should also know my weaknesses, too. For instance, Weston constantly complained about the time I took with patients, or the pro bono cases—"

"I'm not interested in Weston's opinion." Zack practically growled the words. "As for pro bono, unfortunately, neither you nor I have the authority to do that here at the hospital, though we have a new administrator who has been known to write off some of the debts of hardship patients."

"Good. But I might have difficulty keeping up when it gets busy."

"You didn't before when you moonlighted here. We're busier than we were, but we can often pull from fourth-year med school students to help out when it's crazy, and our mid-level providers help a lot."

"Are you trying to talk me into taking the job?"

"Isn't that what you're here for? You didn't expect me to make you beg, did you?" He grinned, leaning forward, elbows on knees.

She resisted the sudden urge to retreat as it hit home how difficult it would be to work with him regularly, see him every day. Being this close to him only brought buried emotions to the surface once again.

He sobered and leaned back. "I'm definitely not denying it'll probably be difficult for both of us after we watched all our plans for the future crash and burn."

She nodded, unable to speak.

"I can't believe how glad I am you're back, though," he said.

She nodded. "So am I."

She watched the light enter his eyes again. She could drown in those eyes, the deep tenor of his voice, the humor that lurked just below the surface, which could charm a frightened child or an elderly patient who might prefer an older physician. His mature sincerity always put patients at ease.

She shouldn't even consider what she was considering, because the pain of the first breakup was bad enough; she couldn't risk it again. But what if she could discover exactly what caused him to break their engagement? If she knew, she would most certainly never do it again. Would she?

After yesterday, with Joy's whole world being turned upside down once again, she knew her emotions were a little raw, but Zack had treated her with kindness. She recalled that their fights last year had been an anomaly. In fact, they seldom ever fought.

"Molly told me she thought she might have to drag you here," he said.

"She didn't even ask my permission," Joy said. "Same old Mom."

"You two'll get your kinks worked out. Was she happy to see you last night?"

Joy began to relax a little, and she knew that was Zack's intention. He'd always been able to draw her out, get her to talk about anything. Almost anything. "I think she was. She even gave me a couple of hugs, which was a huge thaw for her. I never could understand why she was so unhappy with my job choices."

Zack's smile dimmed momentarily. He stared down at his hands. "You two always planned to have your own clinic here in Juliet."

"Sure, but setting up shop takes a lot of time and money,

and we had neither. Notice she was fine with me applying for a job here in the ER. This isn't family practice, either."

Zack picked up some paperwork from his desk. "I know Molly can sometimes forget to explain herself, but I've never known her to voice her opinion without an excellent reason. Her behavior is typical of a mother with an only child."

Joy remained silent, unwilling to begin yet another argument.

Zack looked thoughtful as he fingered the papers in his hand. "Okay, forget I said that. Molly isn't typical of anyone else I've ever known."

"You've got that right."

He met her gaze, the warm humor back in his eyes. "Neither are you, though."

She raised her left shoulder in a half-shrug. "I have, however, learned how to retaliate."

"Oh?"

She grinned. "I made an appointment for Mom to see Dr. Abernathy for a complete physical this afternoon along with the tests you wanted her to have last night."

He whistled and rested his elbow on the desk. "She agreed?"

"She had to. The showdown wasn't pretty, but we dared each other to cancel our respective appointments."

"How do you know she won't cancel now that you've followed through on your promise?"

"Mom doesn't break promises." Joy leaned back in her chair, relaxing further. "Plus I told her that if she backed out, there was no way I'd take this job...if you offer it to me."

"No problem there." He handed her the papers.

Relief flowed through her so suddenly she could barely grip the papers.

"Since you worked for the hospital before, we just need updates on the application and CV," he said, all business. "If you want you can just hand write new info, and someone here will enter it into the computer."

She reached for a pen in a cup on his desk and scooted forward to use the front ledge.

"How's Tressa's poison ivy?" he asked.

"Worse. I gave her a steroid injection this morning, and we're both staying at Mom's for at least a few days, so I can keep an eye on her. Mom, however, doesn't look so great. I heard her wheezing last night from across the yard. What irony it would be if tests revealed an allergy to cats. And what a relief it will be if Dr. Abernathy discovers that's the only thing wrong with her."

Zack leaned forward with his elbows on his knees. "I wondered about toxoplasmosis. With all those cats, you know. But her blood work was fine. She obviously has a great immune response."

Joy added her most recent work information to her curriculum vitae, then glanced up at Zack again to find him watching her. A spark of mischief lurked just beneath that aura of strength and wisdom. She swallowed and looked down at the papers again. How was she going to focus on caring for patients if he was nearby? Her heart rate always increased and her palms grew moist whenever she was near him. Nothing had changed in all the time she'd been gone.

But she needed a job badly, and it wasn't as if they'd be working side by side. They might see one another during shift change if they overlapped, but that was all.

She crossed out an old phone number and wrote in her new one.

~

Zack watched Joy renewing her paperwork and wished he'd taken the chair behind his desk. The more time he spent in her presence the more desperately he wanted to rewind everything eighteen months into the past to prevent the breakup—but that, he could not do.

He still didn't know everything that took place in that research lab. She'd walled herself away from him and he'd been unable to do anything about it. There were still secrets she kept from him, from Molly, from everyone. He understood the need for HIPAA rules, privacy and security in the workplace, but the hyper-vigilance she'd developed when they were together had convinced him Weston Cline was drawing her away.

"How busy are you here now?" Joy asked. "Has there been a drop in patient load?"

He shook his head. "We're busier. I'd say at least a 15,000 volume. After losing the residency program the school focused on increasing the student population by twenty-five percent, generating more jobs in the community. I would estimate that the hospital's census has increased by at least three thousand in just the past year."

"Even with Düsseldorf folding?"

"That's a recent incident, and I doubt it's a permanent situation. Besides, the majority of their workers are seasonal."

"Maybe Mom will eventually have her job back, if we can get her healthy."

"Actually, she's applied for work as a medical assistant in local clinics."

Joy had eyes so deep brown they were practically black except for the few golden striations that gave them warmth. The gold showed especially well when she was surprised. "She never told me that."

"Stick around a while and you'll have time to catch up."

He knew from past studies that the darker a person's irises, the more attractive they were to the opposite sex because the darkness made the pupils look enlarged, which made them appear friendly, open, interested.

He broke the stare first, once again wishing he could kick himself. Why did he have to make a science out of every emotion he had, every verbal exchange they shared?

"I'm glad you remained friends with Mom," Joy said.

"So am I." He'd always admired and adored Molly, but sometimes a small voice told him he remained in contact with Molly in order to maintain some connection with Joy.

"I've heard through the physician network that you've earned yourself a reputation for handling difficult cases," he said. "That kind of care takes longer, but it'll also be appreciated in this community. Too bad Weston Cline didn't appreciate what he had."

"Thank you, Zack. I didn't realize how badly I needed to hear some reassurance. Sadly, Weston isn't a happy man. His life fell apart when his son died four years ago. I believe his recent bad behavior, his divorce, his estrangement from Tressa, stems from that loss."

"And you're still defending him."

She raised her eyebrows.

"Sorry if I'm being unprofessional," Zack said. "You always did show compassion for even the worst of scoundrels."

She laughed.

"And there I go again. For some reason, when it comes to that man, my lack of professionalism knows no bounds. I'm betting he wasn't easy to work for."

Now he sounded as if he was fishing for information, and he wasn't. Was he?

She clasped her hands together on her lap and leaned forward. "I defend Weston to his daughter, because she's his offspring, and for her sake, I won't defame his name to her. But just between us, he's a genius with money and business, and someone I hope I never have to see again."

"You once told me you'd like to accept Weston's job offer for two years, pay off your school loans and save enough to come back and start a clinic with me."

She stacked the pages and slid them onto his desk. "I told you I was tempted, but until I lost my job I told him no. We could have eventually saved enough right here in Juliet."

Knowing Joy as well as he did, he couldn't help suspecting that Weston had lied to him last year; now that he was looking into those open, trusting eyes, he couldn't believe she'd behaved the way he'd been led to believe.

"Zack? You have that look." She waved her hand in front of him. "What's got you so serious all of a sudden?"

"He told me I was holding you back."

"From what?" she asked. "I had everything I wanted right here."

"He said you had everything it took to make a name for yourself—and beauty was part of it. That's the reason he slapped your image on those billboards. You do have one of the best bedside manners I've ever seen in a physician, and you built the clinic much faster there than you would have here, where the patient population is limited."

"Then I could have moonlighted in the ER until I paid off my school loans," she said. "Weston pulled the bait-and-switch. He made me sign a five-year contract and then made arrangements for me to get the loan on the monstrosity of a house while I wasn't thinking straight."

Yes, the more he thought about it, the more convinced he was that Weston Cline was a king among liars. Joy wasn't the only one who could be manipulated, obviously.

"So tell me about staffing," she requested.

Zack took the hint. She didn't want to discuss the heartache of the past nine months.

"Mid-level providers are here from ten a.m. to ten p.m." he

said. "You probably noticed when you came in that we have three nurses on duty, plus a secretary and two paramedics, and as I said, med students can help out if we need them. It's great coverage, and right now that's all the hospital can afford. Adding two new physicians for double coverage at peak times would break the budget."

"I'd like to officially apply for the temporary position."

Zack smiled and picked up he completed papers. "Admin will require all the accoutrements and make the final decision, but they listen to me. As far as I'm concerned you're on board."

The square shoulders rounded. He could practically see the tension drain from her face. "When do I start?"

He laughed, feeling as relieved as she obviously was. "You haven't asked what kind of a boss I am. For all you know, I could be a tyrant."

"Should I have interviewed the staff before offering my head on the chopping block?"

"Too late. You've already given me the paperwork."

"I haven't signed the contract." She allowed gentle teasing into her voice, and he remembered that had often been the default tone of their conversations. Before the fights began.

She was handling the loss of her job with much more aplomb than he would have expected if, indeed, her heart had been set on the "brilliant career in the city."

He looked down at his hands for a few seconds, then back up at her. "Joy, last year was a painful time for both of us. But I know you, and I think you know me well enough from long years of friendship that we'll be able to make the transition."

She angled hear head, eyes narrowed. "You never actually explained why—"

"I know."

"And you obviously aren't ready to tell me."

He reached across the space between them and laid his hand

on hers, loving the soft feel of her skin. He'd been in love with her since the first year they met. "Someday we'll talk." Once he got over the shock, himself. "Let's take this new development a day at a time, if that works for you."

She smiled into his eyes. "It does."

He released her and sat back. "One thing concerns me. Weston Cline is too cunning a businessman to just throw away all the money he spent on his prized physician."

She paused, studying the items on his desk as if looking for an answer. "He called me twice while I was driving here last night, but I deleted his messages this morning without listening."

Zack gritted his teeth. Of course.

"I'm not going back." She leaned forward, emphasizing her words. "I was miserable. Not long before you called yesterday, I had a patient scream at me so loudly the whole clinic heard him accuse me of sleeping with the boss to get my job. He didn't get the endless supply of narcs he wanted."

"You might get that kind of treatment here from time to time. We do get drug seekers."

"You don't advertise this department as a pain clinic, and my new boss would never attempt to take advantage of his authority by trying exactly what I was accused of doing to keep my job."

Zack's teeth were getting a good grinding down today. He wasn't surprised. He actually would have been surprised if Weston hadn't attempted to seduce her, but her words assured him that her former boss had not been successful. That filled Zack with overwhelming relief, but a fury so deep he wished he had time to drive to Corrigan and punch Weston in his pretty face. Last year the man had actually convinced him—

"Sue him." Zack could only blame himself for listening. Where had his head been last year?

"It would be my word against his. Plus, he could make things much more difficult for Tressa staying here, even though her mother has custody."

As always, Joy thought of others first.

"When I think back," she said, "I recall that he spent unnecessary time with me." She looked at Zack. "I didn't even think, at the time, about how that might look to you, and I'm sorry."

"You were an innocent. I, on the other hand, was an idiot." Zack had allowed his jealousy to control their fates. At what cost?

"At the time," she said, "he talked for hours about his plans for his clinic, and when I suggested taking pro bono cases, he assured me I could do a number of those. I was more interested in planning the clinic because I was still dreaming of starting our own clinic here."

Zack closed his eyes and drew in a deep breath, let it out slowly. "You didn't get a complete job description onto the contract, did you?"

"I was accustomed to men like you, open, honest, readable, so I took him at his word without studying the contract as closely as I should have."

He gave her a wry smile. "Dark and mysterious I'm not."

"I thanked God for that every moment we were together. I never liked darkness, and mystery in a man is like he's living behind a façade."

Zack leaned forward. "Does he know Tressa's here?"

"Not yet."

"Joy, be very cautious with this man. He had the power to make your name regionally famous, but with the kind of money at his fingertips he can also hurt that name."

Joy's eyes clouded over with worry. Zack would be kicking himself for the rest of his life at this rate.

"Of course, he can't hurt you here," he said. "Not under my protection at the hospital."

"He might try. His own daughter has warned me not to underestimate him. When do I start work?"

They decided she would begin her first shift on Saturday as he walked her out of the office. "I'm sorry about what you're going through," he said.

She shrugged. "I made some decisions that have backfired on me. Mom raised me to have faith in God's providence."

He leaned forward. "I know you quit Molly's church before you left here, but I don't think you've lost your faith in God."

"Well, I don't exactly feel the love, if you know what I mean."

"You don't have to feel it."

"I think it might be nice, though."

"No. You're going through a time of pruning in your life, Joy, when God removes some of the excess to allow you to bear better fruit. You've been raised by a qualified vintner, and so you should know what that's all about. For good or ill, your response to the pruning may affect the rest of your life."

She shook her head. "You sound so much like the old Zack. You sure you shouldn't have gone into the ministry?"

"I've chosen the ministry where I can bear the most fruit." After the pain of last year, he knew all about being pruned. His only question was if God had removed Joy from his life completely, or if it was only for a time, so they both might grow.

"Remember anatomy lab?" Her voice distracted him from his thoughts.

"It's where we first met. Of course I remember."

"When some of the other lab students made crude comments or gave their cadavers unkind nicknames, you named our cadaver Mrs. Addison."

"That was in honor of a teacher I admired in high school, because our cadaver had offered her body to train new doctors. Therefore, she taught us well."

"That kind of thinking was why we were friends," she said.

The phone buzzed, and a voice came through the speaker about some test results.

Joy stepped out into the wide hallway. "I need to hunt down some scrubs. I didn't pack with the intention of starting a new job, so I'll need to contact the clinic secretary in Corrigan to fax my file to the hospital."

He joined her at the door. "I'll call you as soon as I get the go-ahead, but if you can come in on Saturday, unless I tell you otherwise, the shift is seven A to seven P."

He wanted to touch her hand one more time before she left, but he stood back and watched her walk down the hallway, entranced, eager, anxious. "Lord," he whispered, "what wild ride do you have us on?"

Chapter 13

Late Thursday afternoon Tressa sat at Molly's kitchen table, hands clenched, paralyzed by fear as Joy and Molly shouted quietly at each other.

Joy placed a printout of Molly's test result onto the table. "Mom, you should have let Dr. Abernathy admit you—"

"Not paying for a hospital stay."

"Which means you're leaving me to pay for your funeral."

"Stop with the guilt—"

"We're not playing games here. You refused the meds—"

"I'm taking the insulin until I get the sugar under control, but don't think for a minute I'll touch a statin."

"Sometimes even the most evil drug can help—"

"It won't help my liver. I'll get the cholesterol down." Molly nodded toward Tressa, who wished she was anywhere but here. "Our young friend's been nagging me for months to let her help me with a diet. I'm game. I'll even take niacin for the triglycerides, even though I know it'll double my hot flashes and give me a permanent sensation of sunburn."

"It won't be so bad if you start slowly." Tressa hadn't realized until yesterday that the foundation of her life that had been tested these past four years would threaten to crumble completely in one single week. She knew how Joy felt.

Sometimes, on the worst nights after Keegan died and Mom and Dad divorced, Tressa had laid awake at night wondering what would happen if her mother died. And she'd cried so much her pillow was too wet to sleep on. Joy probably wanted to cry right now.

"I knew it would be bad, but I didn't expect this," Joy murmured.

Molly crossed her arms and sighed. "I haven't had heart damage."

"Yet."

Molly glared.

Tressa caught Joy's attention and gave her a warning look. *Don't lecture her, let the numbers speak for themselves.* Molly was not in the mood to be open to suggestion, especially from her daughter. Tressa knew how that felt, too. Mom never listened to her.

Joy cleared her throat and took a deep breath. "Mom, the stress test shows a problem."

"Not an MI. And I've agreed to one med to control the blood pressure, but three? He's gone overboard. I'll take the one med I can afford until I can control it with supplements."

"Which don't work nearly as—"

"Molly, I've been thinking." Tressa stood up so suddenly she nearly knocked her chair backward. *Just keep talking.* "You know that cooking class I took with my mom a few months ago? Well, I was going to take over the kitchen at home for the summer and experiment with all these healthy alternatives to the recipes we learned in the class, but you've got an even bigger kitchen. Why don't you let me play chef? I mean, I shouldn't stay here for free, and if I cook for you over the summer, those numbers can—"

"You both *do* know what these numbers mean, don't you?" Joy asked.

"That I could die someday?" Molly got up from the table and pulled a pot from a lower cupboard. "Who isn't?"

"I know this isn't good, Molly." Tressa pointed to the test results. "But we can get these numbers down if we try. In school, I'm—"

"Of course we can get them down," Joy said. "What you need to do is fill all the prescriptions Dr. Abernathy gave you, not pick and choose."

"No insurance," Molly said. "And I haven't sold out to big pharma the way you have."

"Of course you have insurance." Joy's voice was heavy with sarcasm. "Everyone has it now, remember?"

"Which means I especially can't afford all the meds now."

"It'll cost even more later," Joy snapped, "when this progresses to a heart attack or stroke, or when you lose a leg or go on dialysis for diabetes."

Molly gestured to Tressa. "I think you were interrupted. What were you saying?"

"I know a special diet plan that helped Mom."

Molly nodded as she turned on the faucet to fill the pot, but Tressa could see the distaste on her face. No more junk food for Molly. This was going to be a challenge. Good thing Tressa liked challenges.

"The worst thing about dieting is the work involved. But I can do that work for you. Ask Joy about my healthy sandwiches. Low carb. I can even do gluten free, and desserts you won't even be able to tell are good for you."

"She does know how to make a killer sandwich," Joy said, "and not in the literal way. But Mom, first you're going to have to take steps to lower those numbers. I can help pay for—"

"Don't say it."

"I was going to suggest that I float you a loan. Zack says you're looking for a job as medical assistant."

"Sure am, but being qualified and being hired are two different things. Ever heard of age discrimination? No one admits it, but it's alive and well everywhere I look."

"So let me help you until you do have a job."

"Okay, then just hush and let Tressa talk," Molly told her.

"Mom, this is your life we're—"

"Exactly." Molly turned to narrow her eyes at Joy. "My life, not yours. Aren't those the very words you used on me when I thought you were making a mistake last year?"

"We weren't talking about life and death then, and I wasn't making a mistake. I gained a lot this past year." Joy nodded toward Tressa to emphasize her point. "Are you saying having her in my life could have been a mistake in any way?"

Molly stood staring at her daughter with her mouth open. She looked at Tressa and closed her mouth.

"And even if I hadn't met Tressa," Joy said, "I'm still alive to land a new job, which you won't be if you don't do something now, immediately, to change those numbers."

Molly turned off the faucet and carried the pot to the stove.

Joy crossed her arms. "So…?"

"So you're not buying any medications for me, you're not loaning me money. If I can't take care of myself, then I'm sure as thunder not going to let my daughter do it for me." She turned on the gas burner. "However, there is a medicine I can take that is known to not only lower cholesterol, but also blood sugar."

"Something besides what Dr. Abernathy prescribed?"

Molly reached under the counter and pulled out a bottle of dark red wine. "If you're so bent on seeing me healthy, I'll do it my way or not at all."

Joy groaned as she spread her hands out to her sides, then dropped them helplessly.

"I'm not calling this wine, my dear. It's medicine. And just like medicine," Molly said, pointing at Tressa, "too much can be deadly. I made this myself. I was just experimenting with my own grapes, letting this age a little, but there's enough for me to have four ounces a day."

"And you can eat fish," Tressa said. "And lean meats and low carb breads and lots delicious salads and my special desserts with nuts and everything. You'd be surprised what—"

"Gotcha," Molly said. "You're going to wow me with your delicious food replacements."

Molly would see. They'd both see how good healthy food could be. "So do I get the job?"

Molly sank back into her chair. "If this experiment doesn't work, and if something happens to me, you'll blame yourself."

"I promise not to."

Joy reached for the bottle. "Is there more where this came from?"

Molly nodded. "Why? Do you suddenly feel like you need a swig?"

"No, but I'm going to pour this out if you don't listen to me for a minute." She held the bottle up. "This might have helped keep your blood sugar at lower level before you developed diabetes symptoms, but now it won't help. Where's the rest of it?"

Molly walked to the table and leaned toward her daughter. "I'm not telling. Because I plan to drop this weight and recover from the diabetes."

Tressa braced herself for another uncomfortable standoff. She loved Joy and Molly, but even though they'd both softened a little since last night, they still clashed nearly every time they were in the same room.

Before more fireworks could begin, Joy's cell phone rang.

Joy looked at the screen, then at Tressa. "I'd better take this. It's your father."

Tressa watched Joy step out of the house, and she suddenly felt sick to her stomach.

~

Joy stepped onto the front porch before answering Weston's call. If this got ugly, she didn't want Tressa to have to witness yet another uncomfortable exchange today.

She took a deep breath and allowed the long-familiar peace of the Missouri River below to calm her for a few seconds, then, before the call could go to voice mail, she answered. "Hello, Weston."

"Where are you?"

"I'm sorry?" He knew her destination last night.

"Why didn't you answer my calls?"

"I received several calls." She stepped from the porch and strolled toward the cliff several hundred feet away. She wanted to tell him she hadn't felt it necessary to jump through her former employer's hoops barely two hours after she'd been fired. She bit her tongue. Not the best way to proceed with Tressa's immediate future hanging in the balance.

"Now that I have you on the phone anyway, why don't you tell me what you think about my proposal?"

She slowed her steps. "I apologize. I didn't make myself clear. I didn't listen to your voice mail, I deleted it." Dial back the attitude, Joy.

There was a pause and a sharp exhale. She waited quietly for him to get his temper back under control.

"I'll help you with that. I suggested you show up at work tomorrow at your regular time, and we'll disregard the papers I gave you last night." His words were precise and clipped, as if speaking to a recalcitrant underling. "It would be perfectly legal, and we can move forward quickly from there. I don't think you realize quite how hard it would hit you to lose this job."

"I'm sure I do. I could lose money, and lots of it."

"I can do things for your career that few people can even come close to doing, and I doubt they taught you how to market yourself in med school."

Joy sighed. Yet another game. But this time Weston had overplayed his hand. "I'm sorry, it would not be possible to return to work with you."

"Why not?"

"Did you know that one of the signs of insanity is attempting to achieve a specific result using a method that has already proven to be a failure? We failed, okay? It didn't work."

"Then you tell me what you really want, and I'll make your dream come true."

"My dream is to work far, far from the city, and I can't see myself luxuriating in that beautiful mansion you chose for me while knowing I can't reach out and lift up others who can't afford my exorbitant fees."

"I'll have a new contract drawn up allowing you an agreed-upon number of pro-bono cases per month."

"Weston, I'm sorry." She didn't want to anger him, but she didn't want to play games, either. "I'll allow the equity in the house to revert to you if you'll take over the loan and take my name off the papers. That money can be used to help pay you back for my med school loans. Perhaps a nice severance package would help, since there was no good reason for me to be fired."

"Why? You were jobless when I hired you."

She gritted her teeth, appreciating more with every step the honest, kind relationship she and Zack had built together. "I was working emergency medicine part time." That wasn't exactly true. A couple of shifts a month was practically jobless.

"I spent too much time building the patient base at your clinic when I could have been building my own."

There was a long pause, and then a quiet sigh. "Where is my daughter?"

Joy caught her breath silently, at first shocked, and then outraged. He already knew? Why on earth hadn't that been the first thing on his mind when she answered? "She's here and she's safe."

He swore under his breath. "I want answers, and let me warn you they'd better be good ones. Tressa's mother couldn't climb out of bed long enough to pick up her phone today. I had to hear about Tressa's absence from school from one of her teachers, Mrs. Moore."

"I'm sorry you had to find out that way." Mrs. Moore needed to be reminded who was the custodial parent. "I think if you'd tried you could have reached Sylvia quite easily. I did. I spoke with her about the situation this morning."

"And you didn't think to call me, as well?"

Joy's steps lengthened as she neared the cliff. "Tressa isn't due to visit you for several more days, and without me there you'll be at a loss when it comes to conversation." They both knew his level of nonparticipation in his daughter's daily life.

"What did you do," he snapped, "drive straight to Sylvia's to pick up Tressa after you left here yesterday?"

"Nope."

"You needed your pound of flesh, didn't you? You think you can hold my daughter hostage to get what you want from me?"

She stopped as if he'd slapped her. "Is that something you think I would do?"

"Didn't you?"

"You think I'd use your daughter in a tug-of-war just to get back at you? What kind of a monster would do something like that?" She turned to march along the rim of the cliff, silently answering her own question. But monsters were made of pain and fear and loss as much as they were formed of greed and hatred and revenge.

"Let me ask you this one more time. Why is my daughter with you?"

She gritted her teeth at the threat in his voice. As if he cared. She held the cell phone out and was ready to snap it shut, but she glanced over her shoulder toward the house, and saw Tressa hovering at the open doorway. What would be best for that embattled child?

"Unbeknownst to me," she said, keeping her voice calm, "she was in the backseat of my SUV when you fired me, Weston. I believe she would have announced her presence otherwise. She stayed with me, without my knowledge, to make sure I was okay during the drive, though I assure you that I am perfectly fine."

There was a short silence during which Joy could picture him closing his eyes and forcing himself to take a step back and think about the situation more clearly—as he'd often told those in his employ to do in his condescending way.

"Joy." His voice was suddenly much gentler. "I'm sorry I hurt you. It was an awful day for all of us."

Joy didn't acknowledge that. She was beginning to understand that yesterday might have been one of her most successful days ever. She'd even ended up with Tressa, and she was no longer legally tied to Weston Cline in any way.

"You know how much I've depended on you this past year to help me communicate with her," Weston said.

Joy waited for the 'but."

"Your influence in her life has counteracted the awful influence her mother—"

"I don't want to hear it."

"Yes, I know, I've heard the sermon. Tressa needs her parents to get along."

"Strange that you don't seem to listen, and neither does her mother."

He remained silent.

"Though I regret she'll miss the last two days of school," Joy said, "you can rest assured she is well cared-for and well-loved here." Unlike in Corrigan, where she basically raised herself most of the time.

"Here being…?"

The question irritated her, but she retained a calm demeanor over the phone. "I made it clear where I was coming last night. It's one reason we argued, remember?"

Yet another silence. She could almost hear Weston's mind working. He might still be angry with her, but he trusted Tressa with Joy more than with Sylvia. And he certainly didn't wish to take on the task of parental supervision because, in the first place, he was seldom home. In the second place, of course, he was helpless in the face of the female adolescent psyche.

"I've thought quite a bit about our conflict," he said at last.

"The conflict we had over the way you treat Tressa? Or the conflict about my coming home to help my mother?"

"The one about your job," he snapped.

Joy stumbled in a hole. Moles. One would think the multiplicity of cats at this address would take care of that problem for good. Too bad they couldn't take care of the mole at the other end of this line. "A job's just a job, Weston. Another one will come along." Such as Saturday, if Admin agreed with Zack's recommendation. "Right now Tressa's situation is more pressing. She's a tender-hearted young woman."

"Look, Joy, I know we don't see eye to eye about Tressa. I don't know what I can do to change what I am."

"Oh, I have plenty of ideas about that. It wouldn't hurt to try kindness."

He ignored the remark. "I also realize that you and I disagree about clinic finances, but as your employer I had the right to expect certain services for payment."

She bit her tongue. Certain services? "You're right. The typical employee doesn't speak to her employer as I did to you yesterday."

"Exactly."

"The typical employee also isn't expected to be an after-hours companion on every visitation date with his daughter." Not that she'd ever minded. She enjoyed Tressa's intelligence and sense of fun. "Another thing a typical employee isn't legally compelled to do is sleep with her employer to keep her job. In fact, there are very strong laws against such coercion." Now she was breathless with the exercise she'd expended to keep her temper under control.

There was a long pause, in which she heard him sigh. "I'm sorry. I had too much to drink last night, and we know that seldom happens."

Always with the excuses. "Many of the most successful companies disallow office romances. I know why."

"I always felt there was more than simple business between us. At least, that was how I read you when you came to work for me."

She closed her eyes, regretting those few kisses, the sweet, chaste caresses she'd allowed early on. Yes, there might have been a superficial need to be reassured of her acceptability due to Zack's rejection of her, and Weston's charisma and physical male beauty were legendary. The initial attraction died a quick death, however, when she discovered the darkness in him. When Tressa alluded to it later, it became obvious.

"Joy?"

"My contract stated nothing about a requirement for physical involvement with my employer."

"Would you just tell me what changed?"

"I discovered that we wanted different things, Weston."

"You took my countersignature on the mortgage for your house quickly enough."

Interesting that he would always remember things he wanted to remember. She, on the other hand, recalled standing outside the overlarge media room, staring at the indoor pool, and thinking what a waste the place would be for a single woman. "Funny, but I don't recall telling the Realtor I'd take that albatross. You were the one who told her that."

She glanced toward the house and saw Tressa standing on the porch, obviously wondering what her best friend could be talking to her father about for so long.

And then Tressa's arms crossed over her shoulders. She leaned forward, grabbed the post beside the steps, and collapsed on the top step. Something was wrong.

Joy rushed toward her. No way could she tell Weston what was happening. Molly stepped out onto the porch and sank down beside Tressa.

Best not to alarm Weston in any way. She slowed her steps, still watching the two on the porch, and listened as Weston rambled on about the changes he might be willing to make in her contract if she agreed to return to Corrigan. For the moment, she played along, and she hated herself for it.

Chapter 14

Tressa sent God a silent thanks for the drama class she'd taken this past year, because she sure needed it now. She placed her head between her knees while the whole world darkened around her like one of those hideous carnival rides Mom's third—no, wait, it was the fourth—boyfriend took her on.

She threw up that day, not because she was afraid of the ride, but because she found out the hard way that Mom had the poor sense not to ask the man why he was divorced. Later Tressa found online that there was a court order keeping that jerk away from his own children.

To Tressa's dismay, Mom discovered soon after Dad left that singles groups were the best places to meet men. What she didn't realize was that some of them were as messed up as she was, and because they shared some of the same problems, they didn't realize why their fresh, new romances never worked out. Why was it that Mom always tended to date molesters and abusers?

The porch door closed, and heavy footsteps came up behind her. "Tressa? It's going to be okay, you know. Joy can handle your Dad." The boards of the porch creaked when Molly sank down beside her. "You feeling all right?"

Like throwing up. Like crying. Like dying and getting out of everyone's way. Without her, Mom and Dad wouldn't have anything to fight about. Neither would Dad and Joy, and from the looks of it a few hundred feet away, they were going at it. Tressa never knew Joy could walk so fast and get so much mud on her pants without noticing.

"Maybe that steroid injection's just now kicking in," she told Molly. "I don't like needles." She focused on swallowing, not puking. Had to breathe in the cool, fresh air through her nose and let just the air and nothing else drift from her mouth. She still couldn't stop the darkness from surrounding her, but when she looked up the sun was high in the sky without a wisp of cloud.

"How about a nice, cold cloth across the back of your neck? That helped when Joy had an upset tummy."

Tressa couldn't do much more than nod, but that was all it took for Molly to heave herself up and go back into the house.

Trippurr butted Tressa's shoulder and bulldozed onto her lap, purring so loudly she thought Joy might hear it out in the field. Uh-oh, Joy was watching as she walked toward the house. She looked worried. What was Dad saying now?

The darkness obliterated Joy's image, and Tressa snuggled Trippurr, feeling the vibration of the cat's purr. Worf climbed onto her lap, as well, and just before Molly came out with a wet cloth, some of the darkness lifted.

"Faint much?" Molly pulled Tressa's hair from the back of her neck and laid the cloth against bare skin. At first it chilled her, then it felt good. So good.

Molly tapped her on the shoulder. "I asked you a question. Joy might be the only doctor in the family, but medicine has been my passion all my life. What's going on with you?"

"I always faint easily, but right now I think it's just hormones because I finally got my period."

Molly sank down beside her. "Cramping?"

Tressa nodded.

"Like I always told Joy, take a brisk walk—"

"I know, I know, but don't overdo."

"So my daughter did listen to me sometimes. Hmm. Well, that's a nice little surprise."

"I might go lie down a moment."

"Not with cramps. You need to breathe the fresh air. Come on, you and I both need to take a brief walk."

Tressa didn't know how much further she could push the acting routine, but the darkness was lifting slightly. "I think I'm feeling better."

"Of course you are. It's the cats. They climb all over me and purr, and pretty soon I'm feeling so much better." Molly helped Tressa to her feet as Trippurr and Worf tumbled off, landed on their feet and sauntered away. "Are you up to it?"

Tressa looked up into Molly's dark eyes. They were caring eyes, focused on Tressa alone, not on anything else right now. "Yep, let's go."

Molly gave her shoulders a quick hug and turned to walk away.

"Um, Molly?"

"Yeah, babe?" The steps didn't slow.

Tressa cast off the final vestiges of darkness and caught up with Molly. "How did you manage to raise Joy so well all by yourself, when I have a full set of parents who don't know what to do with me?"

"Brass tacks?" Since they'd begun to email back and forth over the past few months, Molly always asked that when she wanted to know if Tressa was ready for some hard facts.

"Okay."

"First of all, your set of parents are more shattered than I ever was, and there are two of them, which means there's a lot more mess to deal with when there's double the mess. I know it's because of Keegan's death—"

"And not only that, he was illegitimate, and Dad's side of the family always looked down on Mom, so when Mom wouldn't get an abortion and Dad had to 'do the right thing,' I don't think he ever forgave her."

Molly's steps slowed a little. Her breath came in small puffs. "Joy's illegitimate. That didn't stop me from loving her just the same. I figured since she was going to be the most treasured part of my life, I would find a father to treasure her even more than I did."

Tressa stopped walking. "But you never got married."

With obvious relief, Molly stopped, too. "Nope, as hard as my family pushed for me to find someone and get married quickly so I wouldn't live in total humiliation, I refused."

"Good for you."

"I did something more important. I found the true Father to us all." Molly took a few more deep breaths, then nudged her forward. "Come on, I need the exercise even if you don't."

Tressa lingered, strolling slowly, listening to Molly's labored breathing.

"I ignored my family's interrogations and attempts to shame me," Molly said. "I also ignored the town's self-righteous words and name-calling."

"You didn't get a lot of support, did you?"

"No, but I did became involved with a group of people who knew about sin, but also knew about grace. Even though I didn't tell them the whole story of Joy's conception, and even though I refused to walk to the front of the church—as some members insisted I do—and repent of the most obvious of my sins, most of those folks accepted me as family. As Joy grew, my parents couldn't help loving her, and all was forgiven. Time heals a lot of wounds."

"Why did you refuse to repent?"

Molly glanced over her shoulders, sweat dripping down her face. "Because I wasn't guilty of that particular sin, and I wasn't about to repent of something I didn't do."

Tressa stopped again. "What are you talking about?"

"And no, she was not an immaculate conception, simply a forced one."

"Molly? You were raped!"

With a raised hand, Molly glanced around. "Hush, okay? You have to promise never to tell anyone. For Joy's sake. You're only the second person I ever told, and it didn't go so well the first time."

"Joy doesn't know, then."

"Solemnly swear."

"I do."

Molly flipped the sweat from her face, her breath coming in gasps. "For Joy's sake, right?"

"But shouldn't she know you didn't intentionally…you know…do that."

"How would you feel if you found out your father was a rapist?"

"I already know what my father is. People can rape in different ways."

Molly grimaced, nodding. "And as for your poor mom, you do realize people can also *be* raped in different ways."

"I guess I never thought about it like that. Molly, I think we should go back to the house. You don't look so good."

With a brief nod, she turned back. "Just remember you swore."

Tressa hung back, fighting a return of the blackness. "Don't overdo."

Molly fell into step with her. "How're you feeling now?"

Now wasn't the time to upset Molly. "Better, thanks. You and Joy seem to be getting along better."

"I'm just beginning to realize I'm doing to her what my family, and this town, did to me when I returned home from college two months pregnant. I didn't think I owed every shop clerk and self-righteous old biddy or cocky old rooster an explanation about what really happened in my life. Joy's a grown woman, and no matter how disappointed I am that things didn't fall into place the way we planned, it's her life, not mine."

"So it's working? You know, to look at things that way?"

"Depends on my mood." Molly chuckled and patted Tressa on the shoulder. "Having you here helps a lot, but I don't want to make you a referee."

"I don't mind." Some folks might not think Molly Gilbert was a normal person, living with dozens of animals, caring more for them than she seemed to care for people. But those people didn't take the time to get to know her. Molly was the kind of person who might possibly care too much. Was that why she hid herself away out here amongst the trees and went grocery shopping during the hours few people shopped? She cared, and that was a lot more normal than Tressa's parents.

"I wish I could stay here forever."

Molly smiled and winked at her. "You won't always feel that way. Eventually a girl grows up and wants to make her own way."

"But you weren't allowed to do that."

"Oh, I made my own way."

"You could have had an abortion like Dad wanted Mom to do. After all, Joy was a product of rape."

"That didn't make her any less an image of God. Joy was never a product. She was a child. Why should she lose her life because of one man's evil?"

"You could have carried her to term and found a couple to adopt her."

Molly shook her head. "She was part of me, and no matter what others thought of me, I knew the truth."

"But you wanted to be a doctor."

"I figured if God allowed her into my life—no matter the circumstances—then it was up to me to raise her. I couldn't do both, and I've never been sorry."

"Is her… is the father still in Juliet?"

"I see him occasionally."

"He ruined your life! Don't you want to make him pay?"

"For what? The happiness of raising a precious life? Of helping her reach for the stars I thought I'd grasp? All I wanted was for him to never know about her."

"That's another reason you don't want me to tell, right? He's a sadistic monster."

"Actually, he was quite drunk at the time, and possibly high on something besides alcohol. Had I known that the clothing I wore and my overly friendly attitude made him think I was willing, I'd have worn a feed sack, but I was young, underage, and had been raised in a protected environment. I didn't know much about the monsters some men can be."

"Like my father."

Molly raised an eyebrow at Tressa. "Honey, believe it or not, you're at the age when a child is more likely to resent a parent. I've been there, I know."

"I don't think so. *Your* father didn't fire *your* best friend because she wouldn't have sex with him."

Molly stopped walking, and her face lost some color.

Tressa grabbed her arm. "You okay?"

Molly closed her eyes and nodded. "I'm fine, honey. This best friend of yours, she told you what happened?"

"Didn't have to. I was eavesdropping. And what would you have done if your mother started bringing men into the house to spend the night, but those men wanted you instead?"

"I'd have done exactly what you did, sweetheart." Molly flicked a length of hair from Tressa's cheek. "I think I owe Joy a huge apology. She was meant to take that job with your father."

"But he fired her."

"And in the process, you came to stay with us. Your parents are wandering, lost, damaged almost beyond any kind of repair they might receive from human therapy. They can't help you when they can't help themselves."

"You're talking about God stuff now."

"Something like that. But no one can follow God if they don't know Him. Let's get back to the house before you have to drag me home."

~

Joy held the cell phone out from her ear as she watched Mom and Tressa stroll along the lane toward the house. They looked serious. Tressa glanced toward Joy. Hmmm. False alarm? She looked like she was fainting for a moment there.

"Scribes and nurse practitioners could take some of the load off you," came Weston's voice. "That would give you time to see more patients, and you'd only have to spend five minutes per appointment..."

She shook her head and let him talk. He was welcome to talk himself hoarse. She wasn't returning.

"Dr. Hearst is history, too," he said.

That announcement, barely heard, brought the receiver back to her ear. "You're firing the only physician you have?" Had he lost his mind? "Are you also closing the clinic?"

"Why would I do that when we have the best?"

"Weston, the only physician the clinic has is Dr. Hearst. The only reason patients ask for me is because of those ridiculous billboards and TV ads. Plaster Dr. Hearst's picture over mine, and all will be well."

"You want to give kids nightmares?"

"You're being unkind. She's a perfectly attractive physician."

"There's not enough airbrushing in the world to—"

"Fine, then, if you're going to be picky, replace a single headshot with a group shot. Utilize the whole staff if you're so concerned about appearance."

"Not even the best marketing can keep a practice successful when the physician doesn't have your charisma."

"What I have is compassion. Charisma and compassion are two different words entirely, and the clinic won't survive without compassion." Though it was nice to finally have him admit his efforts weren't what made her a success. "Dr. Hearst is a compassionate doctor."

"Not according to what I hear from patients. I would suggest a reconciliation would behoove both of us."

"I'm much more interested in reconciliation between you and your daughter, and to a certain point, her mother—"

"We're discussing your future right now, Joy. You're my best asset."

"Your most precious asset is your daughter. Let's discuss her."

She grimaced at the tense silence.

"Might I remind you that I have limitless resources from which to draw to ensure you don't have a future in medicine if you refuse to cooperate with me?" He said it in such a casual tone.

"Excuse me? I don't think I heard you correctly."

"Have you not considered the power of wealth I have at my beck and call? I could sue you for wiping your nose and you couldn't win because you don't have a penny to your name—except those few measly thousand you managed to finagle from the bank before your assets were frozen."

She stopped walking. Apparently she'd pushed him too far. His claws were extended. He knew nothing about the wealth her grandfather had been building all these years with his ownership of thousands of acres of rich riverside property. All Weston knew was about Molly's penniless state, not her stubborn pride, which kept her from accepting help from her parents.

After enough time had passed for his warning to sink in, Weston continued. "I would consider developing a new contract that spells out more specifically your duties as a physician in my employ."

"Hold it. Let me get this straight. You think you've just terrified me into kowtowing to your every whim because you have money?"

"Money moves the world, and you're the jewel that will decorate mine."

"Yeah, you just go ahead and let yourself think that. As for the money you supposedly spent on *my* career, it would seem to me that you exploited my appearance, and by that, I mean the ridiculous 'beauty queen' looks I'm supposedly known for, and which mean nothing to me or my career." Of course Joy knew why her face was still on those billboards—because she took after her mother, and Mom was a beautiful woman by any standard. Joy had been told too many times by too many people that she should enter a few beauty contests to earn the money for med school.

"As for a lawsuit," she said, "my face is still on those billboards along major Kansas City thoroughfares, and though it was implied in my contract that I would cooperate with anything you felt necessary to promote the clinic, I'm no longer bound to that contract. You're using my image without a signed consent for my likeness to be exploited." *You self-satisfied weasel.*

"I paid off your school loans. I can demand immediate repayment."

"Fine. I'll pay you back."

"How?"

"With money. That's how it's usually done. Of course, that would be after we have a CPA decide how much extra business those billboards and the television commercials have brought for your clinic, from which I would never benefit."

"We have a non-compete clause."

"I checked the contract this morning. I'm not allowed to work as a pain physician for two years after leaving your employ, but that's only within a fifty mile radius, and that's taking for granted I would ever wish to become a drug pusher again. I'm not pushing, and I'm nowhere near you now, so we're not in competition, unless, of course, you wish to take me to court, in which case I would surprise you if you think your money can ruin me. I'm not as helpless as you might think. I suggest that instead of wasting your time on me, you turn your attention to your daughter."

Silence. The soft sound of fingers drumming on his desk. "What competition? You can't possibly have another job already."

Joy was glad she'd slapped the man last night. She still wished she'd punched his nose. "I no longer answer to you. Let's talk about your daughter's wellbeing. I think she could use some extended time away from the hostilities between you and Sylvia this summer." He should be happy about that, at least. He wouldn't have to interact with Sylvia about Tressa.

"Sylvia's the least of my worries."

"Which is one reason why I won't come back to work for

you. You share a child with that woman, and yet you never have a good word to say about her to Tressa."

"That *woman* needs to be committed."

"And yet the courts you seem to be so capable of purchasing have decided she's still more capable of caring for Tressa than you are. What does that say about you, when even money won't talk for you?"

Joy paused, wincing. She'd gone much too far. Taunt the animal and he will extend his claws again. "Weston," she said more gently, "Sylvia's mental difficulties after Keenan's death and your divorce are simply manifesting in a different manner from yours. You attempt to micromanage everything in your life now."

"Don't try to preach to me about—"

"Sylvia has lost her ability to manage at all. Tressa hasn't received extended counseling for the horrific losses she's experienced, and she needs input from whole, healthy adults to guide her right now."

"If you were back in Corrigan I might be willing to put more effort into some kind of a truce—"

"What? Hold it! You're using Tressa as a bargaining chip?"

"I'm simply trying to work out a truce that would benefit both of us."

"If you love your daughter, you wouldn't use her well-being to get what you want." Somewhere along the way Joy's eyes had been opened to the wiles of the man. She thanked God that happened before she allowed the relationship to go too far.

She glanced over her shoulder toward Mom and Tressa. The child had more common sense than both her parents, and yet what would become of her if she had to continue to be subjected to their lifestyles of desperation?

But despite Weston's character, somewhere inside he truly did love his daughter. So did Sylvia. Maybe it was the love they feared right now after the pain of losing Keegan. Still, it was there.

"If you don't care about Sylvia's welfare, then please consider helping her for the sake of your daughter."

More silence.

"Weston?"

"Sylvia is perfectly capable of picking up the phone and making an appointment with your friend, Myra. She has plenty of income from me already for the fees if she would find a less expensive place to live."

Joy cut back across the grass toward the house once more. Time to end this, and she knew how to do that. "Would you like to speak with Tressa?"

"Does she want to talk with me?"

Joy hesitated a little too long.

"I didn't think so." He said the words softly, and Joy heard vulnerability at last instead of the hard, businesslike voice he used to intimidate. Yes, he deserved what he was getting, but he hadn't deserved what he got as a child—a cold, unloving mother, the death of his brother, and later, as an adult, the death of his son.

"If you'll excuse me," she said, "I'm in the middle of a situation here. You can call to check on Tressa any time you want, and I highly advise it if you want to retain the love of your child, but right now I'm needed elsewhere." She said goodbye and disconnected before he could reply.

Chapter 15

"You've got purple hair." Five-year-old Dakota stared up at Joy, his eyes unfocused as she completed a suture repair on his forearm.

"It'll change colors again before long." She winked at his mother, Sherie, who stood beside the exam table looking pale, eyes red-rimmed. "The medication," she explained. "It won't be long now."

Joy's suturing skills had improved exponentially since coming to work in the ER two weeks ago, which was a good thing. She'd forgotten how many accidents could happen in farming and fishing land. Seasonal laborers weren't quite as adept with their tools of the trade as their permanent counterparts.

There was a knock at the exam room door, and Zack stepped in wearing his typical navy blue scrubs and white coat. Looking hunky. And delectable. Unfortunately, seeing him regularly for the past two weeks hadn't done a thing to cure her attraction to him. Joy refocused on her work.

"Hi Sherie, Dakota." Zack closed the door behind him as he eased over to Joy's side. She could almost feel herself being pulled into his orbit.

"Hey, big guy," he said to Dakota, "that arm looks pretty good. What happened?"

"I fell down the steps," Dakota said. "You look weird."

Zack chuckled. "I bet a lot of things look weird to you right now." He nodded to Joy. "Dr. Gilbert, your shift was over thirty minutes ago. I can take over for you if you have plans."

"No plans for me, and I'm just finishing. Sorry I didn't get to the other three. You know how things are at shift change."

He stepped back to the door, looking pointedly at Joy. "Dr. Gilbert, I need to speak with you as soon as you're free."

"I'll be right there." Joy finished tying off her last suture and made sure a nurse would be in to watch Dakota as the drugs wore off. She joined Zack outside the door. "Something wrong?"

"Not sure." He glanced along the empty hallway, then touched her shoulder and urged her forward. "Let's talk in my office.

She fell into step beside him. Yep, it was absolutely a conundrum she'd applied for when she filled out the information for this job. Even after two weeks here was no denying the frisson of heightened tension she felt when she was close to him, especially when he touched her. She'd not been able to get him out of her mind, and she knew it was no silly crush. Zachary Travis was the real deal, and having the opportunity to compare him with the handsome and magnetic Weston Cline, she was more convinced than ever that no one could ever fill Zack's place in her heart.

Working and living out of town these past months had at least given her enough distance from Zack to recover from the raw cut of their breakup. Being close to him here in Juliet brought back the wrench of that loss. But with that pain was blended a small amount of hope that maybe the break wasn't permanent, after all. She didn't allow herself to dwell on that hope for long.

"Good job on Dakota's arm." Zack entered his office and

motioned for Joy to have a seat. "What did it look like before you cleaned it?"

"Like he fell down concrete porch steps. Why? Are you concerned about a fracture?"

"I'm not questioning your care." He sat down in the chair beside hers. "Any concerns about abuse?"

"None at all. Sherie looks as if she's been crying, and Dillon didn't show any signs of discomfort with her. Is there something I'm missing?"

"We don't have a prior record on him, so it's not like this is a common occurrence. Sherie was a single mother in our church when she married Ray last year. Several of the ladies in the church tried to talk her out of getting married because he doesn't share her faith. She seemed happy at first, but her smile has dimmed progressively over the months."

A jab of irritation surprised Joy. She'd struggled with self-righteous church ladies in the past. "And on that you're basing the possibility of abuse?" Sharp. That was too sharp. She needed to back off, and fast. She'd already lost one job because she'd been too outspoken with the boss.

Zack leaned forward, elbows on his knees. "Of course not, Joy. Dillon's a playful, active little boy, so the occasional skinned knee or elbow is normal, but he's had bruises on his arms a couple of times when he came to church. That raised my suspicion."

"You've observed this yourself?"

"I've...yes. It's been pointed out to me."

"Oh, really? And since when did these pointers start watching for evidence? After Sherie married the wicked man who doesn't attend the right church?"

"I'm sorry, I didn't make myself clear. He doesn't attend any church."

"So that makes him dangerous? I don't attend any church,

either. Maybe he's been hurt by an abusive church, as well. I don't suppose anyone happened to notice a skinned elbow or knee or scrape or bruise before the wedding?" Joy bit her tongue, but too late. Now it sounded as if she was accusing his church of being a bunch of gossips.

"Joy?" Zack looked dumbfounded.

"Sorry." Back down, back off, be nice. "I think this is hitting a little too close to home. I recall too many times in my own church when the ladies all thought Mom needed to know every time I whispered to my girlfriends during a sermon, just because I didn't have a daddy."

"That wasn't fair. I understand what you're saying."

"Still," she said, "I'll check it out, and if I find sufficient evidence I'll report it. I just haven't noticed anything suspicious."

"I'll be glad to talk to Sherie if you would prefer it."

"At least trust me with this, Zack. Besides, it'll be less embarrassing that way, since you're a member of her church, and all."

His eyebrows went up. "I hadn't thought of that. Good idea." He turned to leave. "By the way, I'm sorry about sticking both feet in my mouth. I do remember you took a verbal beating when you left your old church."

"Some of the members still won't speak to me when I see them in town. I'm anathema to them. Seems if I don't belong to their sect—er, denomination—I don't belong at all."

"There are always tares among the wheat in this world. Don't let the tares take over the church."

"I think they already did at my old church. Mom even left later."

"I know it's hard, but don't let the hypocrites steal the faith you have in God."

"I think too many people believe they speak for Him."

"If they don't speak from the Bible, they don't speak for God."

Joy nodded. "I could've simply switched churches quietly, but I'd seen the way that group of self-righteous bigots treated Mom for so many years. Not all of them, but too many. I wanted to make a statement."

"What kind of statement?"

"I wanted them to see that their behavior made me want nothing more to do with people who used God's name to give them power over others."

"I don't know if they got the message, but I did."

"So...that wasn't one of the reasons you broke our engagement?"

He frowned. "You actually thought that?"

"What was I supposed to think? You never told me."

"Okay. Maybe it's time we had that talk, then."

"I'll go see if I can speak to Sherie and make sure Dillon's doing well before I release him." She stood up.

He joined her and opened the door. "Is this how you earned your reputation? Hanging around long after quitting time?"

"This 'reputation' you keep talking about comes from marketing in high quality and quantity, with my face plastered on billboards. Myra told me yesterday that those awful pictures are still up in KC."

"I hate to admit it, but Cline is a shrewd businessman. No picture of you could be awful. He recognized a quality physician, but he also realized your other qualities would bring the patients to the clinic in the first place."

"As if."

"That man really got to you, didn't he?"

"It's not easy to be told I'm skating through life on my appearance, especially since I worked hard to learn the skills I know."

"Um, forgive me for noticing, but you seem to have a weird hang-up about your appearance." He grinned.

"You noticed that, huh? And I've tried so hard to be subtle."

"Never doubt your quality, inside and out," he said softly. He raised his hand as if he would touch her cheek, but drew away.

She hovered in the doorway, glad she was wearing her purple scrubs, the color of which might mask the blush she felt rising on her cheeks. "So you think I'm cute, huh?"

He blinked. His skin color deepened. "Cute doesn't quite cut it. I believe that would be 'significant beauty.'"

She turned back and nudged him with her elbow, grinning. "And you have more devastating charm and good looks in your pinky than Weston Cline ever dreamed of possessing. You're missing one vital quality when it comes to competing with Weston, though. Deceit."

He walked beside her down the hallway. "Speaking of whom, has he been in contact since you left Corrigan?"

She glanced at her watch as she strolled down the hallway toward the ER proper. It would take Dillon a few more moments to fully recover from the meds she gave to relax him. "He called the day you hired me. He threatened to ruin my career if I didn't return to the clinic, but I held my own. He's called since then, ostensibly to ask about Tressa, but he never forgets to mention the contract he has waiting for me to sign."

"He really wants you back, and believe me, he's willing to do anything it takes to get you."

"And you know that how?"

"He called our administrator, Mrs. Jackson."

Joy groaned. If Weston couldn't get her to cooperate, he'd do an end-around. What disturbed her was that he'd already proven his willingness to use Tressa as a pawn, knowing how much Joy cared for her.

"What did he say to Mrs. Jackson?"

"He asked if you were an employee here," Zack said. "She told him sweetly that her list of personnel was no business of his. He reminded her that his family had funded the research department of the school. She thanked him for his generosity and hung up on him."

Joy laughed. "Um, not the wisest thing to do to a man like Weston Cline."

"Mrs. Jackson isn't from around here, so she doesn't worship the Cline family name the way others do."

"So she doesn't know about his attempts to win me back?"

"Oh, she knows. He called her back and attempted to put her in her place. When she tried to shut him down again, he informed her of a certified letter you should have received yesterday with a new contract for you to sign."

"I'll have a talk with her."

"He told her there was no way she could compete with his terms. He proudly announced how much he had increased your pay, gave you more control over patient load, and gave you authority over other physicians he might persuade to come to work for him in the future."

"He thinks that will tempt me?"

"I told Mrs. Jackson that Weston Cline doesn't really doesn't know you very well."

"I hope she's convinced."

"She will be."

"I need to have a talk with Sherie. The subject of Weston gives me heartburn."

Zack watched Joy leave, her steps long and fast, as if escaping. He followed and nearly caught up with her by the time she reached the entrance to the ER proper. It had become obvious in the past two weeks that something about her had changed. She wasn't as chatty and easygoing as she used to be, and though he thought he'd detected a certain interest from her beyond the professional interaction, there was also an occasional defensive shell he couldn't seem to crack. Perhaps it was the awkwardness of his authority over her.

The shell wasn't there every time they spoke, but tonight he could practically swim in it as he followed her to Dillon's exam room. He entered behind her.

When she went to Sherie, he spread his hands as he stood in front of Dillon. "Do I still look weird?"

The child giggled. "You changed. You're skin colored now."

"Good. That means your medicine's wearing off. Do you like dinosaurs?"

Dillon's eyes brightened. "Yeah!"

Zack reached for him and lifted him from the exam bed. "Why don't we go to the play table while your mom finishes with all the boring paperwork?"

Dillon took his hand and followed without hesitation, eyes bright with curiosity. He didn't look like a child who had been intimidated by an angry stepfather. When they reached the children's waiting area, the boy rushed to the bright blue stegosaurus and took a child-sized chair. "I don't have one of these."

Zack glanced around the empty room, then back at Dillon. "Do you have a lot of toys at home?"

"Uh-huh, and my new daddy helped me build a toy box for them, but I have to put everything away at night before I go to bed."

"Your new daddy sounds like fun."

"Uh-huh, he takes me fishing, just him and me, but Mom says he isn't safe."

Zack pulled out another chair and perched uncomfortably on it. "She doesn't want you to fish with him?"

"Yeah, she does, but she wants to get him safe so he can be in heaven with us. I told him I want him safe, too."

Aha. Sherie wanted her husband saved. "What did he say?"

Dillon frowned. "He told me I'd have to love him just like he is."

"And do you?"

"Sure." Dillon picked up a red brachiosaurus. "I don't know how else to love him."

The door opened and Sherie stepped into the waiting room, followed by Joy. The women seemed to have formed a bond. Joy placed her arm around Sherie and murmured, "You're doing a wonderful job with him."

"I wish you had your own practice here," Sherie said.

"So do I, and sometimes dreams come true."

As Sherie and her son left the waiting room, Zack thought about the wise advise he'd just received from a five-year-old.

Joy deserved to be loved for who she was, with no other expectations. And why should there be? Their friendship never held expectations, it just was. Last year Zack failed her. Would he have a chance to right that wrong?

Chapter 16

The sound of laughter echoed through the house as Molly whipped up a simple batch of pancakes on the griddle. This was the first time since her diet began over two weeks ago that she trusted herself to cook these fluffy delights without snarfing them down before they could reach their intended plates. Tressa didn't know what a treat she and her playmates were in for.

"Ouch! Queen, stop it!"

Molly glanced in the middle of the dining room floor, where Tressa lay on her back and allowed three tiny bandits to nose through her hair and nudge her arms. The orphaned raccoons were growing quickly. Nosey, Rascal and Queen made the cats nervous, and so Worf was the only one still inside the house, hovering over the milieu on a ledge far above. Molly couldn't blame the others; a grown raccoon could easily kill a cat. It was a good thing these three were small. Molly would reintroduce them to the wild when they were old enough to fend for themselves.

"Dinner's ready," Molly called.

The raccoons abandoned Tressa on the floor and made a scramble for the kitchen table.

Red-faced from laughter, Tressa got up and followed them.

"This smells great, but are you sure you don't want me to make some pancakes you can eat, Molly?"

Molly set the plates out, leaving the butter and maple syrup on the kitchen counter while she divvied up the fluffy, starchy temptation, one small pancake in each raccoon plate, two larger ones in Tressa's. "I'm sure. Let me keep one sacred food that hasn't had its ingredients reorganized in deranged and wicked ways." She nudged Nosey off the edge of the table. "Chairs only, please."

"You're really going to feed them pancakes?" Tressa asked.

"I don't do it often, but sometimes. A few days before you arrived and helped me to see the error of my ways," Molly said, looking over the top of her glasses at Tressa, "I was eating my own pancakes with real butter and pure maple syrup along with these guys. They, of course, were given no condiments. Queen took a look at my plate, noticed there was a difference, and started chattering at me." Molly smiled at the memory of those three pairs of black eyes set within bandit masks, staring at her food. "They refused to eat unless I shared my butter and syrup with them. So I took their pancakes and fed them to the goat."

Queen, Nosey and Rascal had learned that lesson well. As Molly had taught them, each sat on a chair and picked a pancake up with deft front feet. Though they glanced toward the syrup on the counter, none of them chattered. Tressa served herself. Molly bowed her head and said a quick and silent prayer. When she picked up her fork to dig into her wonderfully delicious and healthy salad—may she lose the sense of taste and smell so she could force herself to eat the broccoli—Tressa was watching her.

"Have you always said grace before meals?"

"Only since Joy was born."

"But you don't go to church?"

Molly poked at a piece of asparagus—wasn't this stuff

supposed to be cooked? "I started going to church when I was carrying Joy because I wanted her to have a spiritual influence in her life, something I never had as a child. We went to church every Sunday, Sunday night, Wednesday night—practically grew roots in that old wooden floor—until Joy left for college."

"I've never seen her attend in Corrigan."

"She left the church for good last year, even asked them to remove her name from the church rolls. I quit going soon after she left Juliet." The cauliflower tasted dry. Molly reached for more buttermilk dressing.

"We attended before my brother died." Tressa took a sip of milk, watching the little ones as they continued to munch with contentment, and only an occasional look of envy at Tressa's extra toppings.

"You don't attend anywhere?" Molly asked.

Tressa shook her head. "I've gone with friends a few times. Why did you quit?"

Molly stirred her vegetables around the bowl. She'd misplaced her appetite. She needn't worry that it would return. "I lost my faith."

"In God?"

"In people. I guess I'm too much of an idealist. I expect people who claim to believe and follow a certain standard of behavior to actually follow that standard every day of the week." Molly reached over and nudged Nosey back to his chair. "I expected Christians to be loving with Joy even after she had her name removed from membership, but I saw with my own eyes that several of the members snubbed her, as if she was suddenly the enemy. That just isolated her further. I think she picked up on the deep-rooted hypocrisy of that particular church before I did, and I admire her decision to leave."

"Did you tell her that?"

"I think she figured it out when I told her I quit, too. Some groups call themselves churches when they're really just legalistic social clubs."

"How can you tell the difference?"

"Well, first you read the Bible for yourself, and then you read it again and again, and if anything is preached in a church that isn't taught in the Bible, then that's not the church for you."

"Did your church hold it against you when you didn't repent of having a child out of wedlock?"

"They 'allowed' me to be part of their congregation, though I wasn't the proper Christian they believed I should be. How could I be when Joy didn't have a father living in the home? I worked harder than any other member on committees and I visited the sick every time I received a call. Oh, I never was allowed to teach a class, and I especially couldn't work with children, but I could certainly do the janitorial work for free. I took Joy to every function, trying hard to please them." She flicked a tiny raccoon paw. "Queen, that's not your pancake."

"Didn't you please them?" Tressa asked.

"Well, that's the problem. I was trying to please the wrong ones. I was seeking acceptance from folks I thought were God's people more than from God. After Joy had her name removed, it seemed all I ever heard the church members talk about was the sin Joy was indulging in, which of course had to be the reason she quit the church."

"What kind of sin?"

"It seems she was seen more than once with her employers at a local diner. Since those employers were both men, and she was a woman alone, they decided Joy quit the church because she couldn't continue to face righteous people when she was living in sin, especially since her fiancé wasn't present at those meals."

Tressa gasped. "Haven't they ever heard of a business lunch?"

"Of course, but since Joy is a beautiful, successful woman, it was too much fun to jump to conclusions. I wish I'd shouted them down right then, but at the time I had my own reasons for wanting her out of that spider web in the research department, so I made the mistake of adding my voice to theirs, and even shared my concerns with Zack."

Tressa whistled. "No wonder Joy left town."

Molly stopped pretending to eat and dropped her fork. "Never try to control someone else's life, even if you think you know what's best for them."

"I don't think she blames you." Tressa pulled off a corner of her pancake and fed it to Nosey, who took it gently and ate it with great delicacy.

"No, because my daughter was always a more kindhearted girl than most of the people in that church. People can jump to erroneous conclusions."

"No kidding." Tressa fed another piece of pancake to Queen.

"Some people in the church were kind, but one too many members made too many snide remarks about the mystery identity of Joy's father after she left. The implication was that I was to blame for Joy's 'fall from grace.'"

"So they think she's going to hell now because she left their gossipy little church."

"I imagine they think we're both going to hell, since I got tired of working myself to death as their slave. Don't get me wrong, there are good churches in Juliet where they don't allow one small-minded family make the rules for all of God's people, but wherever you see God at work, you're going to see Satan attack that work."

Tressa poked her fork into a syrup-soaked bite of pancake, but she didn't lift it to her mouth. "Why didn't you try to find another church?"

"I don't know, sweetie. I'm kind of like a turtle who retreats into her shell when she feels threatened."

"You feel threatened?"

Molly paused. Much as she adored this child, now wasn't the time to delve too deeply into the darkness of the past. "You know I was hurt once, very badly. It was an injury I'll never be allowed to forget."

Tressa grew still. "I'm so sorry that happened to you."

Molly smiled and patted the girl on the cheek. "I can tell you've been spending a lot of time with Joy."

"And you, Molly. I spend a lot of time with you."

"Have some more pancakes. The butter is the real stuff, and so is the maple syrup."

Tressa scooted back from the table and picked up her plate just as Nosey reached for it. "Oh, no you… "

The plate clattered to the floor. Tressa stumbled backward and fell against the kitchen counter. Her face turned pale. She started to slide sideways.

Molly lunged forward and reached for her. "Honey? Tressa, what's wrong?"

"I don't feel…it's going black."

"Sit back down. Put your head between your knees."

Grasping Molly's arms with shaking hands, Tressa did as she was told, her hair cascading over her face like a curtain of pale silk. "Whoa, that was…wicked."

~

Joy's favorite time of the day at Juliet Community Hospital had always been after evening rush—if that rush ended before midnight. Tonight was quiet as she strolled outside beneath the elderly oak trees, through a maze of scented juniper. The sun had settled past the horizon an hour ago. She knew Molly and Tressa would be wondering about her, but she still wanted to soak up some of the ambience that hovered through this place where she'd spent years dreaming about her future.

This was where she'd come after a particularly difficult test in med school, or where she'd brooded over a case during residency training. Something about the vaulted halls and ivy-covered buildings gave her glimpses into a higher thought process. The grape arbors through which the walkway meandered served to ground her, reminding her of her mother's job at the vineyard. Humble beginnings.

She'd been unable to get her mind off Zack's questions tonight. Had she failed a little boy? She didn't think so. Talking to Sherie had given Joy no indication that mother and child were in any kind of danger. In fact, the new husband sounded like a gentle man who enjoyed spoiling his stepson.

Some experts insisted that if the subject of child abuse arose in any way, the physician was mandated to report it. Joy thought some of those self-proclaimed experts needed to have untrue accusations dumped on them a few times; they might be less eager to plunge innocent families into nightmares of harsh oversight and expensive legal jeopardy.

"Missing the city?"

Joy stumbled on the sidewalk and swung around to find Zack seated on the concrete bench nestled within the shadows of the outer wall of the bricked building. Totally in shadow. "Good way to get slugged, startling people like that."

"Sorry. What're you doing here so late?"

"Charts. I don't want to get on the bad side of Medical Records."

He stood up. "I don't think there's a way around that. This new computer system has a lot of glitches. I'm pretty sure our night secretary could design a better program than the one we have." She couldn't see his expression clearly in the low lights, but he already looked tired, though he was just two hours into his shift.

"It takes twice as much time per patient as our old T-sheets did," she said. "That keeps me from spending as much time with each patient as I would like."

"I'd go back to the paper system in a New York second if Admin would allow it. Sorry I didn't warn you about that. Maybe I was subconsciously afraid you'd turn down the job."

She gestured toward the empty ER parking lot. "I hope you can catch some sleep tonight between patients." She remembered night shifts when she'd hovered in the twilight between wakefulness and sleep, trying to get comfortable on a hard twin mattress while waiting for the phone to summon her back to work. "I never understood why ER docs don't work set shifts like the rest of the staff. That way they'd become accustomed to working nights and sleeping days instead of switching back and forth."

"I wondered the same thing until I started making out the schedules. No one wants to live like a vampire. Life happens in daylight."

"So you work the bulk of night shifts?" Why should she be surprised? Zack didn't ask someone else to do something he wasn't willing to do, himself.

"Not the bulk, just the extras."

"You have every right to dump those shifts on the new-hire, you know."

He grinned down at her and nudged her forward. "I can't afford to scare you off. The computer system is bad enough. Want to stroll?" He took her arm, his touch gentle. "Remember how uneven this sidewalk is."

She walked with him, recalling the evenings after classes, after work, between shifts, when they'd done just this. How close she'd felt to him then.

"So...the city," he said. "Do you miss it?"

Right now she didn't want to think about it. "Why would I?"

"I always considered you a country girl. Until you weren't."

Her light mood tilted downward a little. "What made you think I changed?"

He shrugged. "I apparently jumped to some wrong conclusions when you left with Weston."

She gently removed her arm from his light grasp and inched away, resisting a flash of anger that blindsided her. "*With Weston*?"

"Let me rephrase that. You...well...you did go to work for him in the city."

"Excuse me, but I moved *myself* to the city to work in his new clinic, which just happened to be the only job open to me at the time. I didn't move *with* anyone, so let's be clear about that."

"I'm sorry. I know better now, of course." He continued beside her, perhaps a few extra inches away from her side. "And if I didn't, I'd be sure to wear a helmet."

She couldn't prevent a grin. Good thing she was in shadows right now so he couldn't see it.

"I made some thickheaded decisions back then," he said. "Apparently I haven't outgrown all my bad habits while you've been gone."

"Well, it appears we both still struggle with a few human weaknesses." She sighed dramatically. "When will we be perfect?"

"I just hope it's never that bad again."

"Understatement of the decade." And since he'd been the one to bring up the subject, she tested the waters. "I don't know about you, but our breakup changed the whole course of my life."

"But you're back," he said. "At least you learned a few things while you were gone. I feel as if I've been on hold, and I don't have the heart to move on."

Those words soothed her. Time for a little more honesty. "Weston pretended to be doing me a favor when he hired me, but the real favor came when he fired me. That forced me to return to Juliet and face my monsters."

"I promise not to tell Molly you called her a monster."

She grimaced at Zack's attempt to lighten the mood. "Tell her that and you die. You think I miss Kansas City life? When did I ever love shopping or partying or professional ball games? And crowds? Really? My favorite pastime is still reading or canoeing or strolling along the river's edge. My idea of rush hour traffic is still being the third car following a tractor during farming season."

"And the monsters you mentioned?"

"Debt was one, and now I've landed right smack in it again, only it's deeper now unless I can intimidate my former employer a little."

"Remind me to have you hauled away in a straitjacket before you attempt something that foolhardy."

"As you've implied, I've learned a few things while I've been gone."

"So what other monsters met you when you returned?"

"Facing all the people who were angry with me for leaving—including the church members who still glare at me in the grocery store."

"I'll take one load off your shoulders. I'm not angry with you for leaving."

Joy looked up at him, curious. "You mean you were? Why?"

He shrugged. "It's complicated."

"But we weren't engaged."

"After you left, it didn't look as if we ever would be again, either."

"You mean you thought we would?"

"Not…well…it was…as I said, it was complicated."

She sighed. The man was so frustrating. He was the one who broke his promise to her. "I never wanted to leave here, and if we had remained together I could have faced the rest." Let him chew on that. His fault. He brought it on himself.

His footsteps slowed. He exhaled a deep sigh. "I forgot myself for a while, Joy. I forgot who you really were, and before I could come to my senses you were packed and ready to leave."

"Oh, no you don't. The buck stops with you, my friend. When you broke it off that changed everything. The Zachary Travis I know doesn't play games with a woman's heart like that. When you called it off, it was off. For good. I didn't doubt that then."

"You obviously have a higher opinion of me than I do myself. I can look back and see how immature my behavior was. I'm sorry about what you've endured, but I deserved the suffering of these past nine months."

She focused on breathing. Wow. Hadn't expected that. "I don't plan to leave again," she said quietly. "Even if that means working in a busy ER with a lousy computer system and a complicated, uncommunicative man for a boss for the rest of my days. That's how bad it was in the city."

"You really know how to charm a guy, you know?"

"Wasn't trying."

"I don't recommend a career in ER. The burnout rate is high."

"Great, and now you're trying to get rid of me. Not long ago you seemed desperate for any warm body you could find to fill the shifts."

"Oh, no, not just any warm body. You think I didn't have a nice stack of resumes in my top drawer?"

"Remind me to snoop through your drawers when you're gone sometime." She stepped over an unevenly matched place in the concrete sidewalk, focusing on it instead of the uptick in her heart rate that didn't seem to want to calm back down. Since returning to Juliet and receiving a more enthusiastic welcome from Zack than she'd expected, she was surprised to find she continued to nurse some resentment toward him. She hated the feeling, but she also disliked what he'd said about her leaving with Weston. She needed a subject change.

"I heard talk that the campus grounds were due to be updated and the sidewalk blacktopped to make it safer," she said. "I hope it'll still meander all around the campus, beneath the grape arbors, the weeping willows, the massive oaks."

"It will. And no, I'm not trying to get rid of you, just warning you."

"You don't have to, okay? I was already close to burnout at the clinic when Weston fired me, but at least I've learned how to spot a drug seeker from a block away. That helps in the ER."

"Until you returned with the news that you'd been fired I thought you were working your dream job."

She frowned up at him. "My dream was always to stay in Juliet and make a life with you." She didn't care that her anger bled through her voice. "Almost immediately after that dream died I lost my job working for Dr. Payson, and it was the only position I'd been able to find close to home, if you'll recall."

"Other docs make a longer commute to larger towns, then return home at night."

"Juliet was a hostile home back then. Why should I have stayed? Only one person seemed willing to help."

"Cline." Zack said the name as if it was a foul taste in his mouth.

"At least at first, Weston helped me believe in myself when everyone else seemed to have turned against me." How could she have known he had ulterior motives?

"Who turned against you?"

"Let's just say you got along better with Mom than I did."

"That's because you're so much like her." He ducked, as if she might hit him.

"I was thirty-two years old and still living with my mother. What did that say about me?"

"I wonder who pointed that out to you. Cline? He was born into wealth, so how could he ever understand the need to save money? He offered you what you thought you needed to spread your wings and fly, then convinced you he knew better than you did what flying was all about."

There was no missing the harsh tone of Zack's voice. Joy knew he'd never liked her former employer, but she heard something darker just now.

"Why did you choose sides with Mom against me when I took that research job?" she asked.

He hesitated just long enough to make her suspicious. "Dr. Payson had a reputation for being a career wrecker."

"That's it? That's the whole reason you decided to join Mom in her quest to destroy any confidence I might have had in myself?"

"That wasn't her intention. Or mine. She was right about one thing; Payson has ties with the Missouri State Board of Healing Arts, and he utilizes that connection to backstab any physician who threatens his authority."

Zack wasn't telling her anything she hadn't heard before, and he still wasn't telling her everything, but who was she to hold him hostage to the whole truth when she was holding back, as well? Of course, she was stifled by federal regulations.

"Dr. Payson wasn't the easiest person to work for," she said, "but Mom made it sound as if I wasn't good enough at my job to undergo close scrutiny." Neither Mom nor Zack knew how close they'd come to the truth. And it would have been her fault entirely. Hers and Myra's and Laine's, the colleagues she'd worked with on the research project.

All these months, Joy had wondered why the deadliest move she'd made in her life hadn't cost her license. Or Myra hers, or Laine hers. Only Dustin paid the ultimate price for working under Dr. Payson on the research project. None of them knew for sure whether it had been the MRSA that killed Dustin, or the unauthorized treatment, but the fact that it was unauthorized should have cost their careers. Either Dr. Christopher Payson wasn't the life destroyer he was reputed to be, or something else was going on.

What she wouldn't have given to tell Zack everything. She knew he'd suspected she was keeping some kind of secret from him, but HIPAA regulations prevented her from dragging him into the subterfuge with her.

She'd spent hours trying to convince Dr. Payson to make an exception and file for permission to extend his animal trials to limited human trials for the sake of Dustin Grooms, who was dying of an extreme strain of MRSA. When he turned the team down, she'd appealed to Weston. That was what had her spending so many hours with the men, or with Weston, alone. With a colleague's life at stake she had no choice.

"Since you left, I've done a lot of thinking," Zack said. "I had to take a good look in the mirror before I could move forward. I know the breakup hurt you as much as it did me—at least, I know that now. At the time I thought it was a relief for you because you had uberwealthy and successful Weston Cline to take you under his wing. I thought that was what you wanted."

"Because he had you convinced you were holding me back," Joy said. "Yes, we've discussed this."

He sighed and shot her a look. "Okay, there's more."

"No kidding," she said dryly.

"And just keep in mind that I've already suffered for believing the worst."

Her heart sank lower. Maybe she didn't really want to hear

this, after all. "You're finally telling me why you broke up with me."

"I am. You're right, I have only myself to blame for believing Weston. It seems he cuckolded both of us. It's as if he set out destroy our bond the minute he met you, and I helped. He pointed out to me how broke as I was, trying to pay back my med school debt plus help my mother after Dad divorced her for his assistant. I was vulnerable to suggestion. Cline had so much more to offer you."

What a tragic joke. "More of what?"

As Zack hesitated, the night sounds and scents of moisture from the water surrounded and comforted her.

"I especially recall the two nights your car remained in the parking lot. I knew because I was working a night shift here."

She remembered those nights. She closed her eyes and allowed the pain and disillusionment to wash over her. Zack had actually believed the worst? "That's why."

"I was so wrong." He reached out to touch her.

She stepped away. "You never said anything about it."

"Cline can be a pretty convincing man, can't he?"

She glared up at him. "What do you mean? He told you we slept together? That my car remained in town because I was staying with him? I stayed with Myra in the dorms, Zack. That was right after Dustin died and all of our worlds at the research lab had come crashing down around us. She was devastated. How could he lie to you like that? And how on earth could you possibly believe it?" Her voice echoed against the side of the brick building.

"I'm sorry, Joy. I understand now, believe me."

She wanted to scream the rage out of her system.

"Remember when you suggested we put off the wedding for a year?"

"Yes, because you were working yourself to death trying

help your mother get back on her feet again, and you had two siblings still in college. They needed you."

"Well, maybe I wanted you to need me, too," he said. "Guess who warned me you'd try to postpone the wedding."

"He did that?"

"Weston Cline, mind reader. Or maybe he's more of a mentalist. He convinced you to do that to me, didn't he?"

Joy felt as if she was trying hard to wake up from a nightmare, but she couldn't find her way out. "I assured him when you and I got married we could both work to pay off all our bills. He told me that would drive a wedge between us, because no man wanted to be rescued by a woman." Why was she just recalling this?

"He's a chameleon."

She didn't realize she was crying until tears tickled her chin. "There are a lot of those."

"You never were one of them."

"No, but sometimes, when a guy's own father breaks his wedding vow, the world can feel like a free-fall, and the guy—"

"Meaning you."

"Yeah. He kind of loses his way for a while."

She suddenly found herself aching for his pain instead of blaming him. He was just trying to figure it all out, himself. Why didn't people realize that divorce always caused damage, even to children who were adults, living on their own, making their own lives? What made people think their decisions only ever affected them?

She ground her teeth until her jaw ached. "Weston and your father both caught you off guard."

"Well, that's the thing. I already knew you were tenderhearted and honorable. Weston just took it a step further and convinced me your honor was what kept you from returning your engagement ring and letting him take you as far as you wanted to go in your career."

"He had me convinced that I should get out of debt so my bills wouldn't be a burden to you when we got married."

Though the night was chilly, with moist air blowing across from the river, she felt a hot film of sweat form up her neck and across her forehead. Her fingernails dug grooves into her palms.

She returned Zack's gaze in the glow of an amber security light directly above them. "All you told me was that you'd realized we weren't meant to be together. You never told me why. That wasn't fair. If you'd accused me of sleeping with Weston we could have at least battled it out. You should have known better, but believe me, I'd have convinced you of the truth no matter what it took."

"After everything I'd seen and heard, I didn't think more needed to be said, and I was weary of the fighting."

"Weary of fighting for me?" She focused on breathing slowly in through her nose, out through her mouth, the way she coached patients in pain to breathe through it.

"I didn't think you wanted to be fought for."

"Okay, then, think about this for a minute, Zack. You agreed with Weston that I was honorable, then turned right around and believed him when he apparently suggested that I went home with him the nights my car was in town. How is that honorable?"

"By then I wasn't exactly thinking straight," Zack said. "There's no excuse—"

"You darn betcha there's no excuse."

"Ordinarily I'd have punched the man's lights out when he made the suggestion."

"Don't worry, I got a good slap in on him. You treated patients in your sleep-deprived state?"

"Not intentionally. Herrod didn't show up for his shift, and the director was out of town. I had no choice but to work or I'd have been charged with abandonment of patients."

Tonight's darkness weighed on her until she could barely stand. Weston had taken advantage of Zack's one moment of uncharacteristic vulnerability, and then he continued to play on it by playing Joy. He knew how to manipulate people, and though Zack was not a malleable man, Weston had taken what he could find. Despicable. But it didn't get Zack off the hook.

"That was the day you broke the engagement," she said.

His broad shoulders slumped. "After you suggested we postpone the wedding."

"I was trying to be logical."

"I was convinced by then you were having doubts. It's the worst thing I could have believed."

"I never heard a word from you in all these months."

"I would have returned to you on my knees and begged your forgiveness, but when I showed up at the lab, I was told you were packing to leave and didn't have time to talk. You'd already taken the job Weston offered you."

"You're saying Weston built a fence around me and you didn't bother to fight your way past that fence. Who told you I was too busy to talk?"

"Payson."

"Really?"

"You weren't there."

"Did you even try to find me? I waited for you to call me."

"You were never home when I went to see you, and what I wanted to say wasn't something I wanted to talk about over the phone. I needed to see your face."

"I spent a lot of time with Myra after Dustin died. They'd only been engaged for three months when he died. After the funding was cut she left. I wandered around that lab like a lost puppy for two days."

"Weston cut his funding? A little convenient for him, wouldn't you say?"

Now wasn't the time to tell him the real reason for the defunding. Myra, Laine and Joy could only be relieved it wasn't worse.

"Ignoring the fact that I took heat throughout college and med school for being one of the few virgins on campus, you were willing to believe I'd have spent the night with Weston when I was engaged to you." She allowed him to hear her disappointment.

All these months she'd thought nothing would hurt her as badly as the break-up. She'd been wrong. She blamed Zack, and she didn't much care that his father's defection made him doubt the sanctity of marriage. It didn't matter how much sleep he'd lost; if he didn't know her better than that after all their years of friendship, what hope did they have of ever knowing one another? In fact, what hope did she have of knowing or trusting a man enough for marriage?

"This was my fault, Joy," Zack said. "I'm sorry."

As disheartened as he sounded, as much apology as she heard in his voice, she couldn't let it go.

Maybe his mother's disillusionment had rubbed off on him, made him less able to trust, but that wasn't Joy's fault.

Not totally.

Okay, she could have handled thing with more finesse. Hadn't Mom warned her Weston Cline wanted more from her than an educated physician? But by then Joy had been so frustrated by her mother's need to control her life well into adulthood that she didn't even pretend to listen.

And Mom had been right.

Though Joy had always felt Zachary Travis would be the last man on earth to lose his faith in God, the same could obviously not be said about his faith in her.

"Maybe I was wrong to sign that contract with the hospital," she said. No matter how hard she tried, she couldn't stop her voice from trembling. "Maybe I should write a letter of resignation as soon as I get home. Working with you after all we've been through is more difficult than I imagined." She turned to walk across the grass to her car.

"No. Joy! Don't let him win now." He said it with enough force to stall her steps for a moment, but she kept going.

"Joy," he called after her. "You really slapped him?"

She knew what he was trying to do, tease her out of her mood, but didn't he realize how angry she was with him? How disappointed?

"That proves you can fight back. Don't let him get to you again."

"You already managed that," she said. "Last year." She raised her hand in a wave.

"You can't run away every time something goes wrong in your life," he called. "What'll this make, the third time?"

She looked up at the stars, wishing she lived on one of them.

"You know those monsters you keep talking about? You're going to have to face them someday, Joy, or they'll always follow you."

She pulled her keys from the pocket of her lab coat and hit unlock, listening to Zack's soft footsteps coming toward her through the grass.

"Joy." He was almost directly behind her.

Her cell phone rang. She glanced at her watch, and realized her little family at home must be worried. She flipped open her cell. Before she could answer, Mom's shout startled her.

"If you're on your way home, get back to the ER now! Tressa keeps losing consciousness. We're coming in."

Chapter 17

Zack stood beside a silent Joy Gilbert at the ambulance bay, watching for Molly's headlights. "All she said was that Tressa was passing out?"

Joy nodded.

"Have there been any prior symptoms?"

"No." Joy pulled out her cell phone and walked away from him across the grass. He heard only one word, "Sylvia," before she was too far away for him to hear her.

Never in his life had he hated himself so completely. It seemed Joy shared that opinion and he couldn't blame her. The day he met Weston Cline last year, the man had looked at Zack as if he was gum on the bottom of someone's shoe. Joy, however, was the exquisite main dish.

Zack had grown accustomed to that over the years he'd known her. She seldom wore makeup, didn't wear revealing clothing, never flirted, and yet since the day they met on their first day of med school in anatomy lab, most of the men in the class made total fools of themselves over her. It never ended, but she'd apparently learned to ignore it sometime when she was a preadolescent, because she took everything in stride. She didn't pretend to be unaware of her beauty, but she didn't take credit for it.

And yet Weston Cline was in a totally different league from most of the men Joy knew. His self-confidence and audacious charm had thrown Zack off his stride. The man could even come across as compassionate and sincere. Zack had never been taught to beware of people like that.

His mother took him and his kid brother and sister to church every time the doors were open, and he'd grown up with some of the kindest people in the world, attended university at Cape Girardeau, learned a lot about ethics and compassion. He'd had an ideal childhood except for those times when he'd arrived home to find his mother in tears. He never knew why until Dad filed the divorce papers a decade later.

According to his parents, they'd remained together for the sake of their children. Mom had been so damaged by Dad's activities with other women that it was almost a relief to see the ties cut. Dad's selfishness and his treatment of his wife would always leave its damage.

How could Zack have made it into his thirties without learning discernment? And how on earth could he have been fool enough to allow the enemy to destroy the relationship he had with the most important woman in the world to him?

He sent a silent prayer toward heaven. Wisdom. Discernment. Those were qualities he needed desperately, and soon. He didn't plan to go through life as vulnerable as a dove. He needed the Biblical wisdom of the serpent somewhere in the mix, as well, and could have used it the day Weston Cline had appeared to ever-so-gently confide in him about Joy. About Joy's hopes for the future—a future that suddenly didn't include Zack.

If he hadn't already blown it, now was the time to match wits with Weston Cline, to stand beside Joy and be a man instead of the dolt he was last year. But first, he had Weston's daughter to treat.

The snap of Joy's flip phone reached him at the same time

the set of Molly's old Plymouth wagon headlights raced into patient parking. Zack stepped close enough to the automatic ambulance doors to make them slide open and called for the staff. He grabbed the gurney and shoved it toward the car, where Joy already had the passenger door open.

"No, honey, don't move," she told the bedraggled blond teenager. "We'll give you a ride."

"But I'm fine now. Really."

Molly shot out of the car and ran around the front to join Zack and Joy. Her short, dark hair stuck out in several directions, and she wore a nightshirt over baggy jeans. "She was laughing with the raccoons one second and fainting on me the next. At first I thought she'd just stood up too fast, especially when she got some color back into her cheeks. Then it drained away again and down she went."

Zack and Joy eased Tressa onto the gurney despite her protests.

"Tressa, have you been eating okay?" She was slender, but appeared well-nourished.

"You kidding? I was just having pancakes with the kidlets. Molly makes the best ones in the world, and that was my second meal of them today."

Zack frowned. "Kidlets."

"The raccoons," Tressa said. "You know, I didn't even black out completely, just got dizzy, okay?"

Molly leaned forward and tapped Tressa on the arm. "You'd have blacked out if I hadn't shoved your head between your knees." Molly walked beside the gurney with her hand on Tressa's arm as Zack and Joy pushed Tressa toward the sliding doors, where the staff had come out to take over and start running vitals.

Zack pinched the skin on the back of Tressa's hand, and it immediately flattened again. No sign of dehydration. "Any nausea, vomiting, headache?"

"A little headache, maybe."

"Have you had fainting or dizzy spells recently?"

Tressa switched her attention to the blood pressure machine being attached to her via the Velcro wrap around her left arm. A tech attached an oxygen saturation reader to her finger. "I've never been in a hospital as a patient."

Zack looked at Joy, who tapped Tressa on the arm. "Miss Tress, I'm pretty sure you heard the question."

"Can't you see I'm okay now? Molly worries too much."

They pushed her gurney into the first exam room and pushed the in-room cot out of the way. Mary, the RN in charge, moved Zack's portable stand with laptop to his side.

"Draw blood," he told her, and gave verbal orders for a complete blood count, electrolyte check, EKG, blood sugar and heart enzyme numbers. "Get her on a cardiac monitor. I'll enter the orders on the computer in a moment."

With an economy of organized movement that Zack had always noted in more mature, experienced nurses, she reached for supplies she'd already gathered in anticipation of his orders.

"So Tressa, let's go over the question again. Have you experienced bouts of dizziness or blackouts in the past?"

"You might as well tell us everything." Joy took the girl's hand in both of hers. "I've called your mother and she's going to have your medical records sent to us in the morning. So, fainting spells? Dizzy? Heart palpitations?"

"If I tell you, does that mean I'll have to go back to Corrigan?"

"Why should it? Your mom trusts me to take good care of you, and I've assured her Dr. Travis's the best."

Zack's gaze flicked briefly to Joy, then back to his notes. The vitals were perfect.

"Even better than you?" Tressa's voice held a teasing tone.

It was impossible not to like the kid, even if she was Weston Cline's offspring.

"He graduated top in our class, and the school has always had tight restrictions. Only the best get in here. He's brilliant, tested highest in logic, and I would trust him with my life."

Zack glanced at her again. "Talk like that could go to a guy's head." Of course, she might trust him with her life, but apparently not with her heart. And why should she? "So Tressa? Come clean."

Tressa rolled her eyes. "Okay, yeah, I did have some dizzy spells but I thought it was, you know, hormones kicking in." She gave Joy a "Help me out" look.

"That was over two weeks ago."

The monitor beeped, and Mary punched some numbers into the machine. "Dr. Travis, blood sugar's twenty-nine. Blood pressure's a hundred over sixty."

"I need an amp of D-50." He looked at Joy. "We're already getting a few answers."

"She's had some hypoglycemia, but nothing like this," Joy said. "But the steroids I gave her for her poison ivy could have caused too strong an insulin response in her body."

Tressa's eyes closed, her face paled.

"Honey?" Joy grasped her hand.

"I keep thinking about the fit Dad will throw. He'll use this to get back at you, Joy."

"Why would her sugar drop so low when she was eating pure carbs?" Molly asked.

"It can tend to run in families," Zack said. "I want a few more tests, keep her on a monitor overnight. I don't like everything I'm seeing here," he said, watching the monitor. "Nothing alarming. If everything else checks out, we'll watch her, order more tests in the morning and see what turns up.

Meanwhile, Tressa," he said, patting her arm, "it looks as if you're stuck with Molly on her diet."

"No more pancakes?"

"That does it," Molly said. "I'm throwing out all carbs from the house as soon as we get back."

"What about the raccoons?" Tressa asked.

"They like fish. We have fish." Molly looked at Zack and Joy. "I'll be keeping a close watch on her when she gets home. She'll feel as if she's in prison."

"I believe you, Molly," Zack assured her.

"You haven't been emptying litter boxes, have you, kiddo?" Molly asked. "I told you not to get near them after you had that steroid injection for your poison ivy."

Tressa hesitated. "You know, I feel fine now, and the litter wasn't that dirty."

"Miss Tress," Joy warned.

"Okay, you know the day Molly wasn't feeling so great and her tests all came back bad and you two were fighting like—"

"Okay, so a little over two weeks ago," Joy said.

"I didn't think it was a big deal, and we were worried about Molly being too busy so I emptied the boxes a couple of times."

Molly groaned. "Tell me it isn't so. You behave just like my daughter did at your age, never listened, never—"

"If you're worried about toxoplasmosis from the cats," Zack said, "unless there's an underlying issue, we shouldn't have too much trouble treating her even if she does have it." Zack glanced at Joy. "She's not showing any of the usual symptoms. For the sugar, we'll do an A1C test. We'll want a urine for the usual." It was standard procedure, and he knew both tests he would have run on the urine would be negative.

Joy gave him a look he knew well. She eyed the door and turned to walk out of the exam room. Zack excused himself and followed.

"She doesn't do drugs."

"I'm sorry, I know, it's just knee-jerk. The urine test will rule that out so there'll be no doubt, same as pregnancy test."

"And she's a virgin. I know this because we talk about all kinds of things, and that's one of them. She's unhappy about her mother's lifestyle, and is determined not to follow in her footsteps. I know Tressa, and she'll never touch drugs. She'll barely do aspirin."

He waved his hand in front of her face. "Hello? You do realize I know this? Not doubting her for a moment so let's get onto more important things. Family history of seizures? Diabetes? Low blood sugar?"

"I'm not sure, but I do believe there's some kind of genetic disorder."

A tech walked out of the exam room with her cart of blood samples. Joy glanced up at her, then glanced around the rest of the empty ER. "Her brother died suddenly four years ago. Keegan."

"How?"

"His heart stopped. It was blamed on a tiny amount of cocaine, but I was never convinced of it."

Zack didn't have time to consider the ramifications of encountering a high risk complication on the daughter of a man who wouldn't think twice about suing for everything Zack had. Which was nothing. "They blamed the cocaine?"

"Yes, and of course I didn't know them then or I'd have argued. The boy was fifteen, IQ off the charts, prepping for Harvard entrance exams, and for the first time in his life he gave in to pressure from classmates so he could stay up all night and hit the books. He took a very small dose of cocaine to remain sharp, not to get high. This was a serious boy who was far ahead of his class in every way."

"Was there an autopsy?"

"Yes, but nothing conclusive except for the trace amount of the drug. Tressa swore to me he never did drugs except for that night and I believe her. They were close. She would have told me about a drug problem if there'd been one."

Zack cracked the door and peered inside to find Tressa awake and taking all the attention with great aplomb. At least for now she seemed okay. He needed those test results asap. He closed the door again. "What else did she tell you?"

"Weston's younger brother died before the age of ten. Also, Tressa once told me her great-grandfather also died suddenly at a young age. I only wish I knew more about their lifestyles, what kinds of foods they ate, that type of thing."

"I need to talk to Weston and Sylvia to see what else I can dig up on family medical history."

She shrugged. "I agree. I'll check them out if you wish. The doctors said Weston's younger brother's heart simply stopped, and if his sugar dropped low enough that could have caused it."

"Try not to antagonize Weston, okay?"

"I'll try."

"Were any autopsies done?"

"No one mentioned it. They don't about the deaths much, but I think they'll be willing to talk if they realize Tressa's life might depend on it."

"Where did you find all this information?"

"During Christmas break we had major roof damage at the clinic from ice and snow, so I found myself free for a couple of weeks. I decided to catch a cheap flight to Vegas, rent a car and drive to Death Valley for a week of hiking and camping. Tressa invited herself along. All we did was talk, hike, roast weenies and marshmallows and read. It was wonderful."

"But you never noticed her becoming dizzy or blacking out with the marshmallows?"

"No, she was fine, but then she ate hot dogs and burgers

without buns, so the protein would have kept the sugar from affecting her so dramatically."

"I've heard you mention she's quite a chef. I've noticed that a larger percentage than normal of patients with eating disorders are in the food industry."

"But Tressa wouldn't be one of them. She's practically a fanatic about healthy nutrition. She's amazing."

Zack grinned. Cline didn't deserve a child like Tressa. He also didn't deserve to lose another child, though.

"Her parents were comfortable about allowing her to go with you on this trip after knowing you for such a short time?" he asked.

"Sadly, I think they were relieved."

"Okay, I'm sorry, but I have to ask—is she adopted, by chance? I thought there was some kind of unwritten law that divorced parents must fight over who gets the kids for holidays and birthdays, thus ruining said special days for each other, and for those kids, forever."

"I know she's not adopted, but I wouldn't know about the rest. It never happened to me since there's been no divorce in my extended family, and my sperm donor apparently never knew anything about me. Mom and I never went anywhere for holidays, we just celebrated together with whatever animals we were caring for at the time."

"So the Cline family flew apart after Keegan's death, and Tressa slipped through the wide open cracks."

"Weston hasn't a clue how to interact with Tressa," Joy said. "He practically bribed me to attend visitation dinners and weekends with her after I went to work for him. She and I hit it off much better than he and I ever did. I reached out to Sylvia for Tressa's sake, because I could see the poor kid was struggling. I felt the family needed some kind of human bridge to keep them communicating."

"How'd that work out for you?"

"It's why Sylvia's comfortable having Tressa stay with me this summer. We're friends. She trusts me."

"So...back to Death Valley."

Joy looked up at him, eyes narrowing. "What are you thinking?"

"You hike together much at other times?"

"Only day hikes. It's something we both enjoy. She's not your typical teenager, and I think the adult attention does her good."

"Do you ever go anywhere buggy?"

Joy gave him a funny look. "Buggy."

"You know, with bugs. Like where you would encounter ticks or chiggers."

"Sometimes. You're thinking Lyme Disease?"

"It's a possibility, but Lyme isn't the only nasty little poison those critters carry around here. Also, remember when I went on that medical mission trip two summers ago?"

"Belize. Yes."

"I discovered a particularly nasty bug that bites its victims without causing pain, and sometimes it takes up to twenty years later for the worst symptoms to show up."

"I remember hearing you talk about it. Chaga's."

"That's just one of so many others. It works kind of like the sleeping sickness in Africa, but its most deadly symptom is heart block. It can be so sudden that no one can do anything about it."

Joy shuddered. "You do know how to make a girl feel comforted. But it's only been a few months, not twenty years. And we weren't in South or Central America, we were in nice, sunny Death Valley in the winter. The temps were perfect."

"There are bugs like that in the Southwest. You didn't notice anything?"

"No."

"Wouldn't necessarily matter, since they could be painless."

"Our tent was top of the line, zipped completely. No bugs that might cause Chaga's could get in."

"I'm still not convinced."

"Glad you're thorough. You go ahead and follow that line of thinking while I call Sylvia back and do some more research into the Cline family genetics."

"We'll keep each other updated about what we find," he said.

"Thanks, Zack. Three unexpected premature deaths in one family? It's just a little too coincidental not to be inherited. If not for the other deaths, I might have suspected a bite of some kind, too, but we need to cover everything."

"And we can't play guessing games. If we focus on the wrong thing her life could be a risk."

"You're getting the EKG readings tonight?"

"Will do. I've already reached the best electrocardiologist in the state, and he'll read it as soon as I get it to him."

"I'll have a talk with Tressa and see if there are any other symptoms she decided to hide from us to keep Weston out of our lives."

He put an arm across her shoulders. "You're always telling everyone I was top in our class, but you never tell them I only beat you by half a percent. Don't forget that. We can do this together."

~

The anger Joy had felt only moments ago had dissipated from memory. This was the Zachary Travis she would trust with her life, with Tressa's life. Maybe even with her heart.

She returned his hug and pulled out her cell phone. "I need

Sylvia digging up as much information as she can get. She knows what's at stake. I'll have Weston dig into his family history and emphasize the importance of it."

"You think you can get them both here without setting off a family feud?"

"If I can get them to cooperate, I might see if he'll allow her to be the courier."

"That would be best. Will he take you seriously?"

Joy closed her eyes. "He once told me my job was to help patients with pain, and not to do the heavy lifting. Anything else we send to the specialists. What does that tell you?"

"If he doesn't change his tune he could overlook your skills and cut us out of her treatment completely. If he depends on his 'good ol' boy' contacts, he could place his daughter's life at risk."

She flipped open her cell phone and left Tressa in Zack's care.

Chapter 18

Barely twenty minutes after talking to Sylvia the first time tonight, Joy was in the process of calming her down again, praying she hadn't overwhelmed the poor woman. Sylvia sounded as if she was barely holding herself together, but when Joy suggested she call a friend to drive her to Juliet, Sylvia declined.

"You'll be there when I get there, won't you?"

"Of course, but we have a few complications, and you might need to hold off until you can dig up more information before coming down here. Does your family have a history of diabetes?

"No, but the Clines do."

"Tressa's blood sugar was low."

"Then she doesn't have diabetes, right?"

"Diabetics can start out with low blood sugar problems, so that doesn't rule anything out. We're thinking the low sugar might have been why she blacked out, but we have other concerns." Joy waited, hoping Sylvia could hold it together. "You still okay?"

"If you're still okay, I'm still okay. If you start to lose it, I don't know what I'll do," Sylvia said. "Joy, you're my lifeline, and if you trust Zack, then I know Tressa's in the best hands possible."

"Good, because I trust Zack. He's keeping her in the hospital overnight just to make sure she doesn't have another episode, but so far she's doing well. Great appetite, laughing with the nurses and asking about you."

"She is? Asking about me, I mean?" Sylvia's voice was hoarse, as if she'd been crying. It also held a new force of desperation.

"She's looking forward to seeing you."

There was a soft, wobbly sigh. "I'll be there as soon as I can. I found a file box filled with Keegan's medical information in the basement. I'm bringing everything with me, but I'll call all the docs for the complete files for the kids."

"And for you, please."

"Of course. Anything, Joy."

"You can stay with us if you're not allergic to cats."

"I love cats."

"I can't think of anything that would be more healing for Tressa than to have you with her. You have an open invitation to stay with us." Just like all Mom's other strays.

There was a brief silence. "How do you do it?"

"Do what? Find extra beds? I have a rather large extended family, so—"

"Silly girl." There was affection in Sylvia's voice. "The first time I met you, there was a certain…I don't know…a sort of openness about you. A sweetness. At first I thought you were just wanting to be friends with me because you had your eye on Tressa's father and didn't want any trouble from me."

Joy chuckled. "Now you know better."

"Halfway through our first conversation I began to wonder if he'd turned back into the old Weston. You know, that maybe he found he could love again. It didn't take long for me to realize you just liked Tressa and wanted to meet her mom. Tressa told me she thought he might be serious about you because he stopped going out of town so much, and she never saw him with another woman after he hired you."

"Oh. That's so sad, because—"

"Yeah, I know." Sarcasm dripped from Sylvia's voice. "My heart breaks for him because you don't return his affection. I still don't know why you put yourself out for people the way you do. I know you love Tressa. I mean, who wouldn't? But you can't help seeing that I'm not much of a mother. You know how I live and yet you've never made me feel like a second class citizen."

"No woman can say how her life would change if she ever lost a child, until it happens."

"I still have one child, though, and I should know better. Yet you've never looked down on me."

Joy winced, recalling the times she'd been irritated with Sylvia's lifestyle and disregard for Tressa's welfare.

"I'm an awful example for my daughter," Sylvia said. "Why else would she leave?"

Joy hesitated. "It wasn't to get away from you." She wasn't sure how much to say, but since Sylvia was no longer seeing Porter, Tressa shouldn't get too angry about one shared secret. "Just know your daughter loves you."

There was a pause. "Okay, out with it. You know something I don't. See? My own daughter doesn't even trust me with the truth."

"Okay, let's just say she's glad you're no longer seeing Porter." Tressa might kill her, but this would be better than letting Sylvia believe her daughter hated her.

"I've never been good at choosing men, and that man was draining me dry."

"That wasn't all he was doing," Joy said. "Now that he's out of your life, I think I can tell you without the threat of horrible punishment from your daughter, but I'd appreciate it if you wouldn't tell Tressa what I'm telling you unless absolutely necessary."

"Joy Gilbert, what are you saying? Did that scumbag do something to my daughter? Because if he did, I'll—"

"He never touched her inappropriately in any way. I know she would have said so. She knew how lonely you were, and you know how tenderhearted she is. All Porter did was invade her space—in her bedroom—pat her hand, let his eyes wander. He asked her all kinds of questions that were none of his business when all she wanted to do was kick him out of the room and go to sleep. She even woke up one morning to find him sitting on that rocking chair across the room, just watching her.

"That gives me chills, Joy. What if he decided to kidnap her for a ransom? Do you think that's why he was dating me?"

"No, he dated you because you're a beautiful woman and you were generous."

"You mean because I slept with him while my daughter was in the same house."

"She mentioned the personal questions just the other day or I'd have been more concerned."

"But if I'd known—"

"If you and Tressa could get some counseling together to learn how to communicate better, that would be a good start."

"I thought we had a good relationship until she left in the middle of the night."

"According to my friend and shrink, Myra Maxwell, even the best of relationships can be improved. Since you've had the wisdom to break things off with Porter I think you and your daughter have a chance for a new start."

There was a quiet sigh over the line. Joy waited. Sylvia had considered counseling before, but since the court ordered

Weston to pay for her treatments, he set her up with an appointment to speak to one of his psychologist friends. She refused to make the appointment, and Weston had held that over her head to manipulate her, knowing she was terrified of losing custody of Tressa.

"Do you think this friend of yours would have time to meet with me this summer while Tressa's staying with you?" Sylvia asked.

"Of course." Joy suppressed a shout of triumph. "You don't mind if Tressa stays with us the rest of the summer, then?"

"She's safer with you. I want to find out why she's fainting, and you've got me scared. You're what, a mile from the hospital?"

"Yes, and when I'm working, Mom's here. Not only does she know more about medicine than some doctors I've known, she's a certified medical assistant. Meanwhile we'll continue testing her until we find some answers."

"Then I want to be a healthier mother for her when she comes home this fall."

"I need all the records you have, as well as anything you can get from Weston's family. I don't want to scare you, but I'm concerned about all the premature deaths in Weston's family history. If this could have anything to do with Tressa, I want to find it before it can affect her."

"You're saying it's something genetic."

"It's one of several things Zack and I are discussing right now. I'll call Weston and—"

"No, let me call him and his mother. I want you with Tressa."

"Dig as deeply as you can, and stress to Weston and Izetta how vital this is." She paused. "I still need everything you can find on Keegan. I know it's going to be hard for you, but the tiny amount of cocaine found in his system couldn't possibly have caused his death. That small amount of cocaine would only have set off a time bomb that was already poised to explode."

There was a long silence, and Joy was afraid she'd said too much.

"Sylvia? Are you okay?"

"His father said the cocaine might've been cut with something caustic."

"Whatever it was, I need to see those files, all I can find. Also is there any way I can get my hands on information on Weston's maternal grandfather?"

"I'll call Izetta. She can barely stand the sight of her own son, especially since Keegan's death, but she and I get along well enough. She adores Tressa."

Tressa had obviously never noticed that. "Why is she so hostile toward Weston?"

"I think she's resented him since his little brother, Arthur, died. Arthur was her favorite."

"I need the files on him, too. How did he die? I heard his heart simply stopped."

"Well, I've never been the sunshine of the Cline family, so nobody tells me much, but I saw Izetta corner Weston at our own son's funeral. I slipped close enough to hear her, and she was sloppy drunk. I could have sworn I heard her accuse him of intentionally killing off the rest of the competition. As if he'd killed both Arthur and Keegan. She's in dire need of counseling."

Fingers of ice clutched at Joy.

"That was when Weston changed," Sylvia said. "At one time I would have told you we were the perfect couple. Shocking, isn't it?"

"No, honey. Keegan's death changed everything."

"Things went downhill fast. Let me tell you something, honey, you think I'm depressed, but I'm a bowl of cherries compared to poor Izetta. Not only did her father die from a sudden heart attack when she was still a teenager—and to hear her tell it, he was the only saint who ever walked the earth—but she lost her favorite son, and then her grandson died. I feel as if I married into a cursed family, and divorce was no escape, since Tressa's also part of that family."

"It sounds that way, doesn't it? But when you talk to Izetta and Weston, find out as much as you can about family health. Since Arthur died suddenly, as well, I'm thinking it might even be the same thing."

"Then maybe we can convince Izetta that her only remaining son isn't a murderer."

Joy shuddered. "I can understand a parent losing control after the death of a child, but to blame Weston for Keegan's—"

"I know. There've been times I've blamed that man for all the problems in my life, but not that."

"Just remember I'm an ER doc now, Sylvia. I have been trained to automatically rule out the worst first, so don't let me alarm you. Please don't panic. I just don't want to take any chances at all with Tressa's life."

"If anything happens to her you might as well shoot me between the eyes."

"We'll do everything to make sure that doesn't happen," Joy said. "And remember, she's been healthy all her life until her menses began two weeks ago. It could be something hormonal, and we're panicking for nothing. But she's in one of the best places possible if there is a problem. Though it's no longer a teaching hospital, it has all the latest equipment, and she has one of the best trained physicians on staff."

"That would be you, right? I want you and Zack to be her doctor."

"You've got it."

"But Joy, no other doctor on earth loves her as much as you do."

"That's the problem. When a physician is too emotional about a case it's difficult to be objective."

"It also makes them try harder to save the patient."

"I'll do everything I can, but I need Dr. Travis helping me."

"I'll start calling now. If I can't gather everything tonight, I'll continue the search first thing in the morning."

"Then please get some sleep, okay?"

"Will do. I'm most afraid Weston will decide Tressa needs to be moved to a larger hospital here in the city. I want her with you. I've seen too many big shot specialists with their high salaries who refuse to see past the edges of their own training. I don't trust them."

"Tunnel vision," Joy said. She knew some good ones, but she knew a lot who thought their specialty meant they had superpowers, which actually made them weak in other areas.

"You have custody, you call the shots," Joy said.

"Not if he can have me declared incompetent, and he'll use that missed appointment with his psychiatrist friend if he has to."

"Then call Myra now and get an appointment as soon as possible. I'll let her know it's necessary. She'll make time for you. That way Weston's weapon of choice will be impotent."

"Wow, I could use some of your backbone," Sylvia said.

"It's time you started healing and believing in yourself."

"I heard you slapped him the night he fired you."

"He told you?"

"Tressa did." Sylvia chuckled, but the humor became a soft sob. "Oh, Joy, please protect my daughter."

Joy looked upward into the dark sky and mouthed a sincere prayer of entreaty. They could not lose Tressa.

~

Zack was doing yet another blood smear on a patient who now appeared perfectly healthy and was chattering to Molly in what seemed to be raccoon language, and they were both laughing so hard he feared for Molly's blood pressure.

"Queen is definitely the boss, and she lets them know it," Tressa said. "You chose the right name for her."

The staff had moved Tressa to her own room ten minutes ago.

Joy walked in to find Tressa entertaining the staff with impressions of the baby raccoons begging for butter and syrup when they knew Molly couldn't see or hear them.

"They know if she catches them they'll lose pancake privileges for that day."

"And worse," Molly added, "they know where I keep the syrup. We've caught them helping each other up into the cupboard twice, but hadn't yet figured out how to open the lid."

"Well, we won't have to worry about that anymore, will we?" Tressa asked. "You said we're getting rid of sugars and carbs."

"Yep, and I already miss my old friends."

Zack caught Joy's attention and raised his eyebrows. She jerked her head toward the hallway and left their patient in good hands.

"I'm leaving her on the monitor overnight. Remember Dr. Allen?"

"He taught a couple of my classes, but didn't he leave?"

"Went into private practice in Columbia specializing in electrocardiology."

"You think she has a heart block of some kind? What would low blood sugar have to do with that?"

"I'm still putting the puzzle together. I had a friend with low blood sugar, and his symptoms weren't the same as Tressa's. Typically, he would wake up in the morning confused and terrified, not knowing where he was. Tressa's symptoms might mean she has something not quite so simple."

"Have you checked for toxoplasmosis?"

"Yes. I'm not ruling anything out, so if you happen onto another theory let me know."

Her cell phone rang. She looked at the caller ID. "Wow, Sylvia didn't waste any time." She answered. "Your daughter's safe in her own hospital room with two doctors watching over her."

"Fine, but do those two small-town doctors have any idea what's wrong with her?" It was Weston. Using Sylvia's phone? Since when?

"Low blood sugar. Were you able to gather any of the information Sylvia's asking for?"

"Not for your hospital."

"So you don't share the regard your grandfather had for our excellent medical school, which still turns out some of the best trained physicians in the country?"

"I have friends who know more about their own specialties than you do."

She forgave his harsh voice considering the stress he was under. "Your golfing buddies? But how will you know which of those specialists to send her to? Let the wrong one get his hands on her and make the wrong decision and you'll have lost your last child." She winced as she said the words. She sounded so arrogant and cold, but he needed to be shocked out of his grab for control.

He didn't reply.

"We know her case now better than any of your friends," Joy said. "Zack has the CDC on speed dial." She gave him an overview of some of the tests they were running on Tressa. "If you want to talk to her, I'll hand her the phone. We're keeping a close watch on her sugar, and if that's all that's wrong with her, it can be controlled by diet."

"Sylvia made it clear that she is choosing to leave Tressa in your town, under your care." The typical charm he used over the phone was gone. "I could get custody in just a few hours if I want to play dirty."

"What's ever stopped you from doing that? You know you don't want custody of your daughter, because she could tell the court she doesn't want to live with you."

"If you or that ex fiancé of yours make a single miscall on my daughter, I'll see to it that you never—"

Joy disconnected, folded her phone and slid it back into her pocket, in no mood to be abused by Weston Cline's empty threats. He'd called to see how his daughter was, and her reassurance was all he needed. Why he felt the need to intimidate, she'd never understood, but she wasn't going to be easily intimidated by him again. Maybe he was fighting an internal battle with fear. He'd already lost so much: his little brother, his mother's love, his son, his marriage. His fear had him losing control, and that was something he feared most. What frightened Joy was how he might act out against that fear.

Chapter 19

The moon peered through the lace of tree limbs outside, where the air was cool and bracing about an hour after Tressa went to sleep, monitor in perfect rhythm, blood sugar normal, Molly sleeping in a recliner beside her bed. Though Joy knew it was silly, she found herself still arguing with Weston's derision of the Juliet Medical Center. He obviously didn't share the wisdom of his grandfather, who saw the importance of selecting and teaching the best students in the nation.

She stepped over to a wooden bench that had been built around the largest and oldest oak tree on campus by the Juliet high school shop class. She sank onto the polished wood and rested her head against the smoothed back of the bench.

"Room for two?" came a familiar voice behind her, and she looked up, still brooding.

"Or not. I can come back later," Zack said.

Joy patted the spot beside her and smiled, wishing she could rub the fatigue from her face. "Please. It's been quite a night, and I could use the company."

Zack sat so closely beside her that she could feel his warmth; that old familiar tremble reasserted itself, switching the direction of her thoughts. It was a nice change.

"Everything got so crazy with Tressa," Joy said, "we never did compare notes on Dillon and Sherie. What did you find out from Dillon tonight when you took him to play?"

"That he's a perfectly normal child." Zack rested his arm against the back of the bench, barely skimming her shoulders. "He taught me something profound."

"Oh?"

"His new dad takes him fishing, built him a toy chest, and he isn't trying to buy him off, he's teaching Dillon how to take care of his things."

"Imagine that," she said dryly. "And he doesn't even pray."

"I never said that."

"Oh, that's right, he just isn't a churchgoer."

"Dillon told me his new daddy isn't safe."

She looked up at Zack, but couldn't read his expression in the shadows.

"He probably told his Sunday school teacher the same thing," he said. "She didn't understand it for what it was—that Sherie wanted her husband to get 'saved,' to become a believer."

"So the Sunday school teacher decided Dillon was being beaten?"

"She jumped to the wrong conclusion. Don't we all do that from time to time?"

"I overheard the gossip," Zack said. "I must have, and it lodged in my memory." He moaned and slapped himself on the forehead. "I'm a boob."

She chuckled and nudged him. "Then it's a good thing you went to the source instead of relying on well-meant gossip. You're a quick study."

"But when will any of us learn?" He took her hand and gazed at her. "For instance, you and me. I took a very wide, wrong turn last year."

"I knew you were struggling, and I thought postponing our wedding would help."

"In the words of the brilliant but occasionally clueless Joy Marie Gilbert, I could have handled anything with you by my side, but when you withdrew to give me my 'space,' I lost my way. There, will that sufficiently lay the blame on you?" He placed his fingers on her lips. "And before you reply, might I just say that you have the darkest, most beautiful eyes that have ever entranced me?"

"You mean other eyes have entranced you?"

"Never. And you have so much wisdom."

"Zack, we both know that isn't true."

He didn't reply, just continued to look at her. "You are beautiful, but that's not why I fell in love with you."

Her mouth fell open. He gently touched her chin and closed it. "That's not the best look for you."

She rolled her eyes. "And *that* was one of the reasons I fell in love with you. No pedestals. I never appreciated being placed on a pedestal, and you never have. But weren't we discussing patients a moment ago?" She pretended to suppress a yawn, when really her heart was rapping hard against every rib in its cage, and she had to force herself to breathe normally. Had he just implied he still loved her?

"We already had that discussion, remember? Dillon's fine as long as his new daddy doesn't run away screaming because of all the well-meaning members in his wife's church watching his every move."

She slumped more deeply into her seat. "I spent thirty-two years listening to too many clueless people who don't even bother to read God's Word placing words in His mouth." She shook her head. "Sorry. That old story again. Tell me about Dillon."

"I saw the affection the boy has for his stepfather. I'm no

child care expert, and I'm certainly at a loss when it comes to relationships—"

"I'll have to agree with you there," she teased. "But I can identify."

"Dillon knows his mother isn't happy because his new stepfather didn't get saved the way she expected him to."

"It seems to me there's a good reason Christians are warned not to marry unbelievers. So what did Dillon say about his mom and stepdad?"

"He said he didn't know any other way to love his stepdad except just the way he was."

"Smart child." She smiled in admiration. "Amazing that God's way is the way of a little boy. If you can't love someone just the way they are, without trying to change them, you don't love them."

Joy contemplated those words, recalling the song she knew by heart because she sang it in church practically every Sunday, *Just as I Am*. She glanced sideways at Zack again, where the amber glow of the security light set Zack's features in sepia, outlining his strong chin, nose. His brows were darker than his light hair. She realized he was also watching her. Waiting?

"She's already married to the guy now," she said. "What's she going to do, divorce him because he's not doing what she wanted? Everyone deserves a second chance."

"Even me?"

She felt that old familiar squeeze around her heart. Did other women feel this way when they were falling back in love with the men of their dreams? "Especially you."

He reached forward and squeezed her shoulder. "I needed that. What did you find out from Sherie?"

Joy succumbed to another yawn, this one the real thing. She tried to shake off the brain fog.

"Joy?" Zack said gently. "You spoke to Sherie?"

"Yes." Joy had to start getting to bed earlier at night. "Dillon was right about the reason for her tears. She and her poor husband had been arguing. She was trying to get him to attend church, and he pretty much told her the same thing he told Dillon. A person doesn't marry another with the intention of changing them. I think I might have helped her understand her own motivations a little better."

"You told her about our breakup?"

She leaned forward and rested her elbows on her knees, rubbing the kinks from her neck. "I explained to her how I felt after I quit my church, and how isolated I felt because I wasn't accepted and loved for who I was."

"I'm sorry."

"We're talking about a patient and a church, not you and me."

"Actually, I think we'll always carry our professional lives home with us. So we really are talking about us, don't you think?"

"Then do you feel you were wise to realize you wouldn't be able to accept me as I was?"

"Never, Joy. I'll always accept you as you are. I've learned my lesson."

She nodded, but until he had proven himself with the worst of it, he couldn't stay that with assurance. "I warned Sherie that pushing her husband to change after marriage would only extend the distance between them."

She thought about that one huge secret she hadn't told him. Of course, as physicians, they had both learned well the excessive need for protecting the privacy of others. What would he say, however, if she told him about the laws she and her research colleagues had broken? He needed to be warned about what they might be up against if they reconnected.

"I saw them when they walked out," he said. "Sherie told me to thank you again."

Joy closed her eyes and recalled her exchange with Sherie. "She hugged me." That expression of Sherie's loving concern for her husband had touched Joy in a way nothing else could have. She wasn't demanding that her husband become a Christian for her sake. She wanted him to understand her faith better, and to benefit from it. She wanted to share it with him.

Joy and Zack might both suffer if their relationship went further without his knowing the possible fallout that could hit them later.

"Speaking of patients tonight," Zack said, "I noticed Molly didn't have one harsh word for you tonight, and vice versa. Are you two getting along better?"

"Tressa has a calming effect on people. Too bad it didn't work for Weston and Sylvia." Joy considered that for a moment. "She still might teach them a little more about relationships. Sylvia's promised to get counseling from Myra, and if Weston and Sylvia realize their behavior is hurting Tressa, even to the point of possibly making her physically ill, they might work on getting along better."

Zack took Joy's hand into his once again. "What do you think about post-engagement counseling?"

She looked up and was prepared to speak when his lips pressed gently to hers, his arms enveloping her. She inhaled the scent of the soap he scrubbed with so often during the day.

He drew her against him. "I never doubted the sincerity of your faith. In fact, I admire the faith you showed when the church you thought you could trust began showing disregard for the truth of God's word."

"I never looked at it that way before."

"I think it's taken us nine months to discover how to better protect what we have together," he said.

Joy looked up at him. "Have? As in, right now? Are we talking about something more than friendship?"

He drew her closer. "I want more, Joy. Much more. I want that same lifetime we dreamed about, with careers and family and a home together we were planning when things fell apart."

"You want to get married?"

"I always have. Nothing's changed. I lost my mind and allowed a divisive, jealous person to plunge me into confusion and hurt us both deeply and cause us a lot of painful time apart, but you've jump-started your career in family practice—"

"No one's driving all the way down to Juliet from the metropolis of Kansas City just to see a doctor, so my career is back where it was last year."

"Not if we get married and pool our resources. We don't need a lot to live on as we pay back our school loans. We can work ER while we build our own clinic, and if necessary, we might even utilize some of the master marketer's techniques."

"You're kidding. You'd splatter my face onto some billboard?"

He chuckled and pulled her back into his arms. "I wouldn't do that to you."

She closed her eyes and relished his warmth, his love, his sense of humor. But her smile died. Zack had shared his whole heart with her—had told her everything, and withheld nothing, even though the telling of it had been painful, and he couldn't have known if she would ever be able to forgive him.

But she'd promised Myra and Laine. She took that oath seriously.

"I think we might have a little more learning to do," Zack said. "But Myra would be a good counselor."

"Not Myra." Joy pressed her fingers to her lips.

"Why not? She's our friend."

"How do you think you would feel if I'd died last year instead of Dustin, and you were asked to prepare them for marriage, all the while you couldn't help remembering that could have been you?"

He frowned. "Joy, what's wrong? There's something else, isn't there? Besides Myra's feelings."

Joy didn't know what to say, and so she didn't say a thing.

"Would you stop second-guessing yourself?" he said. "I want the same things you do, and I want to share them with you, but you're right, we do need to learn more about each other first, do some intentional counseling."

"Agreed." And if he still wanted to marry her when he knew everything, then she would be at peace for the first time in a long time.

~

Despite the euphoria of this sudden reassurance of their love for one another, something kept Zack on edge, and it was the same hint of secrecy that he'd picked up on last year. He certainly no longer doubted her love for him, or her rejection of Weston. That poor man would never have what he wanted.

But even though Zack knew Myra was Joy's best friend, there was something about the way Joy looked away when she mentioned Myra's name.

He took her hand and helped her to her feet. "Joy, I have a confession to make."

She looked up at him as if she wasn't sure she could take it.

"My mother has a job, my father had to agree to pay for college for my brother and sister, and he even had to pay me back for the money I gave Mom. It was that or jail."

"Ouch."

"So I'm moving forward, but I need to know we're moving forward together." He kissed her hand and held it as they walked. "Whatever horrible secret you had to keep last year concerned Dustin's death, didn't it?"

Joy stopped walking. "Yes.""

"Maybe I know you better than you think. I understand the rules, okay?"

"Which ones?"

"The ones that will forever prevent us from sharing everything, particularly whatever happened in the research lab last year. Whatever caused Dustin's death."

She started walking again, her hand tightening on his as if for strength. "What if the incident in question might possibly affect your life someday? Especially if we were married?"

Ah, the euphoria of that thought—being with her for the rest of their lives. Okay, they were discussing something serious. He needed to compose himself. "I...uh...was good friends with Dustin." Zack swallowed. "I saw what happened to him after he was infected with the worst strain of MRSA this hospital has ever seen."

"So he broke the rules and told you."

"He needed someone to talk to, and I was his physician outside the team. I knew Payson applied for permission to use the serum you were using on the primates because of the good results you were getting, but he was turned down."

"So that's why you think Dustin died."

"You're saying it wasn't?" Zack asked.

"Dustin and Myra were as madly in love as we were. What wouldn't you have done to save my life in that situation?" she asked.

He stopped walking. "Are you telling me Myra broke the law and used the serum on Dustin?"

"He wouldn't let her do it herself, but he was too sick by

then to prepare the serum, so Myra placed it next to his bed and he administered it to himself."

"No one told Payson?"

"Laine wrote up the report after Dustin died. We all signed the report because we had knowledge of it. Laine left out Myra's part in it. She had a...special relationship with Dr. Payson, so she volunteered to put it on his desk with a note of her own. The next thing we knew, a furious Dr. Payson was telling all of us that funding had been cut. We knew it worked well on primates, but not on Dustin. We all expected to be reported and lose our licenses, since we were aware of Dustin's intentions and didn't report him ahead of time, and yet Dr. Payson said nothing to us at all."

"Of course, loss of funding is much less destructive for a researcher's reputation than the failure of that research."

"So if I lose my license someday because Dr. Payson belatedly decides to report us—"

"You'll still be the Joy I've always loved, but if nothing's happened yet, nothing will."

"How can you say that? Payson has a nasty reputation for destroying careers, remember?"

"Yes, I've heard that often, but never seen it, myself. If he was going to turn you and the others in to the State Board, he'd have done so already. Since he hasn't, that means he's been keeping the secret, as well. He'll be just as culpable."

She frowned up at Zack. "He's required by law to report everything. He wouldn't risk his reputation just to cover our hides."

Zack took her arm and led her back toward the front entrance. "Tonight we have a living patient to worry about. If she remains stable, there's no reason why I can't have her transferred to my care."

"In ER? She needs a family doc."

He chuckled. "That would be me."

"What are you talking about?"

"You knew I didn't want to remain in ER forever. For the past year, I've been purchasing equipment when I could afford it, and now that my father has paid me back for the money I used to support my family, I was able to lease a storefront office across the street from Dusseldorf Vineyards."

"And you didn't tell me?"

"It was going to be a surprise as soon as I got it set up, but Tressa's needs are more important."

Joy threw her arms around him and kissed him once, twice, three times on the check. Until he turned his head and their lips met.

Chapter 20

A week after Tressa was released from her overnight stay in the hospital, Molly adjusted a Vignoles creeper to grow more securely on its wire. The fresh scent of the leaves and vines, the loamy fragrance rising from the trunk, were aromas she would never grow tired of. The pruning she'd done in May had eliminated the right amount of excess growth. The leaves that remained would protect the fruit from overexposure to the sun. The number of grape berries she had removed would ensure that the remaining fruit would receive what they needed to develop the sugars and other nutrients that produced that distinctive Vignoles aroma and flavor.

Now she just needed to do some refining, keep weeds at bay and build another owl house to attract the larger birds of prey, which would keep the smaller birds from eating the grape berries when they ripened.

If she could produce a good, well balanced flavor in her harvest of Vignoles and Cynthiana this year, she could earn herself a reputation as a solid organic grower. There was more and more demand for organic. Production was more expensive and time consuming, but the investment she'd made of both in the ensuing years would pay off—if everything went well.

Now that she worked her own vineyard for income instead of as a hobby, she had discovered she had to force herself to slow down and continue to enjoy the process. Otherwise, what was the point?

She only wished her daughter would discover the same for herself. The moment Tressa was released from the hospital last week, Sylvia was there to meet her with all the medical files she'd been able to find. Molly knew Joy had been disappointed there wasn't more, but Weston's mother had not turned out to be as helpful as Sylvia expected. Thus, Joy and Sylvia had made a conference call to Weston, and without a single argument, he promised to set his attorneys to work and would bring the medical files, himself. He wanted to see Tressa, anyway.

It appeared even billionaires like Weston Cline had a need to be needed.

Sylvia stayed three nights with them. They'd helped Molly with the vines, asking all kinds of questions about the pruning process, and Molly wished Joy could have been there for a review.

Years ago, Joy knew all about the process of growing things, the apparent loss of pruning, then the rush of excitement to see the vines become enriched because of the removal of unnecessary growth. It was sometimes a difficult lesson to remember, and often one had to learn it time after time.

Last night, Joy had come home from a shift frustrated by the overwhelming volume of patients who had rushed the ER doors barely thirty minutes before shift change. This meant she'd had to stay an extra hour to tidy up. She hated to dump her patients on the incoming physician,

Molly had tried to convince her that the patients shouldn't mind being passed on to another doctor halfway through the case. Of course, Joy had explained with focused patience that shift change left an additional margin for error. Molly's reply was that it also meant the patient would receive an automatic second opinion. Not a bad thing at all—unless the second doctor was wrong.

The debate, unfortunately, had ended abruptly when Joy spread her hands in the air and let them slap to her sides, and walked away. Molly needed to relearn the pruning process, herself.

She still felt badly about last night. Her daughter came in tired from work, and found no peace or solace at her mother's home—only discord.

The sound of laughter drifted up the slope of the vineyard from the garden, where Tressa contended with weeds and curious young raccoons. The young ones had finally become accustomed to sleeping at night instead of during the day, so they wouldn't chatter and cry to get out of their shed every night. Everyone had slept better once they learned to enjoy daylight hours. Molly had at first worried that altering their natural routine might make it more difficult for them to be reintroduced into the wild when they matured, but the clamor and sleepless nights had helped her decide that the raccoons would have to adapt or they'd lose their substitute mommy, as well.

The snap-pop-snap-pop of tires on the dirt and gravel drive drew her attention toward the entrance to her property, where a white SUV crept toward her house. Weston Cline was earlier than expected. It was obvious he didn't want a coating of dust on his car; she could have walked the drive more quickly than he drove it.

"He's here," Molly called down to Tressa.

The girl straightened, her arms filled with a selection of disgustingly fresh and healthy vegetables for yet another salad. Molly had to admit to herself, though, that the diet and exercise were more fun than she'd expected, and Tressa was showing her how to get the most out of the fewest calories. The good news was that Molly would actually have a chance to increase her caloric intake in order to prevent a metabolic slowdown. She couldn't wait. But she still had to eat healthy foods.

Molly left the vineyard and walked down toward the garden, musing, as she had many times in the past weeks, that traversing the slope of the vineyard was easier than it had been six weeks ago. Her muscles, though they had already been strong from carrying an extra eighty pounds with her everywhere she went, were stronger still, more toned. Lately, she'd noticed some definition in her arms from the strength training Tressa had forced on her.

The exercise she enjoyed the most was walking with Tressa. Their long talks reminded Molly of her relationship with Joy when she was that age. She could now walk for hours daily, much to Joy's surprise and Molly's delight.

The car pulled to a stop at the house, but Tressa didn't move to greet her father. Instead, she reached down to nudge Queen from the lettuce.

"Honey, he's here to see you," Molly said quietly as she stepped to the edge of the garden. "You might as well greet him."

Tressa looked up. Smudges of dirt streaked her forehead and the sides of her face where she'd dabbed at the perspiration. Her eyes held Molly's. "What if he tries to force me to go home with him?"

"We'll cross that bridge later. Right now, he's worried enough about you to leave a business meeting and drive here to see about you."

"Where's Joy? She's the one he wants to talk to."

Molly studied her.

"What?" Tressa's typically cheerful, soft voice held a thread of irritation. "It's the truth. Oh, sure, he'll listen to the medical details of the inconclusive lab reports. He'll push her for more tests. And then he'll do everything he can to convince her to come back to work for him, sounding all reasonable about wanting me to be back home with my family. I mean, that's the excuse he'll use. He'll do whatever it takes to get her back."

"And you know this because...?"

"I know my father, Molly. He gets what he wants, and he's a game player."

Molly took the vegetables—lettuce, green tomatoes for grilling, peppers—from Tressa's hands. "Go see him. He's less likely to behave precipitously if he feels welcome here."

"It's your house, you make him feel welcome."

"Joy's at the house."

They looked at each other.

"She can handle it," Tressa said. "I want to wash these under the faucet outside."

"Okay, I have a few more vines to discipline." Molly returned to the vineyard. Last time she'd checked, Joy was on the porch reading up on ER pearls of wisdom from a book Zack had loaned her. When she undertook a project, she put her whole heart into it, and right now her heart was in the ER, never mind what her plans had been originally. Weston would provide a break, at least, from her studies.

~

Joy turned a page, rocking the porch swing just enough to keep herself from squirming with boredom. She was on the final page of the chapter on blunt trauma injuries when she looked up with surprise to find Weston stepping around the side of the house toward the porch. The breeze blew silver and black strands of his hair, and he wore a navy Izod pullover atop a pair of two-hundred-dollar jeans. For Weston, that was slumming it.

She placed the book aside and stood. "Hello, Weston." Though she'd known he was coming this morning, she hadn't heard him drive up, and he was earlier than she'd expected. He carried a briefcase and duffel bag. "Sylvia said you'd found more records. Is that what you have in the briefcase?"

"It is." He held it out for her, then, as if rethinking his gesture, he placed it on the swing and opened it for her. And with every movement, his attention remained on her. "It's good to see you."

She smiled, determined to get through this meeting cordially for Tressa's sake. She only hoped he was also in a cordial mood.

He set the duffel beside the door. "If I'd known this flimsy carrier was all you had I'd have brought a suitcase from home."

"My duffel bag?"

"I thought you'd need your scrubs and lab coats. I think these were the only items in your bedroom that you neglected to pack," he said dryly. "I went by your house on the way to Sylvia's to pick up the extra medical records we were finally able to finesse from the hospital."

Joy eyed him closely. He had never used "we" when referring to Sylvia and himself in the past. And he hadn't said one ugly word about Sylvia since his arrival. Something was making a huge change in this man, and he suspected it had everything to do with Tressa.

"And I don't suppose you had anything to do with procuring those records," Joy said with a smile.

"I made a call to the medical records department at the hospital, asked for the person who had given Sylvia such a hard time the day before, and told her that we needed the records without delay due to the impending death of our daughter, and if, because her staff seemed to have more important things to do with their time than supply life-saving information for our family, the hospital would soon receive notification of a lawsuit that would put them out of business for good.

She gestured for him to have a seat on the padded wicker chair adjacent to the porch swing. "How long before they had the papers you needed?"

He sank into the chair. "Sylvia told me she received a call from them thirty minutes after she asked for my help."

"As I've already told Tressa and Sylvia, I'm now an ER doc, and I tend to look for the worst case scenario in every patient."

"You don't have to tell me that. I know quite well how thorough you are with every patient. Remember? We've engaged in several spats about it, and may I humbly apologize for every one of those spats? I was wrong."

She controlled her amazement. "Thank you, Weston."

"And yes, the prospect of losing my only remaining child has knocked me flat on my back."

"I know," Joy said gently. "And you can trust me that your poor daughter never has any privacy. She's always close enough to one of us so that if she blacks out again, we can bring her out of it." She gestured to the carrier filled with her old scrubs. "Thank you for doing that. It was thoughtful."

He reached for the briefcase and set it on his lap.

"Have you looked at the records?" she asked as he opened the case.

"I wouldn't have known what I was looking at had I done so." He took a folder from the case and handed it to her. "Any new discoveries since we last spoke?"

"All reports show she's a healthy teenager, but she's having insulin spikes. When her blood sugar gets too low, we have fast-acting glucose for her to carry with her, but she recently placed my mother on a diet, and she decided to go on that same diet so her body won't produce so much insulin. It's working very well..."

"I can tell from your voice that you aren't satisfied with the results of the tests Tressa received."

"Zack has his own practice, and he's allowing me to work with him as he runs further tests, but I can't help feeling there's something we haven't found yet. You know how complicated the human body can be."

"Which is why I've decided, after much thought, that I want her here with you. I could hire a physician to be with her twenty-four-hours a day, but I don't know or trust a more thorough physician than you."

"I learned a lot from Zachary Travis. We went through med school together."

"I'm only glad he was willing to take Tressa's case after... Joy, you know I misled him. I caused him to break the engagement."

"We know, Weston. Of course, you know how hard it is for me to control my temper, so let's just say you're lucky you were out of town at the time."

"Forgive me, but knowing what I know now, I might have done the same again. I believe you when you say there's something else wrong with Tressa. There have been too many losses in my family for me to believe otherwise, and as difficult as it seems for me to hold a polite conversation with her, she's my life."

How strange they could behave with such decorum after the horrendous battles they'd had recently. "I spoke with Sylvia earlier this morning," Joy said. "She said she's occasionally had episodes like Tressa's at certain times of the month."

"Do you believe that's all it was? Hormones?"

"I'm afraid not, and I told Sylvia so."

"Naturally, she's very frightened, especially after losing..." He cleared his throat and looked away.

"The blood sugar problem is genetic, but whether or not it's connected to something else, we don't know yet. We're watching that very carefully."

"Yes, I understand. I've gathered all I could. I was relieved to hear from Sylvia that Tressa seems to be thriving here."

Joy shrugged. "Who doesn't love summer vacation?"

The goat bleated from around the corner of the house as three cats wandered from the woods toward the porch.

"In a petting zoo, no less," Weston said dryly. "Who can compete with that?"

She reached for the papers in the briefcase. "Please understand I'm not trying to compete, Weston."

He studied her for a moment. "No, I don't believe you have a competitive bone in your body. By the way, I warned Sylvia how furious I would be if she allowed our daughter to stay with strangers in this hick-town, so I was pretty sure that's what she would do."

Joy laughed. "You know how to pull her strings."

"And she still hasn't caught on that I do it on purpose."

"All this time we thought—"

"That I'd command Tressa to come home." He shook his head. "She's all I have left. I want her happy and emotionally strong, and she's found that with you."

"Did you know Sylvia's alone these days?"

"No. Of course, she wouldn't tell me that."

"And I've found a counselor I believe will be able to help her a great deal."

"You're talking about Myra Maxwell, aren't you? Sylvia did tell me about that. With Dr. Maxwell's experience, I think she might well be able to help. It might be helpful to hold a civil conversation with Sylvia from time to time."

Unable to resist, Joy paged through the stack of papers he'd brought, excited by her find. "This is exactly what I wanted to see."

"I did glance through my grandfather's file. I never knew him, so…anyway, I was surprised to find he was from the Philippines."

Joy's movements halted. "Philippines." That signaled an alarm in her mind for some reason. "I had no idea you had Asian heritage."

He spread his hands. "I'm American. That's all I care about."

Something more stirred in her memory. Asian descendants were susceptible to different illnesses and syndromes than those of European descent. She needed to get started on this right away. First, she wanted to call Zack and let him know.

"Weston, I don't wish to be rude, but I'd like to get that bit of info to Zack."

He looked relieved. "Thank you, Joy." He took her hand and squeezed it gently with both of his. "You can't know how much this means to me. I knew you would be the one to dig deeper and never give up. I can't lose Tressa. Neither can her mother." He released her and turned away to look out across the expanse toward the river. "Some people lose so much throughout their lives that they no longer have any idea about what, or who, they are. Those people will probably never find themselves, but they can make sure what happened to them doesn't happen to others."

"And maybe, in the end, that's what it takes to find oneself again," she said.

She reached for the case, reached inside for her purse, and said a quick goodbye before she rushed to her car to drive to Zack's and take once step closer to discovering what might have killed so many people in Weston's family.

~

Molly watched her daughter's SUV rush away, and she knew it either meant Weston Cline had said something to enrage her, or he'd brought the information Joy and Zack needed to research Tressa's problem.

Well, Tressa was right, this was Molly's home, and she should play hostess no matter how she felt about the guest.

She turned toward the house and saw, to her shock, the tall, muscular, handsome Weston Cline making his way toward her between the vines. He stopped from vine to vine, not touching anything, but apparently admiring them.

He looked at Molly. "I believe I'm in the presence of greatness."

For a moment her tongue, her voice, and practically her bladder, failed her.

"Did you grow these vines?" he asked.

"Yes. These are my prized Vignoles."

"I hear you're a master vintner."

"I've won some local awards." She realized she'd been charmed before she could remind herself what this man had done to her daughter. She opened her mouth to invite him to leave, but instead she asked "Would you like a sample of last year's best?"

"I would love it, thank you."

It wasn't until she'd reached the corral that she realized she likely had mud an inch thick on her face. She glanced over her shoulder to find him studying the half-bricked cathouse. If she had any regard for his opinion she might feel embarrassed by what he would see as her silly little hobby. But his opinion meant less than nothing to her. Besides, if she was reading him correctly, he appeared to be studying the brickwork with admiration.

A few moments later she'd scrubbed off a bit of mud and

managed to find some chilled Vignoles and a clean glass. He met her on the porch out front.

"You must have a gift for growing things," Weston said when he took the glass from her and sniffed the bouquet. "This must have been one of your award winners, wasn't it?" He held up the glass, then sipped and savored.

"Have you judged wine?"

"Not me, I'm merely an enthusiast, but I know perfection when I taste it."

Molly thought she could see what had drawn Joy to a city where she had never wanted to live or practice.

There was movement to the side of the house, and Weston glanced that way, where his daughter had taken the raccoons into the small paddock where Captain Kirk ruled over a brown and white spotted milk goat.

"I imagine you handle your animals in the same way you do everything else, with attention to detail."

"Yes, they all have their yearly injections. We have a tenderhearted veterinarian who understands my need to rescue living things."

He nodded toward Tressa. "How did she handle being in the hospital?"

"Actually, I wish she would show a little more concern. She doesn't think we should be making such a big deal about a simple fainting spell."

He watched his daughter, and Molly thought she caught a glimpse of fear in the silver-blue eyes, the clenching of his firm jawline.

"As you can see, she looks healthy as a horse today," Molly told him.

He returned his attention to her, and she suddenly wondered if she'd imagined what she'd seen. "And you, Molly? I trust you're doing better with Joy here."

"Much. Tressa has especially been helpful. She's a genius with recipes, and she's such an animal lover. She has a special affinity with my orphaned raccoons."

He cut a sharp glance back toward Tressa. "Raccoons?"

"Don't worry, they've been checked out by the veterinarian, as well. They're in excellent health and are carrying no diseases. Same goes for the cats, the horse, the goat, the dogs. Tressa also loves to work in my garden. You have quite a girl, there, Weston. I've always thought so."

He turned back to Molly, and his expression had warmed several degrees. He actually smiled. "Thank you. Despite the best efforts of her parents to turn her into a neurotic young woman, I think she's resisted so far. Apparently, miracles still happen." He gave her a self-effacing grin. "Joy's been a strong influence in her life this past year."

"I think Tressa's been a strong influence on Joy, as well. She adores your daughter."

"That's why I was agreeable to this arrangement for the summer, but you must understand that I intend to provide child support. I take it Joy is thriving with her work in the ER?"

Molly hesitated. "Joy thrives where she's planted, as you've seen."

"I haven't had a chance to discuss the job with her. She's always been working when I've called, and today she's eager to get started looking through the files I brought. I know she's dedicated, but is she happy working at the hospital?"

"My daughter is in transition, Mr. Cline. I don't know that anyone is particularly happy in that phase of life." And why was she telling him this? Joy could reveal to him however much she wanted him to know. "I'm sure Tressa will be happy to see you."

"I'm sure she will." He said it hesitantly, as if he didn't quite believe it. "She's had no more episodes, then?"

"Not as far as I know, unless she has a cat allergy we haven't found." She would pull some Sheetrock and 2x4s from her supply in the cathouse and erect a dividing wall in the next couple of days. That shouldn't be too difficult, and then Joy and Tressa could have at least a small amount of privacy. Molly certainly valued her own.

~

Tressa looked up from her work with the weeding, and braced herself to meet with her father for the first time since she left. She even smiled and waved. Dusting her hands on the legs of her jeans, she left her work in the garden.

"Hi, Dad. Thanks for coming, but you didn't have to. I'm fine."

He reached for her, and she stepped into his arms with barely a hesitation. The gesture felt awkward.

"So you've become a doctor these past two weeks?" he asked as she stepped back. "Why don't you let Joy decide how you're doing?"

"She and Zack are on it."

"I spoke with her when I delivered the medical records and some of her work clothing."

Tressa stepped back and looked up at her father. "You did that for her?"

He looked uncomfortable. "Is that such a surprise?"

Tressa glanced at Molly, then back at her father. "Well, yeah. Did you talk to Mom about the medical records? I mean, really talk *to* her, and not *at* her?"

"Your mother and I have spoken a few times about your condition, and believe it or not, we didn't even scare the neighbors. Your mother was concerned that, since I was driving here, something more might be wrong with you than she'd thought, and that I had been told and she hadn't. You might want to call her. I don't suppose it occurred to her that I would simply want to see you after you've been gone so long."

"Three weeks, Dad? Really?" Tressa gave him a knowing smile. "Admit it, you missed Joy."

He looked uncomfortable as he glanced back at Molly.

"Why don't you two take a walk?" Molly suggested. "Tressa, your father might want to explore the vineyard."

As father and daughter walked side by side toward Molly's pride and joy. Dad remarked on the vines without a single sarcastic comment. No wonder Mom was worried. Dad was being nice? There was less arrogance in his attitude, more concern, and a softening of his features. There was also sadness and a very powerful undercurrent of concern that he was attempting mightily to conceal.

"Dad, *is* there something Mom and I don't know? I mean, about me?"

"If there is, I don't know it, either, Tressa, but we're not taking any chances."

She wilted. Here it came. "I feel fine. All I have to do is keep track of my blood sugar and—"

"Slow down. Tressa, relax. Getting upset won't help things."

But she couldn't help it. Her breathing was tight and her heart raced. Was he going to try to take her home with him? Would he force the issue about Joy going back to work for him? He was still being nice, but she'd discovered long ago his niceness could be a Trojan horse. It wasn't as if he had the patience of a monk.

"Don't worry," he said.

She looked up at him. "What?"

"We're doing all we can to make sure you're okay, but I've agreed with your mother, Joy and Molly that you should stay here for the summer. I'm arranging to have a regular support check mailed to Molly from my accountant. Otherwise, I don't think she'd accept."

"You know her that well?"

"I know Joy that well, and Molly seems to have patterned her daughter after herself."

"Like mother, like daughter, right?"

He eyed her in silence for a moment. "Not necessarily in every case."

She couldn't miss the implication. He didn't want her to turn out like her mother. Did he realize his behavior had influenced Mom's most recent personality change?

"My concern, Tressa, is that you've inherited something from my side of the family, not your mother's."

"I know. Zack and Joy have told me all about it."

He walked beside her in silence, but for some reason, this time it wasn't an awkward silence. It was more thoughtful. As if this time, maybe he'd actually listened to her? Wow, what was with that?

He stopped walking suddenly, and she stopped, too. "Dad? What's wrong?"

He raised his hand as if to touch her cheek, then dropped it again. "Tressa, maybe all you have is a case of low blood sugar and you'll live until you're ninety, but this scare made me realize something I wish I'd remembered four years ago, when your…when Keegan…when he…" Dad's voice wobbled, and tears moistened his eyes.

"When Keegan died," Tressa said softly, feeling tears burn her own eyes.

"No matter how long any of us has to live, I'm just now learning a lesson I should have learned a long, long time ago. Nothing is more important than those we love. We might never be able to speak the same language, but no matter what, Tressa, I love you."

Tears flowed down his cheeks. He dabbed them away, then took Tressa into his arms and held her for such a long time. And she didn't even mind it. In fact, she cried a few tears of her own.

"I love you, too, Dad."

Chapter 21

On Sunday afternoon, five and a half weeks since Tressa hitched a ride with Joy to Juliet, she loved the place and the people more than ever. Though she'd had few fainting spells, she was relieved to know that Zack and Joy were spending all their spare time researching whatever might be wrong with her.

She nudged Rascal's pointed nose back through the crack in the door of the shed. He'd grown so much bigger since she'd arrived, but he was still so cute he was difficult to resist.

"I told you, bedtime. It's late. Get some sleep, and I'll see you in the morning." As she turned away she steeled herself, as she did every night, against the pitiful cries of the raccoons. Dad might have once called her a drama queen, but she had nothing on the manipulations of the little bandits.

She chuckled as she walked toward the house in the deepening dusk. Captain Kirk nickered at her from his paddock, and she saw a dark shape flitting toward the front porch. Worf chasing bugs, his favorite pastime in the evening. He often refused to go outside in the daylight, but dusk had him out scampering at every windblown leaf.

She'd almost reached the house when the sky went suddenly dark. She stumbled and caught herself. Something furry bumped against her leg, and then she heard Trippurr's gravelly purr beside her.

This couldn't be happening, not now. She'd endured so many of those needles, had gone to Columbia for every single heart test Zack could come up with, and the only answer anyone could find was low blood sugar. So she'd eaten the same diet she'd placed Molly on last month. The good news was that her skin had cleared. The bad news was that she always had to be within shouting distance of someone else. Zack's rule.

Besides, if she got sick and Dad didn't feel they were doing their best to get her well, what was to stop him from dragging her out of Juliet and pulling every string he could to get custody of her and have her placed in the most advanced facility in the country for treatment? Maybe she should hide her symptoms this time.

She leaned over and rubbed Trippurr's back, and earned another bump in the leg for her efforts. All she needed to do was grab a spoonful of almond butter. That was all she needed. All her tests had come back negative, and though she could tell from Joy's expression and Zack's silent observation that they weren't satisfied, there wasn't anything more they could do. She just had to take it slow and watch her blood sugar constantly. She couldn't return to Corrigan. Not yet. Maybe things were changing, but they needed to change more.

~

Molly wanted chocolate. She *needed* chocolate, and she needed it now. Extra dark, rich, heavy with cocoa, filled with nuts, maybe some dried blueberries. It was, after all, good for the heart, just like the medicine she'd been treating herself with since Tressa arrived to play diet drill sergeant. Molly had done without her favorite food for what...five weeks? More?

This was the fifth Saturday since Joy and Tressa arrived, so this diet was sliding into its second month.

That first month there'd been more than one night she'd slipped out the front door and walked to the hospital to buy a Rice Krispy Treat and chocolate bar from the vending machine. The third time she'd tried, though, someone had rigged an alarm system on the front porch that sent her pitching forward into a mattress at the bottom of the steps with clanging pots and pans.

That had started the dogs to barking, the goat to bleating, and the cats all came flocking from the front door when Tressa opened it and switched on the porch light.

So the last time Molly had slipped outside, she'd had to climb down the lattice from her bedroom window. Unfortunately, when she arrived at the hospital, Zack was waiting beside the vending machine, arms crossed, with his foot tapping the floor.

Tonight she was desperate enough to attempt to eat one of those hideous carb-free desserts Tressa made when Tressa came in the back door, followed by Trippurr the Huge.

"I swear, that cat's gaining all the weight I'm losing," Molly said.

"Huh-uh. I weighed her yesterday. She's sixteen pounds. She was fat when Joy and I got here. I think it's normal for her. You've done better, despite your nightly trip to the vending machine."

"I don't go nightly. Besides, I'd think the walk to and from the hospital would burn off the calories."

"Maybe, but carbs increase your hunger. I stopped craving sweets, and even bread, once I forced myself to cut out anything starchy for the first two weeks. You wouldn't be struggling so much if you'd do the same thing."

"Okay, kid, do you think you could be a little less self-righteous?"

"I'm not being self-righteous, I'm simply trying to help

you with your appetite. If you didn't hit the candy so much it wouldn't be so hard for you to lose."

"I think I'm a lost cause, so why bother?"

Tressa grinned. "You're kidding. You can't tell how much you've lost?"

"I told you I don't want to see how much I weigh. It depresses me."

"Okay, I won't tell you how much you weigh, I'll just tell you that you've lost twenty-five pounds in a little over five weeks. If we start exercising more—"

"What! Did you say twenty-five?"

"Haven't you noticed how your jeans flop all over the place now? If you don't buy some new clothes you're going to lose your pants in the middle of the grocery store someday, and then everyone will have something to talk about again." She winked. "You know, like what a nice, shapely, gorgeous, tight—"

Molly laughed out loud. Of all the things that had surprised her over the years, this pretty much topped the list. She felt the thrill all the way down to her toes—which she realized she could see more easily than she had when she and Tressa began this project.

"Twenty-five?"

"Sorry, I know I wasn't supposed to tell you for another two weeks—"

"I'm glad you did. Now I won't feel so badly for driving to the store for some chocolate."

"No."

"Only a bite. One or two bites of extra dark chocolate won't make me gain anything."

"That's not the way to reward yourself. A cute new swimsuit in a smaller size is the way to reward yourself."

"I really lost twenty-five pounds?" Molly hadn't been this pleasantly surprised since learning of her daughter becoming engaged to Zachary Travis. Too bad they couldn't turn back time.

"Can't you tell?" Tressa asked. "I saw the safety pin on your bra. I thought you said you could sew."

"When have I had time to pull out my sewing machine? When I'm not in the vineyard, you've got me in the garden growing more greens or walking a marathon."

"Half a marathon, and we don't do that every day."

"It all takes time."

Tressa took a handful of the folds of Molly's tee shirt. "You've got a shape under there."

"Round is a—"

Tressa covered her ears and giggled. "No! Not that old lady line."

"I guess I could afford a new pair of jeans, maybe some underwear with actual elastic in it." Joy was paying generously for room and board, and Weston had sent two support checks for Tressa. Molly had asked for none of it, but she wasn't surprised.

"Maybe a dress or two? Something to show off the waist?" Tressa suggested.

"I think it's time to see Dr. Abernathy again. Get my numbers checked. That's what Joy will nag me about."

"After losing that much, your numbers will be so much better. For the price of a lab test, we can get a home testing kit."

"Even better. Make it so, Number One. That way Dr. Abernathy won't force me onto his scales and announce aloud to all the staff how much I weigh."

"Tomorrow. We'll do it tomorrow." Tressa glanced at the clock. "Are you going to need the bathroom in the next thirty minutes? I think I'll take a shower."

"I'm fine. Go ahead." Molly frowned and looked closer at her young friend. She'd been so distracted by that wonderful announcement about her weight that she hadn't realized the girl looked pale. "How are you feeling?"

Tressa rolled her eyes. "The same way I feel every time you ask me. Shouldn't Joy be home by now?"

Molly glanced at the clock. "Sometimes she works late, you know. Especially when Zack has the night shift." Molly looked at the clock. How blessed she'd been by her brilliant daughter once she stopped trying to control Joy's life and every single decision she made. To her amazement, Joy could make good decisions on her own.

"You know," she said, while Tressa puttered in the bathroom, "when Joy was growing up, I was so proud of her that I was incapable of brooding over the circumstances of her conception."

Tressa dropped what sounded like a shampoo bottle in the bathroom, and for a moment Molly was distracted—still hyper alert about the fainting spells that Tressa swore hadn't returned since her night at the ER.

Tressa would be in the bathroom for at least another fifteen minutes, Molly knew from past experience. There was no doubt she was accustomed to much finer housing; her own bathroom was probably four times the size of Molly's single one.

Molly made herself useful at the kitchen sink, washing still more vegetables that someday, she was sure, would turn her skin green or orange or some other unattractive color.

The evening light streaked purple and mauve across the surface of the Missouri River, and Joy sat on a bench alongside a riverside path beneath an elaborate grape arbor. It seemed every spare plot of ground in Juliet held a vine or two. In the autumn they would be loaded with ripe red or black or yellow-green fruit bursting with flavor. Joy thought about the vines she had planted behind the clinic in Corrigan. And then she thought about her patients.

She'd received multiple calls from the clinic about her former patients. Some refused to be seen by Dr. Hearst, and some had cases more complicated than anyone at the clinic was willing to take on.

The calls had left her feeling badly about leaving her patients, particularly the ones with more complicated conditions. Myra had to remind her that Dr. Joy Gilbert wasn't the only physician with a brain in her head or a heart in her chest. Still, it was those patients that the clinic rejected that concerned Joy the most.

With a flick of her wrist, she had her cell open and Myra's speed dial pressed. Maybe for once she wouldn't be working late or out on a midweek meeting—that woman had more activities keeping her busy every moment of the day and night, it didn't take a degree in psychology to realize she was still hiding from the pain of losing Dustin.

"Hey, girl. Did Dr. Hunk release you from the torture chamber for the night?" Myra's rich voice teased her.

Joy grinned. "The ER is not a torture chamber."

"It is for you."

"Well, anyway, more on that later. First, tell me what's going on with Sarah."

"Funny you should ask. You've got some kind of personal radar for your patients, haven't you?"

"Trouble?"

"I wouldn't call a temper tantrum trouble, I'd call it progress. Now, if I can just get her back to my office for another session. She stormed out of here in a rage without making another appointment."

"Is she angry with you?"

"She thinks she is, but you and I both know better. She's just going through the process. Finally."

Joy sank onto a concrete bench beneath the arbor. "Friend, I owe you a steak dinner."

"Lots of people do, honey. I prefer king crab."

"You've got it. I think I'll give Sarah a call."

"You mean we're gonna tag team this one?"

"I just want to remind her she hasn't been abandoned."

"She told me you called her the day after she was released from the hospital. It meant a lot to her, Joy. I think we're cracking this egg. Now, before you ring off, give me a quick download on Zack. You two still playing nice?"

"Not only are we playing nice, but Weston made a visit, didn't say a hateful word, and he's very concerned about his daughter. Mom's been sweet and supportive. Everybody's filled with so much sweetness I'm getting cavities."

"I have his ex's permission to share with you, so I'll just say to be careful. Weston's certainly afraid for Tressa, and he's showing his good side right now, but beware. Also, thanks for sending Sylvia my way. You're good for business."

"I don't suppose you'd be willing to take on the bad one."

"You mean Weston? You're kidding."

"If he's sincere about healing some of the complications in his family, stranger things could happen than for a smart man to try some counseling."

"Very true, but I'm not ready to throw myself into that particular tsunami."

"However, by talking to you—someone smart, who used to work for him, and who is younger—would force him to swallow a whole lot of pride, and that's one of his worst traits."

"I suppose for Tressa's sake I could try it."

"And meanwhile I'll have a talk with Sarah."

"And don't forget the crab legs. King crab. And if I'm going to take on Weston, throw in a bonus steak. Kansas City strip, three inches thick."

Joy was shaking her head when she disconnected.

Chapter 22

The moment Tressa walked out of the tiny, steamy bathroom, Molly placed the back of a hand to her face. "I'm still a little concerned about you. Are you feeling warm?"

"Not now. I got hot in the shower until the water got cold. What is that thing, about a ten gallon heater?"

"You'd tell me if you got dizzy, wouldn't you? I heard you drop the shampoo bottle."

Tressa grimaced. "I just got a little overheated, and you know how sometimes you get dizzy when that happens."

Molly shoved her salad into the fridge and clapped at the little bandits, who came running out from under the sofa, their favorite hideout. "I think we've had enough excitement for the day. Joy needs to check you out when she gets home. I wonder where she is."

"No," Tressa said quickly. "Not Joy, okay? She's been working too hard already, and she doesn't need to treat another case tonight, she needs to relax."

"Then maybe an appointment with Zack?"

Tressa shrugged and reached for Queen. She snuggled the raccoon close and was rewarded by a trill of contentment. "I'm afraid if I even get checked out, someone will say something to my dad and he'll change his mind about allowing me to stay here. At the least, it'll scare him, and you should've seen him, Molly, he was crying. He told me he loved me and everything."

Molly smiled, shaking her head. "So what I'm hearing you say is that you'd rather risk dying than take a trip to the doctor and get tested to make sure you don't die, because you'd rather die than frighten your parents. What would dying to do them?"

"Can I just wait and see if I start feeling better?"

Molly hesitated, then shook her head. "You don't know how much time Zack and Joy are spending to find what's wrong with you. Your health is most important."

"Then promise me you won't call my father."

"If you're okay, I promise. So you'll let Zack check you out?"

"Tomorrow, maybe?"

"Why don't you go lay down on my bed and rest. I don't want you climbing the stairs while you're dizzy."

"I think Joy's education must have infected you," Tressa said as she allowed Molly to lead her toward the large bedroom with windows that overlooked the river. "You sure know a lot about medicine."

"That's because I studied everything I could get my hands on from the time I was about twelve."

Tressa sat on the bed and swung her legs up. "Joy told me you talked to her about becoming a doctor for as far back as she could remember."

Molly sighed and glanced out the window. So many things she would have changed. "Maybe I shouldn't have pushed her so hard. What if she really would have wanted to be a musician or an English teacher?"

"Then she'd have told you. I don't think Joy ever does anything she doesn't want to do."

"Yeah, well, the nut didn't fall far from the tree."

Tressa grinned. "I'm telling Joy you called her a nut. Couldn't you get school loans like Joy did?"

Molly took Queen and motioned for Tressa to lie down. "Supporting oneself as a single parent is extremely difficult for a young girl without a college degree. No loans were available for someone in my condition. After Joy was born, I didn't want anyone else to raise her. She was mine, and mine alone. I stayed here because I wanted Joy to have the influence of family, and of course they never blamed Joy for not having a father. I only wish others had been as considerate."

"So you gave up your whole future for her?"

"Don't you think she's worth it?"

Tressa scrunched the pillow beneath her head. "Sure, but she's living her life now. What about the rest of yours?"

"Aside from my garden and vineyard, I'm still heating up the old computer lines with job resumes. So now we wait." Molly reached down and felt Tressa's forehead. "No obvious fever. Have you been drinking enough water today?" She gently pinched some of the thin skin on the back of Tressa's hand. It immediately smoothed. Her fingertips pinked up nicely as soon as they were squeezed. Good cap refill. "You aren't dehydrated."

"Would you quit worrying about me? I'll call Zack tomorrow and make an appointment to see him. I still think it's hormones. That's Mom's answer to everything."

"We'll see."

"I think my mother feels like you."

"She feels fat?"

Tressa grimaced. "No, silly. She feels like a throwaway. I remember you told me how you felt one time after you got pregnant. Grandpa and Grandma Livingston never had much money. Grandpa was injured in an accident at work in the steel casting factory, and they lived on disability."

Molly sank onto the linen chest in front of the window. "I

remember. We talked about that the day she gave permission for you to stay here. Your mother didn't feel like an acceptable mother for you. That's why she let you stay here. She felt like a throwaway, and that you're better off with us here."

"I agree with her."

"I hope you haven't told her that."

"No. Usually, when I call her, she does the talking. Do you think that's why Mom does what she does? Because she feels she doesn't deserve to be treated with respect? It might help if she respected herself a little."

"Everyone needs to be loved. When she's constantly told by others in so many words that she's worthless, she begins to believe it. I know how that feels."

Tressa slowly sat up on the bed. "I remember Joy telling Mom that day that she was a beautiful, strong woman, and that she raised a great daughter."

Molly smiled. "My daughter, the encourager."

"You're a strong, beautiful woman too, Molly." Tressa stood up cautiously. "And you raised a great daughter." She wavered, and then everything went black again.

~

Zack was still finishing with a patient when Joy returned to the ER, so she stepped back outside and made another phone call, incapable of resisting the lure of Juliet's warm, sensuous summer. She returned to the grape arbor as she punched a memorized number.

Sarah Miller answered her phone on the first ring. Her voice was barely above a whisper.

Joy hesitated for the very reason she had referred this patient to Myra in the first place. She didn't have a degree in psychology or psychiatry. Or in grief counseling.

"Sarah, hi, it's Joy Gilbert."

There was a short pause, then, "She reported me, didn't she?" There was suddenly a touch of resignation in her voice. "I told her to stop asking me. She was really nice about it, but she wouldn't stop trying to get me to talk about that night."

"That isn't why I'm calling. I just wanted to know how you were doing physically. Have you found another doctor yet?"

There was silence.

"Sarah?"

"Are you firing me from your service now?"

"Excuse me?"

"When I called the clinic the other day the receptionist told me you'd be back."

"She did?"

"You're not?"

"Sarah, I'm sorry, no. I was the one who got fired. I'm working full time in the ER in Juliet, Missouri." Why did Lisa tell her that? Time to straighten things out with Weston once and for all.

"So in essence, I'm being released from care again."

"Dr. Hearst would see you."

"I don't think I want to go back to that clinic unless I'm going to see you."

"Remember what I told you?"

"Which time? You told me a lot of things."

"Unless you get to the root of your problem, Sarah, you'll continue to have trouble. How has your stomach been feeling lately?"

"Worse. Especially today."

"Sometimes symptoms will get worse before they get better, but they can get better."

"So you have been talking to Dr. Maxwell."

"Of course I have. She's my friend. That's why I trusted her to help you. I'm glad you took my advice."

"Did I have any choice?"

"I hear it's helping."

"You're kidding. Didn't she tell you what happened today?"

"That's why she thinks it's helping. Anger is one of the stages of grief. You've broken through the wall of denial and are moving forward. Don't worry about Dr. Maxwell. She's trained and capable of taking it."

"I kind of hated myself for yelling at her."

"Don't feel badly. Sarah, you need to keep seeing her."

"I don't want to go through that again, and I can't pay her."

"She's not asking you to."

"So I'm just supposed to go to her office and yell at her some more, and she's letting me do it for free?"

Joy smiled, noting the sound of sarcasm in Sarah's voice. She'd never exhibited even the hint of a sense of humor previously. "She's a closet masochist."

There was a brief, soft sound of polite laughter.

"I can't help feeling that if you continue to see Dr. Maxwell, your physical problems will eventually disappear," Joy said.

"You know what? I understand all that intellectually. Really, I do. I have a college degree, you know. I was working on my CPA when…everything happened. Then I just couldn't do it anymore."

"That's surprising to me, Sarah. Sometimes, after dealing with people all day long, the thought of sitting alone in an office working with nothing but numbers sounds soothing."

"You've never heard of tax season, have you?"

"Okay, any time except January to April."

"Being alone gave me too much time to think. Memories always invaded the silence. That's why I got a day job doing floral arrangements. Putting up with perfectionists can shut out all other thoughts. It's why I work overtime, and even hang around work when I'm not on duty."

"Have you spoken to Dr. Maxwell about this?"

"The subject hasn't come up."

"Why don't you bring it up at your next session?"

Sarah gave a quiet sigh, then paused. "I'm afraid she'll try to force me to try again for my CPA—"

"She won't force you to do anything," Joy said. "She'll just start helping you make your own decisions again, instead of letting the grief determine your future."

"What happens if I don't get another appointment?"

"You stand to lose too much, Sarah. I don't want you to allow those ugly, vile men to determine the direction of the rest of your life."

A sigh…and another sigh as the silence stretched with the strain of a difficult decision. "Okay, well, I guess I could go once more. I should at least apologize."

"That's good. One step at a time."

When Joy returned to the ER, she found no patients. Two nurses sat chatting at the central desk, and the nurse practitioner and receptionist were both working on reports. Joy found Zack in his office on the computer. She knocked at the open door.

He looked up and smiled a welcome, though she thought she detected an eddy of wariness in his body language as he crossed his arms over his chest. "You know those bruises the ladies at church were worried about with Dillon?"

"Oh, no. Not more."

"Yes, and you know why he's getting them?"

She braced herself. If she'd made an error in judgment—

"The poor child has some amblyopia."

"He has a lazy eye?"

"It isn't constant, just comes and goes, according to Sherie.

He fell hard today down some stairs, and there wasn't anyone around to push him."

"Is he okay?"

"Nothing's broken."

"I wish I'd caught it when I checked him."

"Doesn't happen all the time. I've got him on a patch for the problem eye, and all should be well in a few weeks."

"And his stepdad? How are things with the parents?"

He shook his head and leaned back in his chair, staring at the far wall. "Sherie's willfulness is their biggest problem. She's unhappy because her husband won't share her faith, and she seems to be blaming God about it now."

"For a choice she made outside of God's will?"

He shook his head, hands spread, as if he couldn't understand it, either.

She sank into a chair across from his desk. "Zack, all those years I attended church because Mom wanted me to, I didn't do it for God, I did it for her."

He looked up at her. "All this time you've battled with yourself over whether or not you truly ever had faith in God."

"And I'm still battling."

"I was never convinced you rejected your faith when you left that church, okay? You obviously believe in God; a person doesn't fake your kind of faith."

"But I resisted too often."

"Really? I saw you resist your mother when she was wrong, and me when...well, when I blew it. I don't recall you making choices that were intentionally in rebellion to God's will. As I've said before, don't let the ugliness of one poorly run church make you doubt your faith in God. On the other hand, don't claim a faith you don't really have. Both could be catastrophic."

"So tell me what a real church is."

"A true church is the body of Christ, and in my opinion its

members don't believe they can work their way to heaven, and unlike poor Molly's former church, they don't expect certain obvious sinners to work their way out of hell. They place their faith in Christ alone, and this prevents them from becoming self-righteous. I hate that you were raised to believe that the love of God is harsh, judgmental and filled with antagonism. Poor Molly wasn't raised in a home where the parents took the kids to church, right?"

"That's right."

"Then she had to search one out for herself. She did the best she could. Now the next step for both of you to take is to seek out a church that feels real to you, that follows true Biblical principles instead of making up their own."

Joy leaned forward, slowly touching her fingertips together, finger matching finger on each hand, as she considered his words more carefully. Zack apparently did know her well in some ways.

"I don't believe you ever abandoned God, Joy. I know for a fact He would never abandon you."

The intercom buzzed just as he was reaching for her. With obvious reluctance, he turned back to the desk. "Yes?"

"Dr. Travis, we have a patient for you."

Joy's cell phone beeped. She checked the screen. It was the hospital number. When she answered, she heard her mother's voice. "Joy, Tressa's been passing out on me again. I had to bring her to the ER. Where are you? I saw your car in the lot, but—"

"I'll be right there."

Joy and Zachary rushed down the hallway side by side, and she didn't even have time to bask in the power of his words.

This time she wouldn't be able to write Tressa's illness off as simple low blood sugar.

Chapter 23

Tressa lay on the ER exam bed feeling stupid and desperate, and this time she was so scared she didn't even think about what her parents would do. She only worried that she might die and destroy both their lives for good. Just when things had begun to look hopeful...now this.

She sat up. "Molly, does Joy have to call them?"

Molly laid the magazine she was reading onto the chair beside her and stepped to the bed. "The problem's more serious than simple low blood sugar this time, honey. When I checked your heart rate, you were out for thirty seconds without a pulse. I was just getting ready to do CPR when you woke up. They need to know.

"I saw what happened to them when Keegan died." Hot tears ran down the sides of her face.

"Sweetheart, I don't think God's done with you yet, but I'm praying harder than I've ever prayed in my life."

The exam room door opened and Zack stepped in. "Tressa, how are you feeling now?"

The tears still came. All this time she'd told herself her parents were the darkness, but now she knew that the darkness came from whatever lay inside her—whatever killed so many in her family. "I trust you."

Joy came in behind him, and without asking, she knelt beside Tressa's bed and took her hands. And she prayed. And she cried and sniffed. Her voice was so soft and broken Tressa could barely hear her, but there was no doubt she was praying. Molly knelt and laid her hands on Tressa's shoulders. Zack knelt and placed an arm around each of the women doing battle against the darkness. And Tressa imagined she could feel those prayers fighting the battle she'd sensed taking control of her life and the lives around her for so many years.

They'd just finished when the door opened and Mary, the RN, walked in. "Dr. Travis, I just received word from Weston Cline that he's flying down with Mrs. Cline, and they'll be meeting with your cardiology specialist in Columbia. There are clear skies, so they should be there any moment. We have a helicopter coming to pick Tressa up.

"Thank you, Mary. Crash cart?"

"Set up."

Zack sat down beside Tressa and held her hands. "Sweetheart, we've been doing a lot of research lately. The low blood sugar threw us off, but Joy and I have especially been interested in your Philippine heritage, so we've researched certain Asian medical syndromes. Until tonight, however, when Molly witnessed your heart stopping, we didn't know to look for this particular problem. What we're suspecting is called Brugada Syndrome. I called a heart specialist tonight and sent him a printout of your monitor reading, and he wants to see you tonight. Now."

"This syndrome stops my heart?"

"That sometimes happens, and we believe it was what took the lives of your family members, but with you we've caught it in time. If that's what it is, we can have a defibrillator implanted into your heart to keep it from stopping on you."

"B-but all those people in our family. They just died. Little kids, Keegan, my great-grandfather."

"This is a difficult syndrome to find, honey," Joy said.

"If Joy hadn't given you those steroid shots for your poison ivy," Zack said, "your other symptoms wouldn't have alerted us to watch for something more serious."

"And if Zack hadn't forced all those other tests on you to test for Chaga's Disease," Joy said, "which is from a bug bite in the Southwest where you insisted on going with me—"

"And if Molly hadn't been with you to check your pulse at just the right time tonight," Zack said, "then your heart might well have stopped at any time in the future, and no one would have known why."

"Now we know how to stop that from happening," Joy said.

Tressa gasped. "My father. My grandmother. What about them?"

"They'll be checked, too." Zack looked up at Joy. "I'll see to it as soon as we arrived in Columbia. If this is what we think it is, you might have saved others in your family, beginning with your father."

"I want to go with Tressa," Joy said.

"Me too." Molly caressed Tressa's cheek.

"I'm off duty, Tressa," Zack said, "so Joy and Molly will ride with me to Columbia. You'll have a lot of people waiting for you, and the staff caring for you on the helicopter know exactly what to do if your heart tries to stop again."

"And we'll be praying for you," Molly said. "Have you noticed that something seems to have changed your father? Would you ever have expected him to fly to Columbia with your mother to be there for you during further testing and possible surgery?"

"The darkness is lifting," Tressa said. "That's why. He did seem different when he came down the other day."

"Because he knows you're the most important person in the world to him," Joy said. "He told me so, himself."

"Yeah," Tressa said softly. "He's lost a lot in his life. Sometimes people give up when that happens."

"Then he discovered he had more to lose," Zack said. "That's you." He stopped and turned his head, as if listening. "I think I hear the chopper on its way now. You'll be in Columbia in about fifteen minutes."

Joy studied the monitor that had been linked to Tressa's chest soon after she arrived. "I haven't seen a single missed beat. Heart's working perfectly as far as I can tell." She looked at Molly. "It was thirty seconds between heartbeats at the house?"

"I grabbed her wrist before she fell, and held on until I felt the rhythm again."

The helicopter rotors seemed to vibrate the walls as it landed, and within minutes Tressa was strapped into the gurney, looking frightened.

"Joy can't come with me?"

"No room, sweetheart, but we'll get there as soon as we can. Your parents might beat us there."

"What about when I get out? Where will I go then?"

Joy chuckled. "You might be surprised to find that someday you'll want to go home, but if I know your parents, they might prefer you stay with a physician after you're released from the hospital."

"Especially one of the docs who saved your life," Molly said.

~

Joy let her mother sit in the front passenger seat of Zack's car and dialed Myra's number under cover of their chatter, this time adding in her internal calculator how much she was going to owe her friend after tonight.

Tressa's chopper was lifting her up into the night air and carrying her swiftly toward the major medical teaching center in central Missouri. Joy was still waiting for Myra to answer her phone when she glanced at the clock on Zack's truck. It was after midnight. How much money did Weston have to add to the regular bill to get such service tonight?

Myra answered, her voice deep with sleep. "Double dinner for this one."

"I know, I'm sorry. And it's going to get worse." Joy started to say more, but her throat closed. She swallowed back a sob.

"Sweetie?" Then more concern. "Honey, tell me what happened!"

"I'm sorry. I think it's just hitting me, and..." She squeezed her eyes shut and let the tears warm her cheeks. To lose Tressa, who had become like the little sister she'd never have...."

"Joy Marie, is someone there with you, and please tell me you're not driving right now," Myra said.

"Zack's driving, Mom's here, and Tressa almost died tonight." She lost control as everything hit, and she was no longer the doctor in control. She cried the words. "We think she has Brugada Syndrome. She's being flown to University Hospital now."

Mom laid a hand on her head as if blessing her—and she probably was.

There was a moment of stunned silence from Myra in which Joy could visualize her friend's horrified expression. "Tell me that girl's going to be okay. How much can one family take?"

Joy's hands shook so hard she could barely hold the phone. "Believe it or not, Weston is flying himself and his ex-wife to Columbia to meet Tressa there."

"Hold it. This can't be happening. I'm not dreaming, am I?"

The tenor of Myra's words helped to dissipate some of Joy's angst. "The helicopter already picked Tressa up. Zack and Molly and I are on our way to University to meet with a specialist in heart rhythm. He's an old friend of Zack's. I will owe you for the rest of my life, but please, would you try to get there in the morning? I have no idea what condition Weston and Sylvia will be in, but last time I saw them together they were ready to kill one another."

"Okay, well, my date left me high and dry tonight, so why don't I just jump into the middle of a school of piranhas for some excitement?"

"You had a date?"

"Later, my dear. Tressa's well-being is a lot more important, and who can say what this will do to change Weston for the better? It's been known to happen."

"So you'll meet us there?"

"I'll drive. I shouldn't get there much after you do."

"You're the best friend ever."

"Glad you noticed."

"I called Sarah Miller. She's going to give it another try with you."

"And this is the one that'll work. Mark my words."

"Have I ever told you that you're a saint?"

"Yes, and you do recall, don't you, that I've never disagreed with you. Still, you need to stop seeing people in black and white and notice some color every now and then." Myra was chuckling as she hung up. But Joy thought she heard a note of tension in that chuckle. The prospect of encountering Weston Cline tended to do that.

Zack glanced over his shoulder at Joy. "Doing okay?"

She nodded. "It's been a rough few weeks, hasn't it?"

"Divine appointments and pruning."

Joy grinned to herself when she saw her mother give Zack a skeptical look.

He saw it. "I used to preach to Joy that the hard times in a person's life are divine appointments—opportunities to develop character in ways that might never otherwise be developed. A person's choices impact the development of her character, and the closer those choices are to God's plan for them, the better and quicker the development.

"So you're saying we'll all be better after this hardship." Molly's words were filled with doubt.

Joy thought about the change she'd seen in Weston. There was no telling whether or not the metamorphosis would continue, but it was a start. "We can live with regret or we can find forgiveness in our hearts for those who have injured us and move forward."

"I don't get what that has to do with Tressa nearly dying tonight," Molly said.

Joy smiled again, thinking about Myra's accusation that she saw things in black and white, with no color. Maybe Joy took after her mother when it came to right and wrong, black and white.

Settling into her seat, Joy allowed herself to relax while Zack drove alongside the moonlit river. Staring across the softened edges of the foggy midnight, she wished her life could be as productive as the arbors along the cliff side.

The grapevines that grew with abandon on the hillside vineyards above the Missouri River held a mystic place in Joy's heart; in the years she was growing up, they'd given her hope that someday even her rebellious spirit could be cultivated into something fine and acceptable in God's eyes.

Of course, as a child of the vineyards, she knew too well the pruning that must take place during the cultivation process. It kept the life-giving nutrients from being wasted on too many leaves and unproductive branches, or even an overabundance of the fruit, itself. Pruning directed the nutrients, instead, into just the right amount of luscious grapes, making them sweeter.

She understood and appreciated this life-enhancing process, but she'd sometimes found the pruning in her life to be so painful that she felt like the discards, and wished the mighty Missouri would sweep her away and deposit her, as it often did the rain-washed cuttings, onto a distant riverbank where no one knew her or remembered the mistakes she'd made—where even she might forget.

If she had been in Weston's shoes, losing a baby brother, despised by his mother, losing his son, and enduring a vicious divorce, would she have been more likely to behave as he had, taking what she wanted in any way she deemed fit, making money her god?

How could one person blame someone else if she hadn't walked in his shoes?

"Something about Weston Cline's indeed changed," Molly said. "Think it'll stick?"

"I didn't know him before all his losses made him what he was," Zack said.

"He loves his daughter," Molly said. "And for the first time since I've seen them together, he doesn't seem squeamish about showing it."

"Or afraid," Joy said. "I do know Tressa is happier since his visit when he brought more medical files. He went out of his way to talk to her and listen, and she still loves to relive that day."

"It's good to see the happiness in her face," Molly said. "But what I'm asking is, will he change one he's reassured he won't lose Tressa?"

"I know she broods about it sometimes," Joy said. "A girl doesn't want to give freely of her love only to have it ripped from her again."

"I'm probably not the best to judge," Zack said. "He tricked me and I allowed it, and the trick worked for nine months, but he also taught me a lot about myself. I continued to learn about myself so that next time I'm blessed with the love of my life," he said, glancing over his shoulder at Joy, "I'll know how to treat her, and to always place her first in my heart, and never to listen to something someone else says about her without asking her first."

Joy grinned. "Thank you. And if you do forget, you have a backside that will endure some kicking."

"May I help?" Molly asked.

"Molly! You weren't exactly the epitome of kindness and understand last year," Zack said. "I shouldn't have listened to you, either."

"Then you both have my permission to kick my tush if I start to cause trouble."

"Thanks, Mom. I'll hold you to that."

"I don't think we'll have any trouble—okay, we probably won't have a dangerous argument more than once a day. So, is all sweetness and light?"

"We'll get an idea as soon as we arrive at the hospital and talk to Tressa's parents."

Silence fell in the car, and as they left the view of the Missouri River behind, Joy found herself praying that this would make the changes in the lives of the Clines they'd needed for so many years—since Weston was a child, himself. That little boy she'd glimpsed a couple times needed happiness in his life, and she didn't think he'd had much of that.

Chapter 24

Zack led Joy and Molly into the room at University Hospital in Columbia, Missouri, where Tressa was being prepped for yet another test, and likely surgery. He wasn't surprised to find Weston standing on one side of Tressa's bed while Sylvia stood across from him, both touching their daughter's arms, exposed amidst the tangle of wiring.

When the greetings had ended and Sylvia returned her attention to her daughter, tears fell down her cheeks, and Weston placed a comforting hand on hers.

There was no missing the gesture, and Zack saw Tressa's eyes widen, then she looked up at him and winked.

Soon after, a physician came walking in in surgery scrubs. "Well, folks, we have a full night tonight, and Mr. Cline, you will now be joining your daughter as a patient in our hospital, so while you and Mrs. Cline are filling out more paperwork, we want you out of those clothes and into a gown."

Weston's expression of shock caused Joy and Zack to smile at each other.

"I'm sorry, I don't understand," Weston said.

"I called ahead," Zack told him. "Brugada Syndrome has already taken how many members of your family? It stops with you, and with your mother and other relatives as soon as we can get them down here." He held his breath, waiting for Weston's reaction.

The man turned to his ex-wife, pulled out his billfold and handed it to her. "You know all you need to fill out the forms...if you wouldn't mind?"

They looked at each other for a moment, and though Zack wasn't a mind reader, or even a face reader or a reader of body language, he saw something happen between the two. In Weston's expression was humility, in Sylvia's was compassion.

This family might make it after all, if they continued in the right direction.

Zack squeezed Joy's hand and turned to walk with Weston. He knew there would be some explaining to do, but before he could speak, a tech came up beside Weston with a wheelchair.

"I don't really need—"

"Trust me," Zack said, "you might. Don't you dare break your little girl's heart and die on her."

Weston paused only briefly, then removed his sports coat and seated himself in the wheelchair. "Here I am with someone who has every right to wish me dead, and not only have you saved my daughter, you've interfered to save my life as well?"

"I'm a doctor."

"What a horrible curse for you."

"Sometimes it feels that way." Zack walked in silence for a few moments. "You loved Joy, too."

Weston gave a quiet sigh. "More than you can ever imagine."

"I think I got the idea."

"I'm a tough business negotiator, but I have a work ethic. I don't cheat my clients. When it came to Joy, though, ethics flew out the window. When I finally realized she didn't return what I felt for her—and believe me, that's a first for me—I realized I'd done a lot of damage to a lot of people, especially to her."

"But you couldn't keep her working for you and stay away?"

"I could have, but I knew where her heart was. At first, I fired her in anger, but as I thought about it, and realized she was happier in Juliet, and that even my own daughter was happier in Juliet, I realized what a horrible mistake I'd made."

The tech pushed the wheelchair into a room and a nurse came in and bared Weston's chest. She applied electrodes to him, and then she left, promising to return after the readings were taken. The tech gave Weston a gown and left, as well.

"I'll give you some privacy," Zack said.

"Would you first please allow me to apologize properly?"

"I thought you had."

"I need to undo some wrongs. Tell Joy she will receive everything she's paid on the house. I've bought it, then sold it at a decent price, and she will receive the extra. Also tell her that her school loans are still all paid, and she owes me nothing."

"That's generous."

"I took a year from her life and yours, and I might never be able to forgive myself for doing what I did."

"That's quite a start," Zack said. "I'm curious about one thing. Not long after Dustin Grooms died last year, you discontinued financial support for the research project, and yet not a word was ever said about the official report."

"That's because the official report—and I'm assuming you mean the one about the illegal use of the serum on a human being to save Dustin's life?"

"That would be correct."

"Dr. Payson never saw that report. I know his reputation as well as anyone, and had he seen the report left on his desk, Joy, Myra and Laine would have lost their licenses and possibly gone to jail."

"You do realize you could go to jail for that," Zack said.

"I've kept those papers in a safe place, and used that opportunity to offer Joy the job I'd wanted to offer her as soon as

I met her. Now, since you made the call about having me checked in here," Weston said with a slight grin, "you took on responsibility for my care. That would make you my family doctor."

"Lucky me," Zack said dryly.

Weston grinned. "So that affords me the luxury of doctor-patient confidentiality. You cannot breathe a word of this to anyone. And Payson must never know."

"You have my word," Zack said. "I don't believe you owe me an apology any more than I owe you my gratitude."

"What on earth for?"

"I learned a lot this year. I learned that I need to be able to trust the woman I love, and take her word above all others, or I don't love her enough."

"And do you now?"

"Anyone who ever tries to tell me Joy wants to leave me will earn a black eye."

Weston nodded. "Love her well, Dr. Travis. I know of no one who deserves it more."

~

Joy walked beside Zack, hand in hand, in the silent hospital corridor. "So he actually apologized?"

"Everything I told you is true, not a figment of my imagination."

"Wow." Whatever happened from this point forward, Joy would focus on celebrating each day as it came, and living life to its fullest. She would also stop trying to control her own life, and learn to allow Someone Else to gently guide her. That was the most empowering way for a person to live.

When those grapevines were pruned properly, and lovingly brought to fruition, the reward was a joyful abiding. One could feel clean, productive, and have a life filled with sweet, rich abundance. One must only submit to the pruning.

"Here's something else that is no figment of my imagination." Zack stopped walking and reached into his jacket pocket.

She grinned. "I'm starved! You got me a candy bar?"

He hesitated with his hand halfway out. "Um, no, but I will after this, okay?"

"Well, all right."

He knelt in the middle of the empty corridor and took her left hand.

She gasped. "Not a candy bar at all, is it?"

"This is way better than a candy bar. I know this fits unless you've gained a bunch of weight this past year—"

"What!" She drew her hand back.

"But you don't look it! Honest!" He watched that hand with concern.

She frowned. "You sure about that?"

"You did just ask for a candy bar."

"Okay, fine, make it salad if you have to." She held out her hand, smiling, and of course crying at the same time. "How on earth could you still love me after everything I've put you through? But I'm not letting you get this ring away from me again."

He slid it on, and if anything, it was a little loose. "Joy of my heart, there is nothing you could ever say or do that would make me love you any less than I do right now."

She stared at him, quirked her mouth as he looked up at her. "So you're saying you could definitely stand to love me more, then."

"Um, what?"

"You love me less now than you ever will again."

He grinned, then grew serious and cleared his throat. "I

love you more than ever before, and my love for you could only deepen as the years pass."

"Ah, much better. I love you, too, and I've never stopped, and I believe there will be times I'll love you even more than I do right now. Which is amazing. Can we get married next week?"

"I say let's go for it. Anything for you."

"Well, then, how about that candy bar?"